My Heart Belongs

in San Francisco, CALIFORNIA

Abby's
Prospects

JANICE THOMPSON

BARBOUR BOOKS

An Imprint of Barbour Publishing, Inc.

Model Photograph: Elisabeth Ansley/Trevillion Images
Series Deisn: Kirk DouPonce, DogEared Design

Published by Barbour Books, an imprint of Barbour Publishing, Inc.,
1810 Barbour Drive, Uhrichsville, OH 44683, www.barbourbooks.com

Our mission is to inspire the world with the life-changing message of the Bible.

ECPA Member of the
Evangelical Christian
Publishers Association

Printed in the United States of America.

Chapter One

Late April, 1853

"Never underestimate the power of coffee, Neville." Abby lifted her delicate white cup and took a sip of the powerful brew, then did her best to balance it on the saucer. The jolting of the train made the task nearly impossible, but Abigail's expertise with a cup and saucer won out in the end. She managed to place the items on the dining car table without spilling a drop.

"I'm a tea man, myself." The family butler took a sip from his cup and his nose wrinkled. "Not that I would call this stuff the Americans drink tea." His porcelain cup clattered against the saucer, which he gripped until his knuckles turned white. Neville's furrowed brow softened after another drink of the hot beverage. "I spoke with the conductor earlier this morning. We're a mere hour and a half away from St. Louis. Can't arrive soon enough to please me."

"Wonderful. And from there?" Abby glanced out the dusty train window to the vast prairie, which ran for miles.

"We take a coach into the Oregon Territory, where we will join your mother in Oregon City. She will be expecting us in two weeks, if all goes as planned." Neville's sour expression gave away his thoughts on the matter. "I have been told, however, that things ordinarily do not go

5

as planned. We might not arrive until the last week in May."

"All will end well, Neville." Abby took another sip of the hot coffee, assurance rising up within her as the words took root. "Everything will work out for the good. Watch and see. And along the way we shall have adventures aplenty. After a while, you will forget to be upset at me at all."

"Hmm." Neville's brows drew downward into a frown, but he said nothing, at least for a moment.

"Why you chose to travel in late spring is beyond me." He tugged at his collar and swiped beads of sweat off his forehead with his napkin. "This heat will be the death of us."

"Certainly nothing like the weather in Philadelphia, is it?"

"Nor like the weather in Nottingham, which is precisely where I'd prefer to be at the moment." He seemed to lose himself in his thoughts. "Why your father decided to move us lock, stock, and barrel to the States is. . ." His eyes widened and his words ended abruptly. "I'm sorry, Miss Abigail. I've spoken out of turn. Please forgive me."

The train jolted and began to round a curve. Abby held tight to her coffee cup, though the hot liquid threatened to slosh over the edge. "Speaking one's mind is not the same thing as speaking out of turn. And I rarely get to hear your truest thoughts, Neville. I find it refreshing." She set the cup down, reached for a gingersnap from the china plate in front of her, and pondered his words as she took a little nibble of the delicious treat. Of course, Father would balk at the idea of a family servant sharing his thoughts so openly, but Abby didn't mind.

"Refreshing?" His expression softened, and she saw a twinkle in his eye as she glanced his direction. "Interesting description for an old butler, set in his ways."

"Not old at all, Neville. And I wholeheartedly agree. I'd prefer to be back in jolly old England, myself. But Mother has set our family on a westward path, and we must stay the course. No point in turning back now, not when we've made such progress."

"I suppose, but what an unexpected course it is." He paused and took another sip of his tea, as prim and proper as ever. "And I thought the move to Philadelphia was daring."

"Oh, it was, at least at the time. And Father seems perfectly happy there. If only Mother. . ." She bit back the words that threatened to escape then turned her gaze out the window to the expansive prairie. "Anyway, we'll talk her into coming back home. This wanderlust of hers will be short-lived, I pray. A person can't travel forever. By now she's probably bored of spending time with Aunt Eliza and will be ready to be escorted back to Philadelphia."

"One can hope." Neville's words were spoken under his breath, but she understood them just the same. "These last couple of years have brought change upon change, and, as I said, I'm old and set in my ways."

"I know this is hard on you, Neville." Tears welled in Abby's eyes and threatened to spill over onto her lashes. She fought to swallow the growing lump in her throat. "But don't you see? I've got to fetch Mama and bring her back home to Philadelphia. If I don't. . ." Her words trailed off.

"I know, miss." He cleared his throat, his gaze darting to the table.

The train chose that moment to jolt, and a shrill whistle filled the air. Neville's teacup tumbled out of his hand and clattered onto the table below, soiling the white cloth and spilling over onto his jacket. The cup remained intact, but the liquid sloshed all over the plate of cookies.

"Crying shame. Can't believe I did that." Using his napkin, Neville began the arduous task of mopping up his mess.

A waiter appeared moments later with a towel in hand. "Sir, if I may." The young fellow went to work dabbing the moisture from the white tablecloth. Abby couldn't help but notice the handsome stranger peeking at her out of the corner of his eye.

Neville rose and brushed his hands across the damp spot on his coat. "Will you be all right alone, Miss Abigail? I need to head back to my cabin to clean this before it stains. I will return shortly."

"I'm a big girl, you know." She fought the temptation to roll her eyes and, instead, gave him a strained smile. "Honestly. No need to come back at all. I will be fine."

"That is yet to be determined." He responded with a tense nod, then turned on his heel and headed out of the dining car.

The young waiter set his cluttered tray on an empty table nearby and gave her a pensive look as he leaned forward to clear Neville's cup and saucer. "That fella your father?"

"Certainly not. Neville's our butler."

"Butler?" The handsome stranger's eyebrows arched. "Well now, ain't we sumptin'." He held up his pinky finger as he lifted Neville's teacup and pretended to take a dainty sip. "Where you come from, anyhow? Never heard an accent like that b'fore." He set the cup and saucer on his tray, then turned back to face her.

"England, of course. I'm surprised you couldn't place it. Why, back home I could tell from a person's speech patterns exactly where they hailed from, right down to the county."

"Where'm I from, then?" He gazed her way, as if daring her to guess. "C'mon. Tell me. I'll even throw in a fresh plate of gingersnaps if you get it right."

She thought it through before answering, "Kentucky."

His eyes widened in surprise. "How did you know that?"

"As I said, I'm very good with dialects. Yours gave you away at once. 'Ain't we sumptin'' puts me in mind of good country folks, so I determined right away that you must hail from someplace farther south. Only, your tone has a bit of a musical lilt, so I narrowed my guess to Kentucky." She paused as she thought through her next words. "There is a hint of a western dialect, as well. Strikes me as odd, for someone Kentucky bred."

He placed the plate of soggy cookies onto his tray, which he then lifted with ease. "San Francisco. Went with my Pa a few years back. One of the original 49ers."

"Forty-Niners. I've heard the phrase, of course, but don't know much about it."

"We wanted to strike it rich, panning for gold. Settled in the Sierra Mountains and surrounding foothills, but spent many a day and night carousing in San Francisco, our pockets filled with gold."

"Hmm. And yet here you are, working for the Pacific Railroad."

"Did well for myself. So did Pa." The young man's expression shifted, and she thought she saw a hint of sadness in his eyes. "At first, anyway. In the end, he gambled it all away."

"Mercy. Your money, as well as his?"

The waiter released an exaggerated sigh. "Yep. That's the long and short of it. Happens to the best of 'em out there." His handsome blue eyes lit up once again. "But if I had my druthers, I'd head back to San Francisco in a hurry. Plenty of excitement there. You ain't lived till you've seen folks from so many different places across the world, all gathered in one location. It's something to behold. I heard every language you might imagine: Chinese, Spanish, even German."

"Sounds fascinating."

"Oh, it was. Best couple years of my life. So far, anyway." He seemed to lose himself to his daydreams. After a moment, he snapped to attention. "If you ever do make it there, go to the restaurant at the Gold Rush Inn. Opened in '51, just before Pa and I headed back east. Best cook in town. The cherry pie is the best in the West, and don't even get me started on her coffee. Tell 'em Jimmy Blodgett sent you."

"I don't imagine I'll ever see the inside of the Gold Rush Inn, but thank you for the recommendation, James."

"Jimmy. Only my Ma calls me James." He shook his head and continued his work. "So, where're you headed, if you don't mind my asking?"

"Oregon Territory."

"With the family butler?" His right eyebrow arched and he whispered, "Scandalous."

"Hardly." She felt her cheeks grow warm at his implication. "I'm headed there to fetch Mama and bring her home where she belongs." Shame washed over her as she spoke the family's secret aloud.

"I see." Jimmy paused and gave her a look that spoke his curiosity. He leaned in close, the tray still balanced in his hand, his voice still coming out as a whisper. "You sayin' your Ma ran away from home?"

Oh my. How would she ever answer this question? "Not exactly. It might be more accurate to say that she found her life in Philadelphia a bit boring and sought adventure elsewhere."

"Boring?"

"Yes. My father has tried to calm her spirit, even moved the two of them from London to Nottingham when they married. But that didn't satisfy her, so a year and a half ago, he moved our family to Philadelphia to satisfy her wanderlust."

"That didn't work either, I take it?" He shuffled the tray to his other hand.

"Correct." Abby sighed. "She just doesn't seem to want to stay put."

Abby could only picture her father's face, were he witnessing this conversation. Why, he would stop her in her tracks, not just for revealing personal information, but for talking at length to a young man she did not know.

"Did you call it *wanderlust*?" Jimmy asked. "Don't think I know that word."

"Love of wandering. Yes. But Philadelphia wasn't far enough, apparently." The train's whistle sounded and the dining car rocked. Abby gripped the table. "Mother has ventured on to Oregon Territory, where she's visiting her sister. My aunt is married to a banker. From what she says, Oregon is the place to be."

"I'd still choose California any day." He released a whistle as he straightened his posture. "But what a story. Good enough for one of those dime novels the washerwoman reads. Your aunt from England too?"

"Yes, of course. The whole family hails from London. From what I can gather, the women have an insatiable desire to travel."

"That spill over on you too?" The waiter's brows arched as he posed the question.

Abby paused to think through her response. "It's the strangest thing. I don't mind visiting new places, but getting there dampens the experience. I suppose you could say I'm not one for sitting still." She fought the desire to rub her aching backside to emphasize the point. "Up and doing, that's my motto."

"Ah, I see. Well, this job has me beat half the time. I'd rather be being, not doing." He paused and glanced over his shoulder. "Better get back to work before the head waiter has my head on a platter." He nudged the tray a bit higher and chuckled. Then his gaze darted to the window and he very nearly lost his grip on the tray. The dishes clattered as they struck one another. "Oh, did you see that? Buffalo."

"Gracious." Abby turned her attention to the window. "No, I didn't. Not sure I care to."

"Don't get many buffalo up in Philadelphia, I guess."

"Hardly. And never in England."

"Saw 'em all the time in California. Guessin' you will too, in Oregon Territory. Better get used to it." The brazen fellow gave her a wink, then turned on his heel to wait on another passenger. Abby felt her cheeks grow hot. Were all the fellows west of the Mississippi so forward?

Neville returned to the dining car moments later wearing a clean jacket. He took a seat with an exaggerated sigh. "Miss Abigail, are you sure I can't convince you to eat a sandwich or biscuit? Coffee will not sustain you for the journey."

"It will give me the incentive to stay awake until we arrive." She reached for the cup. "Besides, we're not far from St. Louis now. Wouldn't you prefer to eat at a nice restaurant once we get there?"

"I'll be far too busy determining the logistics of the rest of our trip."

"Then eat if you must. I will satisfy myself with a good book." She reached into her purse and pulled out her book by an author named Emily Brontë.

"*Wuthering Heights*?" Neville observed as he glanced at the book's spine. "Whatever is that about?"

"It's a compelling work of fiction that challenges our very strict British ideals." Abby thumbed through the pages, finally landing on the spot where she'd left off. "The story addresses many modern societal issues, including inequality between the sexes."

Neville's eyes widened. "Doesn't sound like a story your father would approve of at all."

"I dare say, Father could learn a great deal from this book. I'm finding it rather fascinating, myself. Enlightening, really, though there are some rather shocking characters. And the story runs a bit on the dramatic side at times."

He gave her a knowing look. "Read it on the train, but leave it behind once we head home from Oregon. That's my suggestion, anyway. Best not to get your father in a dither."

"If leaving home and traveling halfway across the world isn't enough to get him in a dither, I rather think a book won't do the trick." Abby gave Neville a little wink then settled against the seat, ready to get back to her story.

♥

The sound of gunfire split the air. Sam made a run for the kitchen. "Quick, Cookie!" His voice rang out above the noise from outside The Gold Rush Inn. "Take cover. Those fools are at it again."

The rotund older woman swatted the air with her dishcloth, as if unaffected by the commotion outside. "I'm not afraid of a few bullets whizzing by, Sammy-boy. You know that. Used to it by now. And you know those fellas, killing the hours with a gun in hand."

"Killing the hours or killing each other?" Jin, bottle washer at The Gold Rush Inn, spoke up. "Remember what happened last Thursday."

"Yes, poor Mr. Branson, may he rest in peace." Cookie placed her hand over her heart and appeared to lose herself in her ponderings. " 'Wine is a mocker, strong drink is raging: and whosoever is deceived thereby is not wise.' Proverbs chapter twenty, verse one." She shifted her attention back to Sam. "But I'm not afraid of the prospectors, fellas. I'm the best cook in town. They wouldn't dare let a bullet come near me. These men need me too much to kill me off."

"True." Sam relaxed his stance as he thought through her words.

"So, are we opening for lunch today or just standing in the kitchen gabbing?" Cookie reached for a spoon and gave the large pot a good stir. " 'Cause I've got a mess of chicken and dumplings here that some-one needs to eat. Don't think I could manage all of 'em on my own." She laughed and ran her hands over her rounded belly. "Though it might be fun to try."

"Just give me a few minutes before unbarring the door, Cookie. Let the dust settle from the brawl outside and we'll ring the lunch bell."

"If you want these dumplings hot, you'll open that door sooner rather than later. Can't keep this fire stoked all day. Too stifling in this kitchen."

Sam made his way back into the dining room and eased his way toward the front door. From behind him, his father's voice sounded.

"The boys are having a little fun again, I see."

Sam turned to face his father, surprised to find him dressed in dungarees and a button-up shirt, quite a change from his usual suit and tie.

"If that's what you want to call it." Sam fought the temptation to roll his eyes.

"Take it easy, son. You'll get acclimated. . .with time." His father fussed with his belt, a rustic number he must've picked up at the general store.

"That's what I'm afraid of." Sam would just as soon not, thank you very much. In fact, he'd much rather load up their belongings and head back to Independence. Back home, folks didn't shoot at one another in the street. They didn't whoop and holler when they needed or wanted something. They asked politely. And they certainly didn't come barreling into his family's restaurant, sauced and ready for a fight.

"You headed somewhere, Father?" Sam asked, as his father reached for his hat.

"Mm-hmm. Have an appointment."

Sam released a slow breath and ushered forth a silent prayer that his father wouldn't head over to the local saloon. He'd been disappearing a lot these days, often for hours on end.

As his dad slipped out the front door, a passel of hungry customers flooded inside, their voices sounding like a choir in need of practice. No point in showing any of them to a table. They always managed to find their designated spots without effort from him. And with everyone calling out their "Howdys!" to each other, who could hear him anyway?

Before long, the room was filled to overflowing. "Special of the day is chicken and dumplings, fellas," Sam hollered out above the noise. "With blueberry cobbler for dessert."

"Sounds good enough to eat." Jedediah Tucker rubbed his extended belly. He then turned his attention to a spider crawling across the table. "What's this? An appetizer?" A rowdy laugh followed his words.

Sam disappeared into the kitchen, where he took to filling bowls with heaping mounds of chicken and dumplings, which he loaded onto the largest tray he could find. He hefted the tray over his shoulder and made his way back out to the dining room to feed the rowdy crowd. A couple of the men took to brawling, but the smell of Cookie's dumplings calmed them down in a hurry.

These days, with so few rules pertaining to properties, fellas tended to take the law into their own hands. A punch to the jaw seemed a fine way to stake a claim.

Before long, the noise lessened as men swallowed down bowl after bowl of Cookie's tasty dumplings. There was a certain awe and reverence for Cookie's home-cooked foods, which made for a few moments of silence as they ate. Sam always looked forward to this part of the meal. Of course, they took to hollering once again as he dished up helpings of blueberry cobbler.

Most of these fellas would be back for supper, of course. Many would down their food in a hurry then head over to the Watering Hole for several rounds of whiskey, rotgut, and the like. He shuddered when he thought about what went on over at the local saloon.

When the last of the cobbler had been eaten and the fellas disappeared out the door, Sam glanced around the dining room in disbelief. Upturned chairs. Napkins tossed here and there. Bowls overturned. Blueberry cobbler spilled. Those careless ruffians had torn up the place. Again.

What he wouldn't give to return to his quiet life in Independence, to abandon this free-for-all once and for all.

"You all right, Sammy?" Cookie's voice sounded from behind him and he turned to face her.

"Just thinking about home."

"I understand. Think about it all the time myself."

"I miss neighborly folks. Women in sensible clothing. And children. I miss children. Remember how much fun we had, watching them roll hoops at our church picnics? Such innocence."

"I remember, all right. But there are plenty of children in San Francisco, Sammy, just not in our neck of the woods."

"I know. Just reminiscing about home, I suppose. Do you ever want to go back, Cookie?" He posed the question with great care, knowing her answer could lead to actions bent on affecting them all.

Her eyes narrowed to slits. "Sammy-boy, I've known you since you were a baby. Fed and cared for you from the moment you were old enough to chew a crust of my homemade bread. I've walked you through the valley and kept you fed on the mountaintop. Surely you don't think I'd leave you now."

The sting of tears caught him by surprise. Cookie's dedication to the family ran deep, no denying that.

"You've gone above and beyond, Cookie." He slipped an arm over her shoulder and pulled her close. "And I'm grateful."

"It's what your mama would've wanted, me here with you."

"You don't think she would've wanted both of us back home in Independence, leading a less..." He paused to think through his word choices carefully. "Exciting life?"

"Oh, I don't know." Cookie appeared to lose herself to her thoughts. "Your mother was an adventurous soul. Don't you remember that time she made up her mind to go to Africa after a missionary spoke at your church? It took your father weeks to talk her out of it."

"I'd forgotten." Sam's thoughts took a different turn with the memories of that time in his family's life. "If I recall, Dad frightened her off the idea with some story about cannibalistic natives."

"Yes, sir. He did, indeed."

"And yet, here we are, surrounded by savage natives at every turn." Sam's gaze shifted back to the dining room. "And Father doesn't even seem to notice. What's the difference?"

"The difference is, this is his own personal adventure, not someone else's. And, as far as the natives go, at least they're eating my food and not each other." Cookie laughed. "Other than that, not much difference, I'd say."

Sam pondered her words before speaking. "Father has changed, that's undeniable."

"But not you, son. You're instant in season and out, reproving, rebuking, exhorting with all longsuffering and doctrine. Second Timothy chapter four, verse two. Loosely translated."

He shook his head. "Cookie, I don't know how you do it, but you have a verse for everything, don't you? You're a walking, talking Bible."

"Open and ready to be read by all the local rowdies. And I suppose that's a high compliment, seeing as how the good Lord tells us to shine our light wherever we go."

"Even in San Francisco?" he asked, not completely convinced her words were true.

Cookie slung an arm over his shoulder and nodded. "Yep, Sammy-boy. Even in San Francisco."

Chapter Two

Whatever illusions Abby had about wagon-train travel were given up for lost just a few days outside of St. Louis. She found the experience miserable, morning to night. If not for the scenery and the friendships she made with the other women, the whole thing would have been completely unbearable. How mother had endured such a journey to the Oregon Territory, she could not imagine. Her dainty mother could scarcely dress herself without help from a lady's maid, let alone contend with the daily ordeals that arose from wagon travel.

Somehow the days passed, one upon the other. Abby made it through *Wuthering Heights*, not once, but three times. Though she found the story sobering, it helped pass the time. Just two days shy of the trading post at Fort Hall, she began to get her energy back again. Soon they would come to the fork in the road and would take the path north and west to Mama. She prayed her backside would make it.

As they pulled into town, the wagon jutted up and down, back and forth, until every joint ached.

"My teeth are coming loose." Neville squirmed in his chair. "By the time we arrive I won't be able to eat a thing."

"Don't exaggerate, Neville," she countered. "It's not th–that bad."

"Hmm." He shifted his position in the seat, finally reaching for a small pillow and shoving it underneath him. "There. Don't know why I didn't think of that sooner. You should do the same, Miss Abigail. You will thank me for the idea."

She reached into her belongings and came out with a small blanket, which she folded into a pillow of sorts. She attempted to stand but a sudden dip in the trail pitched the coach to the right and she nearly toppled over. The blanket flew across the space between them, landing in Neville's lap.

"No thank you," he said, and then yawned. "I'm too warm already."

Moments later the driver pulled the horses to a halt, and the wheels of the coach groaned against the gravel path in front of the outpost. Abigail startled, nearly jolted from her seat once again.

"Have we arrived?" She peered out the opening at the front of the wagon and took note of the fact that all the wagons in the company had stopped as well.

"Pretty sure we're camping overnight," Neville said. "The two trails diverge here, Miss Abigail, so it'll be northwest from here on out."

"Sounds like music to my ears."

Neville shook his head. "No, that's the sound of men yelling. Not sure what's got everyone so worked up, but I'll check."

He climbed down from the wagon and disappeared in the direction of the wagon master, who appeared to be arguing with someone. Rather heatedly, in fact. Abby stretched her back, eager to get out of the wagon for a few hours.

The sound of voices, followed by angry shouts and what sounded like an argument, convinced her to stay put. She peeked outside to get a closer look. Neville most certainly did not look happy. He stormed back to the wagon and climbed aboard, his expression tight. "Well, this is a fine kettle of fish."

"What happened, Neville?"

"The road to Oregon has been washed out by spring rains. Our wagon master has just received word that we can't move forward."

Her heart rate quickened. "What does this mean?"

"It means we turn back to St. Louis, Miss Abigail."

"No!" She fought back tears of disappointment. "I'm not going back home, not without Mother in tow."

"We can't get to her, Miss Abigail." Neville gave her a fatherly look. "We have no choice but to turn back."

"There are always choices. Always." She released a slow breath and closed her eyes. What would the character in her novel do at a time like this? She would forge ahead, undeterred.

Moments later, her eyes popped open. "We're at a fork in the road, yes?"

"Yes."

"The other road, where does it lead?"

"California, of course. San Francisco."

She slapped her knees, more excited than ever. "Perfect. We'll go to San Francisco and wait until the roads open. No doubt there's a road to the Oregon Territory from there, one Mother can use to meet us."

"San Francisco?" Neville shook his head, the fear in his expression leaving little doubt of his opinion on that matter.

"Yes. Jimmy Blodgett says it's a fabulous town with endless possibilities. And think about it, Neville. Once I send word to Mother, she will be enticed to join us. You know how she is. She will love the idea, I assure you."

"I can't imagine she would want to make the trip. And who is Jimmy Blodgett, pray tell?"

"The waiter on the train. He told me wonderful stories about how beautiful it is in California, how the rivers are thick with gold, and how people come from all over the globe to experience the wonder that is California."

"You'll pardon my asking, but if this fellow found the rivers to be heavy with gold, then why is he working on a train?"

"Well, that's quite another story." She paused to think through her next words. "One that involves a father who preferred to gamble away the family fortune. But the point is, San Francisco is a bustling port town with adventurous opportunities. Mother can meet us there when the roads clear. Don't you see? For all our hesitation about how we would get her out of Oregon, we now have our answer. We will ask her to come to San Francisco for a vacation, and she will jump at the chance. We will see new and exciting things and so will she. Then, when the dust has settled, we'll all head back home to Philadelphia...together. The perfect solution, don't you think?"

"Perhaps. But...San Francisco?" He shivered. "I have not prepared myself for that. I have heard stories, as well, and they are not as...picturesque...as yours. The kind of adventures I fear would involve thievery, drunkenness, shootings, and women of ill repute. Not the sort of locale I would consider safe or inviting."

"One doesn't plan adventures, Neville. One takes them as they come. See? This is a blessing in disguise."

He gave her a look that shared his thoughts on the matter, then a more reflective look came over him. She knew this look well—one of resignation. "If we're to travel to California, I will need to arrange for our travel. This will be a costly venture, Miss Abigail."

"As all good adventures are." She offered a hopeful smile. "Let's look for the silver lining, shall we?"

"Humph. Don't you mean *gold* lining?"

"Gold, indeed." Endless possibilities took root and her thoughts tumbled in multiple directions at once. Suddenly she could hardly wait to get to San Francisco.

❤

"Sam, what can I do for you?"

Sam looked up from the list in his hand as the mercantile owner called his name. Doing business with Marcus Denueve required careful attention.

"Oh, good morning, Marcus. I've come for our weekly supplies for the restaurant."

"Of course. Same list as always?"

"Yes, but Cookie wants to add an extra pound of sugar and three bags of flour. She plans to do a lot of baking, I think."

"And where is Cookie this fine morning?"

"Up to her eyeballs in pastry dough. Couldn't come this time." Sam didn't want to share the rest of the story, that Cookie had sent him on their weekly grocery run so that he could see firsthand just how Marcus had taken to gouging them.

"Well, I'll have Kennedy get your things." Marcus paused and appeared to be thinking. "You want to take care of this month's bill while you're here, or should I send it at the end of the month, as usual?"

"Whatever works for you."

"I'm always happy to be paid." Marcus ran his fingertips along the edge of his wiry mustache. "As one business owner to another, I'm sure you understand."

"Of course. Happy to oblige."

The elderly store clerk, a wiry fellow named Frankie Kennedy, went to work, gathering the necessary items. Sam bided his time, looking over new merchandise. When Frankie finished, he loaded the groceries into a large crate and lifted it to the counter.

Sam snagged the bill and almost gasped aloud as he scanned the amount. Since when did Marcus charge a dollar for a dozen eggs? And why so much for flour? Was the stuff made of gold?

"Hesitating over the bill, eh?" Marcus's words sounded from behind him and stirred Sam from his ponderings.

Sam bit back a retort as he turned to face the man. "A little shocking, if you don't mind my saying so."

Marcus slapped his arm around Sam's shoulder. "Prices are going up. Can't help that, my friend. Such is the cost of doing business in a place like San Francisco. You, of all people, should know that. Won't be long before your father ups the prices at the inn." He gave Sam a knowing look. "It's bound to happen."

Shrugging out of Marcus's embrace, Sam tried to focus on the conversation at hand. "We're already full-up at the inn. Don't need the extra business."

"All the more reason to charge more. You don't have room to grow the building, but you still have plenty of opportunity to grow your income." Marcus's jaw tensed. "Take a few hints from me, my friend, or risk losing your business. There's plenty of opportunity for growth in San Francisco if you charge accordingly. Everyone's doing it, so the fellas will get used to it over time."

"Prices are going up, yes, but this is far beyond what I would've expected." Sam gave the bill a closer look, stunned at the itemized prices. "Why such a big jump, Marcus? Doesn't make sense."

"Gotta allow for a decent overhead so I can keep this place afloat."

Keep the mercantile afloat? At these prices, the place could be painted in gold and adorned in rare jewels. Marcus was already robbing the prospectors by selling pans for ten dollars apiece instead of a quarter. And the cost of his shovels and rakes? Ridiculous. This fellow knew how to rake in a buck by taking advantage of wide-eyed miners and their families. Now he'd decided to gouge the locals too?

Instead of arguing, Sam pulled out the necessary money, slapped it on the counter, and tipped his hat. "Have a good day, Marcus."

"Same to you. . .neighbor." For whatever reason, Marcus's words didn't sound all that neighborly.

Not that Sam had time to think about it.

Outside the door of the mercantile, Mrs. Linden, the pastor's wife, stood with a slip of paper in hand and a laundry bundle under her arm. She glanced up as Sam passed by.

"Oh, good morning, Samuel." Her brow knotted as she glanced back down at the paper. "I'm sorry, I'm a little preoccupied. Almost didn't see you there." She shuffled the laundry bundle to her other arm, nearly dropping it in the process.

"Is everything all right, Mrs. Linden?"

"Hmm?" She folded the paper and put it in her pocket then ran her palms over her skirt. "I'm sorry. I should've waited to pick up my things from the laundry woman after I'd finished up at the mercantile. It's too hard to juggle."

"Here, let me hold that." He took the laundry from her and gestured for her to sit on a nearby bench.

She plopped down with a thud, then shifted her gaze to him. "To be honest, I'm just perplexed by my bill from the mercantile. We've grown accustomed to paying higher prices here in San Francisco. Much higher, in fact." She leaned in to whisper, "But it's highway robbery to charge a person a dollar and fifty cents for a pair of men's underwear. I've never heard of such a thing. Why, if I told Henry, he'd make me take them back. But, well. . ." Her cheeks flushed. "The man is in need of new things." Her voice lowered and the heightened color on her face subsided. "Though you didn't hear that from me, all right?"

"Of course." Sam bit back a laugh. "Regarding the bill, we are like-minded. What Marcus is doing is wrong on every count."

Her gaze shifted to the front window of the mercantile. "Good to know I'm not alone in my assessment. But what can be done about it?"

"Not sure. Something to pray about, I suppose. In the meantime, we all trim back on our purchases. Perhaps that will teach him a thing or two." Sam glanced over his shoulder as a handful of prospectors headed into the store, likely to purchase supplies to carry out to the river.

"He does a good business, even without us locals." Mrs. Linden sighed. "That's half the problem. He doesn't even need our money, though he's happy to take it. But I do agree we should pray. That is our answer, for every problem."

"Even one as big as Marcus Denueve."

"Even one that big." A faint glint of humor lit her eyes as she patted Sam on the arm. "Give my love to Cookie. Tell her I'll stop by when I have a few minutes. In the meantime, you take care of yourself, Sammy."

He smiled as the minister's wife called him by his nickname. She must've picked up on that by listening to Cookie. Before he could give it further thought, Mr. Hannigan, the local barber, galloped by on a gray horse, hollering something unintelligible. Seconds later, a group of rowdies rushed the street in front of them, guns waving.

Sam stepped into the spot between Mrs. Linden and the ruffians, to protect her from harm. She paled and looked as if she might faint. Thank goodness, the men moved on, their shouts and curse words filling the air between them.

Mrs. Linden fanned herself. Sam took her arm to hold her up as she wobbled. "You know things are getting bad when the locals take to assaulting the barber. Mr. Hannigan has never hurt a soul."

"I heard he shaved off Jedediah Tucker's beard by mistake. Poor guy fell asleep and woke up clean as a whistle. Didn't sit well with him, I guess."

"Oh, I see." She reached inside her pocket and pulled out her bill from the mercantile, which she used as a fan. "Well, that's no reason to threaten a man's life."

"More to pray about, I suppose."

"San Francisco keeps the Almighty on His toes, no doubt about that."

Sam turned his gaze back to the street to make sure the danger had passed. "It does, at that. But He's big enough to handle it all."

"True. He's remarkably big." Mrs. Linden rested her hand on Sam's arm. "If He could help David take down that giant, Goliath, surely He can help us here in San Francisco. Just keep a few stones in your pocket, son."

"Stones?"

"Of course. Just a few river rocks in David's pocket was enough to win the battle."

Sam put his finger over his lips in playful fashion, then pulled it away. "Start talking about river rocks, and before long you'll draw in more miners. Can we take Goliath down with something other than stones?"

"Of course, honey. Prayer. Like I said before. That's our best weapon when it comes to doing battle."

Sam tipped his hat as she turned to go her way. He slipped his hands into the pockets of his trousers, half expecting to come up with river rocks. Instead, he found the bill from the mercantile.

With aggravation setting in, he headed back home, to the Gold Rush Inn.

Chapter Three

$\mathscr{T}$he exhaustion in Abigail's body threatened to diminish the excitement as their private stagecoach drew near San Francisco. Still, she fought to maintain control of her emotions for Neville's sake. The man could barely compose himself after so many weeks of travel. Daily, she chided herself for putting Neville through all of this. Poor fellow.

Just as quickly, Abby reminded herself that this was for Mama. No, for Father, really. To bring Mama home would be the best gift she could give her father, wouldn't it? And surely her mother was ready by now.

Oh, but as she gazed out the window, out onto the vast expanse that was California, Abby could understand why Mother loved to travel. The wide-open spaces. The mountain ranges. The magnificent trees in the distance. The sight of the men setting up camp each night. What an adventure, and how unlike their prim and proper life back in Philadelphia.

She spent the final day of their journey composing a letter to Mother, one she would send as soon as they arrived. After folding the stationery, she pressed it into an envelope and put it in her bag.

"Everything all right, Miss Abigail?" Neville opened one eye to peek at her.

"Right as rain."

"Don't speak of rain." He grunted and shifted his position in the seat. "We would be in Oregon City by now if not for rain, remember?"

She smoothed her skirt and forced a smile. "We're almost in San Francisco, Neville. Minutes away, from what I can gather."

He grunted a response.

"I'm sorry, Neville," she said for the hundredth time. "I don't know what to say except for that."

"No need for apologies. I've told you that many times over, Miss Abigail."

"Still, I feel bad." She leaned back in her seat, her mood shifting from light to dark as the words were spoken. "Are you truly unhappy, Neville, or just a little unhappy?"

A thoughtful look passed over him. "I suppose a man—or woman— is as happy as he or she makes up the mind to be. The Bible tells me I'm to be content in whatever state I'm in and I strive to do that very thing."

"Even in the state of California?"

"Or Pennsylvania. Or Nottingham. I don't suppose it really matters where the Lord places me at any given moment. I've got to learn to be content in that place. So, to answer your question, Miss Abigail, I'm working toward contentment. Not sure that's the same thing as happy, but it's enough to get me through."

"Promise you'll let me know if you're ever really, truly happy?" She waggled her finger in his direction in playful fashion. "Because I'd love to see that face of yours light up in a wicked grin."

"Wicked?" An arched eyebrow indicated his surprise at her choice of wording. "Well, that would be something, now wouldn't it?"

"You know what I mean. I'd love to see you toss caution to the wind and enjoy life more."

"Had my fair share of enjoyable moments as a youth, but that's a story for another day." He pulled back the curtain and peered out the window. "Let's have a look outside, shall we?" After a moment's pause, he added, "Doesn't look a thing like Philadelphia, does it?"

"Not at all. Rugged and sturdy. That's how I'd describe it."

"Only wishing I felt the same." He squirmed in his seat once again.

"Stiff upper lip, Neville. Did it ever occur to you that God might've brought us here for such a time as this?"

"Are you trying to convince me that God had some sort of master plan in shifting our course from Oregon to California?" He gave her a dubious look. "Far as I can recall, spring rains washed out the roads to the Oregon Territory. That's how we came to land in San Francisco."

"He's the God of the wind and rain," Abby countered.

"Pity the poor people who are stranded in Fort Hall just so you could be redirected to California." Neville rolled his eyes.

"I'm just saying the Lord has me here, so He might as well use me. Let's see what He has in store, shall we?"

"I sincerely doubt He plans to use me for any purpose other than protecting you, Miss Abigail. But, again, I am learning to be content in any state I am in, as I said before. So, stiff upper lip, and all that."

Before he could say anything else, the coach made a bend in the road and a town came into view.

"Neville, look!" Abby gasped as she saw the wood-framed buildings, the muddy road, and the men. Lots and lots of men.

"Pulling into town now, folks!" The driver's voice sounded from outside the coach. "Brace yourselves for lots of mud and a roaring welcome from the locals."

Abby didn't need the announcement. Off in the distance a noise caught her attention.

"What is that?" she asked, and then gazed out the window at the saloon to her right. A couple of men stood outside of it, arms waving as they hollered at each other.

"From the sound of it, brawling." Neville gave the place a quick look and then clamped his eyes shut. "What have I done, allowing all of this? I have failed you, Miss Abigail. I should have insisted upon returning home back at Fort Hall."

A gunshot pierced the air and Abby let out a scream.

"No reason to be alarmed, miss," their driver called out. "Just the fellas, celebrating. Happens all the time around here."

"Celebrating? With guns?" Abby could hardly fathom such a thing.

"Well, sure." The man turned her way, offering a near-toothless grin. "Ain't that how they do it where you're from?"

She shook her head. "Back in England we usually host a soiree to celebrate."

"A swore-a?" the fellow drawled. "What's that?"

"A party," she explained. "With guests and fine food."

His face lit in a smile. "Same thing, I reckon. Lotsa folks havin' a swore-a. Fellas around these parts are always ready to have a good time, whether it's on the river with pans in hand or in the saloons and such. Anything to lift the spirits."

"I see."

"Learning to be content," Neville whispered, his gaze shifting to his feet. "Learning to be content."

"Now, if yer lookin' fer good food, head on over to the Gold Rush Inn and give Cookie's pies a try. Best restaurant in town."

"The Gold Rush Inn?" Why did that name sound so familiar? Oh, yes. The waiter on the train had said something similar. This Cookie person must really be a fine baker, to garner so many admirers of her pies. Perhaps a good meal was in order, after all.

"Her real name's Helga," the driver added. "Wonderful woman and the best cook in the gold rush territory. You ain't lived till you've tasted her chicken 'n' dumplin's. They've got magic powers, I tell ya."

"Really?" For the first time in days, Neville looked almost interested.

"Sure. Brawlin' men stop cold when the smell of Cookie's dumplin's fills the room. Forget all about their feuding. And don't even get me goin' on her cherry pie. Folks round these parts bring in their cherries by the bucketful, just so she'll bake more."

"Sounds mighty powerful, indeed," Neville responded. "Though I can't imagine why any woman would want to settle here in California. Doesn't seem like the spot for a lady."

"Hard to find a good cook in a town full of men," the driver agreed. "When we come across a gal with talent, we hold on tight to her. I'd be willin' to bet nearly a dozen men have proposed to Cookie in the past year or so, but none have won her heart. It's better fer the rest of us if she spends her life as a spinster. That way she'll go on cookin' fer all of us, not just one fella."

"As if marrying would have to put an end to a woman's career." Abby clucked her tongue. "Honestly, such an old-fashioned notion."

"If she's half as good as you say, I will propose to her myself. Then I will take her far, far away from this godforsaken place, back to civilization." Neville's strained smirk spoke of sarcasm. "All the way to England, if I have my druthers."

The driver shook his head. "Oh, no, sir. She won't leave. Not Cookie. Her heart's planted right here in San Francisco."

"She's not the woman for me, then, no matter how remarkable her cooking skills." Neville shifted in his seat, and she could read the discomfort in his expression. Not that Abby blamed him. She could hardly bear the pain herself.

"After all the meals we've eaten on the road, I'm happy to give her my business." Abby's stomach growled just thinking about it. How many days had they gone, living on dried meats and fruits and such? The idea of a fresh, hot meal sounded heavenly.

"She's not the only woman in town with a thriving business," the driver added. "If you need your clothes washed, take 'em to Maggie O'Callahan at the laundry. She's as Irish as they come and has the best sense of humor in town. You'll leave laughin' every time and your clothes will be clean as a whistle."

"If there's one thing I love, it's a comedic laundrywoman." Neville rolled his eyes. "Now, if you please, tell us about the Ivory Tower. That's where we're staying while in San Francisco."

"I love the name." Abby leaned out and scanned the street, looking for a hotel with that moniker.

"I have one thing to say." The driver gave her a pensive look. "If you're staying at the Ivory Tower, be prepared to empty your pockets."

"Oh?"

"Yes. Prices in San Francisco are sometimes ten or twenty times what you'd pay elsewhere. Or higher. You'll learn that firsthand at the Ivory Tower."

"For pity's sake." Why hadn't Jimmy Blodgett warned her of this? She might've chosen another destination. Her mind went at once to the cash in her bag. She would have to tread carefully, if they were to stay more than a few weeks.

"The town is much larger than it looks at first," he added. "Sixteen hotels and over a dozen banks. And two hundred attorneys." He laughed. "Trust me when I say that, in spite of 'em, lawlessness abounds."

"Goodness gracious."

"Blame it on Gold Fever, I suppose. Of course, we have the Vigilance Committee now. They take care of lawlessness in their own way." His right brow arched. "Ask one of the locals to tell you the story about what happened a couple years ago when a fella tried to steal a safe from a local store." The driver slapped his knee and laughed. "Let's just say he was tried by a jury and hung that same night."

"For pity's sake," Abby said again. "What have I done?"

"Folks have no sense of control. And to think, this all started with a Mormon missionary."

"Really?" She couldn't picture a missionary bringing lawlessness.

"Fellow by the name of Samuel Brannan. Ask Cookie to tell you the story. She's met him in person."

"I will."

Moments later, the driver brought the wagon to a stop in front of the hotel. Abby took his hand to make the jump down into the muddy street. She landed with a squish, then groaned when she realized the mud contained a bit more than she'd bargained for. Horses had recently happened by and left behind manure.

"My poor boots."

Oh well. No bother. Someone at the hotel would help her clean them. Either that, or Neville would do the deed.

She didn't have long to ponder the condition of her boots. A piercing "Woo-hoo!" sounded from behind her, followed by a loud whistle.

"Ain't she a beauty?" A stout fellow ran his fingers along his scraggly beard as he looked Abby up one side and down the other.

"A fine specimen," another called out.

A couple of catcalls followed, and Abby vacillated between feeling humiliated and wanting to slug these fellows upside their heads. How dare they carry on as if she were some kind of farm animal? Did these men have no manners at all?

"Pay them no mind, miss," the driver said. "These poor prospectors ain't seen a pretty face round these parts since the reverend showed up with his wife in tow. And she's an older gal, not half as pretty as you."

She released a slow breath and tried to get her bearings as she pondered the driver's words.

"What did you call the men again?" she asked.

"Prospectors."

Judging from the way several of the fellas ogled her, they saw her as some sort of prospect. A shiver ran down her spine as a particularly seedy man in filthy dungarees looked her up and down.

"It's not too late to return to St. Louis, Miss Abigail." Neville's thoughts came out through clenched teeth. "A good night's sleep, a hot meal, and we can turn right around and head back to where we came from, forget this ever happened."

"But we've only just arrived, Neville. Remember? And you're learning to be content in every state. That includes the state of California."

"Is it too late to take back that sentiment?"

"Yes. And besides, I promised you an adventure. We haven't even had that yet."

"Speak for yourself, Miss Abigail. I've had enough adventure for a lifetime."

Perhaps he had, but. . .As Abby glanced out over the rugged town, as she took in the buildings, the people, the horses. . .she could only come to one conclusion: there were plenty of adventures ahead.

❤

Sam could tell from the whooping and hollering that the fellas must've clamped eyes on a woman, but which one? Most had stopped flirting with Cookie ages ago. Must be one of the saloon girls, out and about. Not that the saloon girls came out much in the mornings.

He glanced up to see what all the fuss was about and his gaze landed on a girl—no, a woman—with loose tendrils of hair the color of honey-wheat, which softened a lovely delicate face. She wore a tailored traveling suit in a shade of dark blue, and her eyes, wide with wonder, darted this way and that as she took in her surroundings. Definitely not a saloon girl. This was a high-class gal, if such a thing could be gathered from outward appearances.

"Easy, boy." Cookie rested her hand on his shoulder.

He turned to face her. "What do you mean?"

"Nothing. Just. . .easy."

He paused before heading the young woman's way, but the rowdy men forced his hand. "I've got to protect her from the fellas, Cookie. You can see that."

"I dare say that highfalutin fella standing next to her will take care of that for you. He's garnering up the courage to punch a couple of those ruffians in the jaw."

Sam shifted his attention to the man—looked to be in his fifties—standing next to the young woman. The poor man looked even more dazed than the young woman, and certainly not capable of handling the crowd of men pressing in on them.

"Her father, you think?" Sam asked.

Cookie grunted. "Doesn't look like the fatherly type, and they bear no resemblance to one another, that's sure and certain. Can't really peg him, to be honest. A little too scrawny for the likes of San Francisco. Not that I'm one to judge a fellow before a proper how-do-you-do. So, I'll just take myself over there and make introductions. That's the only way to get our questions answered. And while I'm visiting with him, I might convince him to shave off those long sideburns. The poor man will never last in San Francisco looking so fancy."

At that moment, one of the men lunged at the girl, and Sam could contain himself no longer. He barreled into the street, yanked the man back, and stepped into place next to the beautiful stranger.

"Back up, all of you," he hollered. "Give her some room."

No one made a move.

"I said, back up!" He raised his voice, surprised by his own confidence. Any minute now one of these men might give him a black eye for interfering, but that didn't stop him from trying. "Make room for the lady."

The men continued their taunting and flirting.

Sam had just about given up when a shot rang out, piercing the air. The men turned at once to see Cookie, who stood on the front porch of the Gold Rush Inn, pistol raised to the sky.

"You heard Sam, fellas. Leave that woman alone or you'll never eat another piece of my cherry pie."

The crowd dispersed at once.

Sam didn't know whether to be embarrassed that he couldn't handle the men on his own, or grateful that Cookie had come to the rescue.

He glanced at the terrified woman, who looked as if she might faint. "Are you all right?"

"I. . .I think so." She gave him a half-smile, but he could read the terror in her eyes.

"These fellows mean no harm, though that might be hard to believe."

"I believe you." She seemed to relax a bit with these words. "I think I'm just weary from traveling. This will all look rosier after I've had some sleep."

"Have you made lodging arrangements? I would offer you a room at our inn, but we're all booked up."

"She can stay with me." Cookie pressed her pistol back into its holster. "Don't mind a bit."

"No, no." The woman looked distressed. "We've made arrangements at the Ivory Tower."

"The Ivory Tower?" Sam had wondered how anyone could afford the place since the owner's most recent price hike.

He didn't have time to ponder this for long, because the woman's knees buckled and she started to go down. He caught her just in time and nudged a hand under each arm to prop her up.

"Hang on, miss." He slipped his arm around her waist and she leaned into him. "We'll get you to the Ivory Tower, and the sooner the better."

♥

Abby slept long and hard in the lush feather bed at the Ivory Tower. She'd never known such exhaustion. When she awoke, the afternoon hours were upon her. A quick glance out the window to the street below showed the city of San Francisco in full swing. Men dressed in rustic attire swarmed the road, many with a bottle in hand. Others hung on the arms of women in bright satin dresses and ruffled skirts. The whole street was abuzz with activity. How she'd managed to sleep through it was a miracle.

She went in search of a bath and located one inside the hotel, meant for guests only. Certainly a finer option than the bathhouse they'd passed as their coach pulled into town. She relaxed in the warm water, feeling somewhat revived. Until her stomach rumbled.

By the time she was dressed once more, shadows of the evening were hovering overhead. Still her stomach would not stop complaining. If she didn't eat soon, she would be ill.

Abby knocked on Neville's door and he opened moments later. She was stunned to discover he had already organized his room. The open trunk was completely emptied, and his traveling suit was pressed and hung on a wall peg in the corner of the room.

"Gracious, someone's been busy."

"Indeed. Preparing for our return trip, Miss Abigail."

"Return trip?"

"Naturally."

"But we've just arrived. And what about learning to be content?"

"I will not allow you to stay in this place of. . .of. . ." His eyes narrowed as he spit out the word. "Degradation."

"Neville, don't exaggerate."

"Have you looked out the window? Have you seen those. . .those. . . women?" He spoke through clenched teeth. "Degradation is the only word to describe the current state of affairs. I cannot, under any circumstances, learn to be content in such a place as this. Your father would be appalled at the way those men treated you upon our arrival and, frankly, terrified to see you in this current situation. I must rectify it at once. I've let this go on far too long, as it is. I have some chance to redeem myself, but I must move quickly."

"Rectify the situation?" Abby shook her head as she pondered his words. "How, Neville? Can you build a road to Oregon?"

"No, but I can most certainly take you back home to Philadelphia, where you will be safe."

"But Mama. . ."

"Will return home in her own time. You must come to terms with that, Miss Abigail. This is not your problem to fix."

"But I—"

"Now, I don't want to be a bother, but we really must make our plans to leave. I've tended to my clothes and will see to yours after dinner."

"But we've only just arrived."

"And have already overstayed our welcome. Look around you, Miss Abigail. Or, rather, don't. Conditions are deplorable. Simply deplorable. I cannot sit idly by and watch these men behave in such an ungentlemanly fashion. I must assume the fatherly role. So, after dinner I will pack your bags and book a coach to St. Louis, where we will catch the train for home. Not that I've ever considered Philadelphia home, but it's a sure sight closer than this."

Anger rose up inside of her. Abby placed her hands on her hips, ready to state her opinion with clarity. "Neville, I'm a grown woman and I can certainly take care of myself. If you're so intent upon returning home, then do so, but please don't presume to tell me what to do. I've come after my mother. She won't budge, I feel sure, until she's seen me in person. I will wait as long as I must to see her face to face." Abby regretted the words as soon as she saw the deflated look in Neville's eyes.

"Miss Abigail, I implore you. . ."

"We will be in a better position to make such decisions after we've had a good meal." She slipped her arm through his. "That's why I came calling, actually, to summon you to dinner."

"Are you sure you're ready to face that crowd in the street again?"

"From what I understand, Cookie's food will be worth it."

He squared his shoulders, clearly standing his ground. "I will not cross the River Jordan, even if the Promised Land lies on the other side."

"Cherry pie."

His eyes glazed over.

"Now, come on, Neville. Let's go eat some dinner, rest awhile, and make plans in the morning. What do you say to that?"

"I say. . .I say. . ." His shoulders slumped forward. "This cherry pie had better be the best I've ever tasted. Otherwise we've traveled all the way from Philadelphia to San Francisco for nothing."

Abby gave him the broadest smile she could muster then guided him out into the hallway. She could almost taste that cherry pie now.

Chapter Four

*D*inner at the Gold Rush Inn was all Abby had expected and more. Not that she could keep her eyes open long enough to enjoy it fully. By the time the last nibble of cherry pie had been swallowed, she very nearly fell asleep at the table.

Neville managed to rouse her long enough to see her back to the Ivory Tower, where she dressed in her nightgown and tumbled into that cozy bed.

All night long, Abby dreamed about cherry pie. She could still taste it, even in her sleep. Images of cherries floated by, followed by memories of that handsome stranger—the one who had rescued her from the rowdy local men. She'd seen him again at the inn, this time hard at work, waiting tables. Funny, that he would land in her dreams as well. Not that she minded. Not at all.

The following morning, Abby awoke with a thousand thoughts running through her head. She needed to send the letter to Mother, of course, and some sort of message to Father as well. He would be worrying about her, no doubt. How would he take the news of their diversion to San Francisco? Only time would tell, but she could anticipate concern from his end.

After a quick breakfast at the hotel, she advised Neville of her intentions and he insisted upon accompanying her to the post office. Thank goodness the main street was virtually void of cowboys and miners this morning. Perhaps they were sleeping in. No doubt the loud music coming from the nearby saloon late last night kept them awake.

Neville seemed in better spirits this morning, though he insisted on keeping a watchful eye on her as she made her way across the street toward the post office.

"You would be proud of the way I worded my message to Mother, Neville. I made San Francisco sound like a glorious adventure, something she won't want to miss out on."

"A work of fiction?" he countered.

"Hardly. I've told her that the city is teeming with life, night and day. That people are arriving daily from all over the world. That San Francisco boasts the most eclectic, diverse people one could ever wish to meet."

"That would be putting it mildly."

"I've reminded her that a visit to California is a visit to the gold capital of the world."

Neville responded with a grunt. "I would prefer to send a note stating that we are leaving San Francisco by tomorrow morning, if it's all the same to you."

After mailing the letter to her mother, Abby followed up with a telegraph to Father. He would, no doubt, be relieved to hear from her after no word since St. Louis.

"I need to make a stop at the mercantile, Neville," she said as they stepped out of the telegraph office. "I am in need of a few personal items."

"Of course." He gave her a curt nod. "And I am in need of a shave and a haircut. I took note of a barbershop just a few doors down. Perhaps I could spend a few minutes inside while you shop."

"Perfect. That will give me time to get what I need."

"If you're sure you can manage without me."

"I'm not a child, Neville," she said for the hundredth time.

He merely shrugged.

They parted ways at the door of the mercantile and she walked inside. What was it about a general store that always made her feel at home? This one had a broad selection of merchandise, things she was familiar with, but odd things as well. Shovels. Pans. Gloves. Things that miners would need.

As Abby perused the merchandise, she was approached by a man in a business suit. For a moment, she almost forgot she'd landed in a rugged western town. This man had all the markings of a Philadelphia gentleman from his styled hair to his tailored attire. The clear-cut lines of his profile caught her attention at once as did the dark hair and trimmed mustache.

A smile turned up the edges of the handsome stranger's lips, revealing two well-placed dimples. This drew her to him even more. "Well now, I don't believe we've met." His eyes twinkled as he fixed his gaze on her. "And I was sure I knew everyone in town." He stuck out his hand. "Marcus Denueve. And you are. . .?"

"Abigail Effingham. Just arrived in town yesterday afternoon. I knew some Denueves years ago, from Paris."

"The town of my birth." He brought his hand to his chest, as if overcome by this news. "But I call San Francisco home now. Are you here to stay?"

"Not at all. Just passing through."

"Pity." He offered an exaggerated pout. "But now that you mention it, I'd heard that a pretty lady had arrived. The men didn't exaggerate."

Abby hardly knew how to respond to such a comment. She tried not to let her gaze linger on the man but couldn't help herself. Dark wavy hair, deep-blue eyes, the color of the dress she now wore. Clean-shaven face, unlike most of the men in town. Father would approve of this man, no doubt. Judging from his dialect, he'd only been in the States a few years, at best. She could still hear the warmth of Paris in his voice.

"Welcome, Miss Effingham." His handsome face lit in an inviting smile. "We trust you will stay on for some time and get to know us better."

She could listen to this man speak for hours. That rich, melodic tone felt familiar, as if she were talking to an old friend from home.

"I hope to stay until my mother arrives from the Oregon Territory," she managed at last. "That can't happen until the roads open up."

"Won't be long now. But we look forward to getting to know you better in the meantime."

By "we" she felt sure he meant "he." Abby cleared her throat.

"I will leave you in the care of my head clerk, Mr. Kennedy." Mr. Denueve tipped his hat and walked away.

The clerk, a wiry older fellow, glanced her way. "What can I do for you today?"

Clearly not French. Midwest, perhaps?

"I need a few things for my stay, starting with ladies' personal things."

"Don't have much of a selection of items for women-folk, but what we have is right over here." He led the way to a lone shelf filled with serviceable items for females.

"Perfect. I'll take two of these. . ." She pointed at the unmentionables. "And four of these." She picked up several handkerchiefs.

He snatched them and tucked them under his arm. "Anything else?"

"Talcum powder, please, and licorice, if you carry it. That will do for now."

She followed him to the counter and reached for her purse. "How much do I owe you?"

"Six dollars and fifty cents."

"W–what?" Abby could scarcely catch her breath. "Six dollars and fifty cents?"

"Yep." He continued the task of wrapping her items, oblivious to her inner wrangling.

"For these few things? I could have purchased them back in Philadelphia for a fraction of that price."

"You're in San Francisco now, and things are a bit different here."

"You can say that twice and mean it." She glanced down at her purchases, her thoughts in a whirl. "Well, in that case I'll have to adjust the number of items. I'll just take one handkerchief, thank you, and skip the licorice."

This news appeared to aggravate the clerk, who huffed as he tallied up her purchases again. She paid the necessary money and turned on her heel, nearly running into Marcus Denueve. She almost lost her bundle in the process.

"Excuse me, Miss Effingham." Mr. Denueve tipped his hand. "Didn't mean to get in your way there."

"Oh, I'm fine." A bit flustered, but fine.

"You are, indeed." This time his words left little doubt to his meaning.

"Well, I should really be on my way. I need to head back to the hotel and get settled in. I'll need to locate the laundry and then the bank."

"I could help you with that."

"Surely I can find them on my own."

"But you're not from around these here parts, are you now?" He gave her an inquisitive look. "You'll need a navigator."

"Nottingham. England."

"I see. Miss Effingham from Nottingham. Very nice." He stroked his chin and appeared to be giving her a solid once-over. "They grow 'em pretty in Nottingham."

"Th–thank you."

"In which hotel are you staying, Miss Effingham?"

"The Ivory Tower."

"Finest place in town, befitting a lovely lady like yourself." He crooked his arm. "Please allow me to walk you back."

She shook her head and rejected his offer of kindness. "Thank you, but I do not require a chaperone."

His expression spoke otherwise. "Clearly you do not know San Francisco."

"Clearly you do not know me." She offered what he hoped would look like a convincing smile.

"I see. Well, watch out for yourself, Miss Effingham."

"I always do. Besides, I'm not headed back to the hotel just yet. I have to stop off at the barbershop first."

"Oh?" His arched eyebrows showed his surprise. "In want of a shave and mustache trim?"

She fought the temptation to roll her eyes at his silly joke. "No. I am meeting Neville."

"Neville?" Mr. Denueve's brow wrinkled in what could only be construed as curiosity. "Your beau?"

She laughed. "Oh, for pity's sake, no. Neville's our family butler. He accompanied me because Father wouldn't allow me to travel alone. He's rather old-fashioned like that."

"Your father, or the butler?"

"Well, both, actually." She laughed. "But I need to go quickly, if you don't mind, because Neville will worry. That's what he does, you see, when he's not got me in his sights."

"I can see why a man would worry not to have you in his sights."

My goodness, but this man could flirt. Of course, the French accent made the whole thing rather enjoyable, but she would never admit that to anyone other than herself.

Abby bid Mr. Denueve good day and walked a few doors down to the barbershop, which was teeming with boisterous men. Within a minute or two of her arrival, she regretted it. Neville was in the process of being shaved—that, she could see through the window—but took no notice of her. The other men in the shop, however, did. Whistles and catcalls followed. Either Neville had fallen asleep or was completely oblivious. He did not stir from his place in the chair.

Just when she'd decided to take a step inside the barbershop, a voice sounded from behind her. "I don't recommend it, miss."

She turned to discover the handsome young man who had come to her rescue in the street the day before, the same fellow she'd seen at the Gold Rush Inn last night. Abby couldn't see past the specks of gold in those beautiful green eyes. He raked his fingers through his blond wavy hair and shook his head. "You'll be taking your life into your hands if you do."

Abby certainly didn't want to risk danger to fetch Neville, but what choice did she have, save the obvious one of standing here, staring into the most handsome face in town?

❤

Sam couldn't believe his luck as he clamped eyes on the beautiful young woman dressed in blue. After yesterday's episode with the men, he had wondered about her well-being. He'd taken note of her at the restaurant last night, of course. He'd seen the way she'd downed that cherry pie. But to find her here, at a barbershop? Seemed a bit odd.

"As I said, I wouldn't go in there, Miss. . ."

"Abby. Er, Abigail Effingham." She seemed to stumble over her own name.

"If there's someone inside you need, I'll be happy to fetch him for you."

"Oh, I don't need anyone to be fetched, exactly. I just wanted to let Neville know that I'm out here, waiting for him."

"I'll be happy to share that information. Just stay put, and if any of those men come around, don't talk to them."

She looked aghast at this notion. Her gloved hand flew to cover her mouth, then she pulled it away. "They will find me unsociable."

"It's best if they find you unapproachable, and that's a different thing altogether."

"Hmm."

He pointed to the bench in front of the shop, and she sat like an obedient child. Then Samuel went inside to fetch Neville, whom he found sleeping in the chair underneath a hot towel. Unwilling to disturb the fellow, he walked back outside to join Miss Abigail. Perhaps this was a stroke of fate.

"Won't be much longer," he said as he took a seat next to her on the bench.

"Ah. Well then, I'll wait."

"And I'll wait with you, if you don't mind. Can't abide the thought of leaving you alone."

"Neville asked you to do that, no doubt."

"Not at all." Sam cleared his throat. "But your saying that he might convinces me that he cares a great deal about your well-being. He's not your father, then?"

"He's my family's butler. His caring can be a bit. . .stifling."

"I'm not sure we've been properly introduced." Sam extended his hand. "I'm Samuel Harris. My father owns the Gold Rush Inn." He gestured with his head to their family-run business across the street. "I believe you had dinner with us last night."

"Best cherry pie I've ever eaten in my life."

"That's Cookie for you. She's top notch."

The young woman clasped her hands together with obvious zeal. "She's renowned. I heard about her in Missouri, you see."

"You heard about Cookie in Missouri?" This caught him by surprise. "Really?"

"A waiter on our train. Do you know a Jimmy Blodgett?" She shifted her bundle to the bench.

"Name sounds familiar."

"He lived here a few years back. Came with his father. Now he works for the railroad. But, apparently, Cookie's good home cooking made quite an impression on him. He sang her praises. Loudly."

"Well, go figure. I'm from Missouri myself."

"I could have placed you, based on your speech." The young woman folded her hands and placed them in her lap in ladylike fashion.

"Really?"

"Yes, but you have the western drawl down, as well. Fascinating mix."

"Drawl?"

"Ever so slight." A smile softened her lips. "Have I offended you?"

"Not in the least." He found all of this intriguing, in fact.

"You seem well acclimated."

"Acclimated?" He laughed. "You have no idea how hard I've worked not to be acclimated to this area. I'm the opposite of most everyone you see here—a fellow with a solid upbringing. No rowdy, raucous free-for-alls. No gambling. No drinking. Born and raised with the same neighbors, same church folks on Sundays."

"Rather out of your element, then."

Her words had a lilt, an unusual accent, one he couldn't quite place. "Say that again."

She repeated the phrase: "Rather out of your element, then."

He did his best not to repeat the words aloud. "Sounds so different when you say it. Where are you from?"

"England, of course. Nottingham, by way of London."

"I wish I had your gift for picking up on speech patterns. Couldn't quite figure it out."

"I'm still speaking English, you know."

"A different version than the English I grew up with in Independence."

"But English, all the same."

The air hung thick between them and Samuel couldn't tell if he had offended her or not. "Can you teach me to sound like that?" he asked after a moment.

Abby cocked her head. "Now I know you're making fun of me."

"I'm not. The Gold Rush Inn could stand a bit of refinement. Let's start with my speech. You turn me into a proper gentleman, and we'll attract a finer crowd."

"I've no need to change you. Why, I barely even know you." She flattened her palms against her skirt.

"You can't picture me in a fine suit with slicked-back hair?"

Her cheeks flushed as she looked at him. "I can picture it."

"Then teach me your ways and I shall be your willing pupil." He did his best to sound formal. "Our patrons will thank you."

Her gaze traveled to the Gold Rush Inn with its chipped paint and crumbling exterior. "I doubt your patrons will care, one way or the other. You'll pardon my saying so, at least I hope you will, but if I had stumbled across an inn with the words 'gold rush' in the name, I might have anticipated something altogether different."

"Oh?" Sam gazed at the inn and tried to see it through her eyes. "How so?"

A thoughtful look passed over her. "Well, the word gold brings to mind refinement. Beauty. Elegance."

He snorted. "Around here, the word gold brings to mind mining, Levis, icy river waters, and panning."

"I see." Her nose wrinkled, and for the first time he noticed a splattering of freckles. "Nevertheless, an inn with such a name might be a little more..."

"Fancy?"

"Tidy. If you'll forgive me for stating the obvious."

Sam gave the building a closer look. "I'll admit, she could use a bit of a fix-up, but Father hasn't had time for that. He's been too busy taking care of the bills associated with the running of such a place." And what bills they were, especially the ones from Marcus Denueve.

"Folks always say you can't judge a book by its cover—or in this case, an inn by its exterior—but I disagree. Folks do judge by outward appearance, whether we like to admit it or not."

"Not the fellas around here, I assure you. As long as they have a pillow to rest their head and a hot meal, they are happy."

She gave him an incredulous look. "But aren't you trying to attract a new crowd, perhaps bring in the type of people who wouldn't ordinarily frequent such a place?"

"Such a place?" Surely she didn't mean to trample on his toes, but the words stung.

At once her expression softened. "I'm sorry. I'm just saying that you could bring in a high-end clientele if you put a lovely facade on the front of the building."

"We're not lacking for business, if that's your implication. We rarely have a room to spare, trust me. I'm not looking for new—what did you call it, again? Clientele?"

"Yes." Abby gave the building another look. "Forgive me. I've overstepped." She turned his way with an apologetic look. "I tend to do that. I suppose you could call me a fixer."

"No harm done. And for the record, I was just joking when I asked you to teach me how to speak. I don't need a facade, and neither does our building. The men around here could care less about formalities. They're looking for serviceable, not fancy."

"Then they will appreciate the handkerchiefs at the general store."

"Beg your pardon?"

"Nothing." She shook her head. "I must agree that the people here are different, but I find them fascinating."

"Half these men come in here wide-eyed, filled with wonder and hope. The other half have watched the rivers play out. They're regretting the money they've wasted over the past couple of years and the gold nuggets they've thrown around like pieces of dirt. Wishing they had it all back."

"Big money, big problems." Abigail released a sigh. "That's what my father always says."

"Your father is right." Samuel gave her a tender glance. "Sounds like a good man."

"He is. Just a little. . .preoccupied."

"With business?"

"Yes. As are many men, I suppose. But Father would have been better served to pay more attention to the goings-on at home. Maybe then Mother wouldn't have. . ." Her words drifted off and her cheeks blazed red. "I'm sorry. I've said too much."

"Folks always say I'm the kind of fella you can talk to about pretty much anything. And as for what you've said, it's a good reminder to keep things in balance, I suppose. I've watched my father do the same thing. I dare say he will have many regrets at the end of his days, having chosen the love of money over the love of family."

"Precisely."

She gave him a sympathetic glance, and in that moment, he felt they probably had more in common than he'd imagined.

"Our fathers are not the only men to set their sights on money." She turned back toward the barbershop window, appearing more anxious than before.

"The town is full of such men. Ever heard the phrase 'chain reaction'?"

"Of course."

"Well, that's what's happened here. That first nugget was found, and word got out. Next thing you know, folks started trickling in. Then they came like a flood. Then, before we knew it, we were drowning in people from all over the world."

"I've never seen such a mix of cultures before, though Jimmy told me to expect it." She pointed to a group of men walking by. "Chinese?"

"By the thousands."

"They've come such a long way to seek their fortune. I do hope they find what they're looking for."

"They have families to feed back home. A trip—however hazardous—to the Land of Opportunity, and they can care for their families' needs for a lifetime. Most have set up shop and earn their gold that way, not from the rivers."

"Wise."

"We've got fellas from Central America too. And Germany. Name your country and it's represented here. San Francisco has become a melting pot of cultures."

"Fascinating."

"One fellow tried to pay me in foreign coins. I had to turn him down. You'll find lots of languages here, but only one common currency."

"The dollar bill?" she asked.

"Gold nuggets. Don't be surprised if the fellas tip in gold. But beware fool's gold. It'll get you every time."

"My goodness. Well, speaking of gold, I've found the prices here to be rather. . ."

"Shocking?"

"To say the least. I'm stunned. I'm not sure how long we'll be staying at the Ivory Tower." She released a sigh and he could read the disappointment in her eyes.

"I'm afraid we're all full up at the Gold Rush Inn, unless you happen to be looking for a job. I've got a room waiting for our new cook's assistant."

"Job?" Those beautiful blue eyes widened.

"Yep. You interested?"

"Oh, no, I. . ." She looked stunned by the very suggestion, and he was sorry he'd brought it up.

"How long are you planning to stay?"

"Until the roads open up to Oregon Territory."

"You've got a few weeks then. Spring thaws always wash 'em out until at least June."

"I see." She paused and appeared to lose herself to her thoughts. "What sort of position did you say you're wanting to fill?" she asked after a few moments of silence. "I'm not saying I'm interested, but in case I stumble across someone who is."

"I need someone to help out Cookie in the kitchen and to help me wait tables. Ever done anything like that before?"

She shook her head.

"Never too late to start. You'd catch on quick."

"Doubtful, but I will keep it in mind." She jerked to her feet and grabbed her bundle. "Now, if you don't mind, I'll be on my way to the hotel. I'm suddenly exhausted."

"What about your butler?"

"If you don't mind, please tell him I've gone on ahead." Abigail turned on her heel and headed down the road toward the Ivory Tower.

Chapter Five

The decision to stay on in San Francisco was an easy one, at least to Abby's way of thinking. Neville didn't appear convinced, and all the less whenever they had to venture outdoors, where the local men caroused the days away. Abby got used to the jeers and even the marriage proposals, and learned to ignore them as she made her way back and forth to the various shops and the restaurant.

One thing troubled her, though. The dwindling finances were a bit of an issue. She could always appeal to Father's good nature, of course. He wouldn't leave her hanging. She knew that in her heart of hearts. He would spring for more time at the Ivory Tower, but she couldn't really justify spending that kind of money, just for a bed to sleep in.

After a full week in town, Abby and Neville settled into a routine that included daily meals at the Gold Rush Inn. On the first Friday in June, they made their trek to the restaurant for breakfast. Along the way, several men hollered their affections, one pausing to bow the knee while he hollered, "Marry me, honey!"

Abby responded with the words, "I'll have to think about it," to which Neville slapped himself on the forehead.

They settled in at the restaurant and Cookie approached their table, coffeepot in hand. She filled Abby's cup and offered a welcoming smile. Then she turned Neville's way.

"I know, I know. Tea, not coffee. I'll have to set the kettle on to boil, so it'll be a few minutes."

"Good tea is worth waiting for."

"Glad you think my tea is good." She gave him a little wink and his cheeks turned red.

"I wouldn't go that far, but it's a sure sight better than coffee."

"Then you haven't tried my coffee." The cook gave him a knowing look. "You'd be singing a different tune altogether."

"Nevertheless, tea it will be." Neville gave her a knowing look.

"Certainly. Tea for the faint of heart." Her right eyebrow elevated. "Now, bacon or sausage, folks?"

"Mmm. Bacon," Abby responded.

"And you like your eggs sunny side up, if I recall."

"You're really good, Cookie." She gave the woman an admiring look.

"Thanks." The friendly cook gave her a little wink and then turned to face Neville. "Don't tell me. Two slices of bacon, crisp, and one egg, poached."

"Please and thank you."

Cookie shifted the coffeepot to her other hand. "Knew I'd get it right. Don't get many orders for poached eggs around here. Now, how are you two managing? Things going well?"

Abby placed her napkin on her lap and smoothed it with her palms. "In one week's time, I've received four proposals of marriage, one indecent offer that I dare not repeat aloud, and a plea from one of the miners to encourage all of my unmarried friends to move to San Francisco at their earliest possible convenience."

"Oh my."

"Indeed." Abby sighed. "These offers are coming at me so fast they're making my head spin. And to think, we've only been in town seven days. I could be happily married by now."

Neville's nose wrinkled. "Your father would be appalled at the very idea of that."

"No doubt. Though I dare say he would be rather proud of me for forging ahead undeterred."

"Sounds like a reasonable fellow." Cookie gave her a nod. "But I still

JANICE THOMPSON

say keep your distance. These fellas are too brave for their own good."

"Oh?"

"I've seen some of 'em win or lose their shirts—and by shirts, I mean their whole fortune—in a matter of minutes."

"By gambling?"

"Yes, and don't even ask how they spend their money outside of the gambling halls." She gestured with her head toward a woman in a dark-green silk dress just outside the open door of the restaurant. "Let's just say these farm boys from the Midwest have made other discoveries than merely gold."

"Oh, I see." Abby did her best not to gasp aloud as she witnessed a young woman walk right up to a fellow and plant a kiss on his cheek, right there in front of everyone.

Abby felt her cheeks grow warm. "Gracious." She fanned herself.

Cookie shook her head. "It's all around you here. You can either close your eyes to it or use it as an opportunity to pray. Me? I've been on my knees for nigh on two years now, giving the Almighty my suggestions for how to fix this."

"And yet. . ." Abby didn't complete her sentence. Instead, she found herself captivated by a familiar handsome man who passed by the front door of the restaurant.

"Keep your distance from that one," Cookie whispered. "Marcus Denueve. Owner of the general store."

"Oh, right. I met him my second day in town. He's a rare gentleman in this town. And so handsome."

"Yes, well, handsome is as handsome does, so they say."

"What do you mean?" Abby asked.

"Let's just say men in California do things they would never think of doing elsewhere," Cookie said ominously. "Shameful things. Dangerous things. But I dare say they would be better off living within the confines of a few biblical rules, starting with 'Love thy neighbor as thyself.'"

She'd no sooner gotten the words out than a man on the sidewalk punched another in the jaw. The second man went toppling backward, hitting a pole and then falling into the street.

"See what I mean?" Cookie walked over and shut the front door. "Love thy neighbor."

"Indeed." Abby brushed loose hairs out of her face. "Is it always like this?"

"Usually."

"Why are they so angry?"

"They're not. They're bored. And intoxicated."

"I've been bored before. I didn't take it out on my neighbor's face."

"You're a young woman with a proper upbringing. A few of these fellas are angry over legal matters—who owns what claim, that sort of thing. They're all just entrepreneurs at heart, I guess." Cookie paused. "Now eat your breakfast, then wait a spell before leaving. Don't want you to get caught up in the fray."

Cookie disappeared into the kitchen. Abby glanced around the room in search of Sam Harris. She located him at last, deep in conversation with the minister and his wife.

To her right, Neville cleared his throat. "Miss, I feel sure all of this would bring your father to his knees, and that is precisely why I have written to him to apprise him of our current. . .situation."

"You wrote to Father?" Abby sat up straight and gave him a pensive look. "But I already sent him a message myself, the morning after we arrived. Remember?"

"Yes. My note has a slightly different tone. There is only so long a person can walk through the valley of the shadow before sensing impending doom."

"Such drama." She fought the temptation to roll her eyes. "And so much for learning to be content, Neville. Honestly."

He snapped his napkin and placed it in his lap. "You will forgive me in time, no doubt. And for the record, I'm quite content with the note I sent your father, so there you go."

"But I asked you not to alarm him." Abby felt her lips curl down in a frown. "I thought I could trust you."

"Trust me?" His eyes narrowed. "Trust me? Miss Abigail, I've proven myself trustworthy to your family since your parents acquired my services when they moved to Nottingham. I've known you since you toddled around the estate in nappies. I was there when you fell out of a tree at age six and I bandaged your knee myself. And did I not protect you from that villainous Morrison girl when you were fourteen?"

"Well, yes."

"Then you must trust me when I say that writing your father was for your good. And mine too. I cannot abide this town much longer."

A couple of patrons entered the restaurant. Through the open door, the sound of a racket in the street drew Abby's attention. From where she was sitting, she could see the two men still going at it. One of the fellows, who no doubt was liquored up from the night before, punched the other in the jaw. This sent the second man reeling backward into the barbershop sign. The barber barreled out of his shop, waving his razor in the direction of the man who'd fallen, only to have the first man punch him in the jaw as well.

Sam rushed over and shut the door then looked her way with a shrug. Likely he felt he was doing her a favor, shutting out the outside world.

Much like Neville was doing by contacting her father.

Did everyone in town think she was a child in need of care?

"If I didn't know any better, I'd think we'd stumbled upon a stage play, a comedy of errors. Only, these actors are real, or as close to real as one can get in a place like this." She suppressed a sigh as she turned to face Neville. "I'm sorry you felt it necessary to contact Father, but I feel sure he will respond reasonably. As long as he doesn't send a posse after us, I think we'll recover nicely from our visit to San Francisco."

"If I know your father as well as I think I do, he will come himself."

"Are you saying he would venture all the way to California to fetch me when he wouldn't go to the Oregon Territory to fetch Mother? Where's the sense in that?"

"He's a smart man. Your father will surely realize that your mother will join you. This will propel him, I feel sure. And think about it, Miss Abigail. When your mother arrives, you will have two for the price of one, both parents in one place."

Why, of course. It was the only thing that made sense. Both parents in San Francisco? She could almost picture it now.

"And as soon as your father realizes you and your mother are here together, he will sweep you up and carry you both back home to the safety and comfort of a lovely place called Philadelphia."

"I thought you hated Philadelphia, Neville. Didn't you tell me, just a few days back, that you wanted to go back to Nottingham?"

"Miss Abigail, if I must choose between San Francisco and Philadelphia, I will go with Philadelphia every time. Now, don't fret. Your parents will come and this nightmare will end."

"It's not a nightmare at all. More like an entertaining dream. I find it very fascinating." She watched through the window as the local sheriff strode into the middle of the street to break up the ongoing fight. "If not a bit messy." A forced smile followed.

"Whatever you say, Miss Abigail. Stiff upper lip, then. Hold steady till troops arrive."

"It sounds like I'm not the one who needs to hold steady."

"Maybe the Good Lord brought you here. Ever think of that?" Cookie's voice sounded from behind them and Abby turned to discover the woman holding a tray filled with plates of steaming food. "If you read the Good Book, you'll see that lots of folks were sent to places they didn't really want to be. Take Moses, for instance. And Joseph. All of 'em, stuck in foreign lands." She set their plates down in front of them, somehow managing to hold onto the tray in the process. Abby marveled at her skill. The woman could cook, serve, and carry on a decent conversation, all at the same time.

"This is a foreign land, all right." Neville pursed his lips. "But don't romanticize this situation, Miss Cookie."

"Miss Cookie?" She laughed. "Honey, if you can't call me Cookie, plain and simple, then use my real name."

"All right, Cookie-Plain-and-Simple. And by the way, you've forgotten my tea."

"It's coming to a boil on the stove, so hold your horses. And guard your words, please." She looked for a moment as if she might want to slug Neville, if not for the tray in her hand. "The name's Helga, by the way. But what were we talking about, again?"

"You were chastising me, Helga." Neville dabbed at his lips with his napkin. "Insofar as I can recall."

"No such thing. Just reminding you that God uses every road we travel to teach us lessons, so keep your eyes open. Maybe He's got a thing or two to share with you both on this journey out west."

"Humph. I'd sooner not learn any more lessons, if you please, and certainly not in this crowd. Send me back to the quiet life and I'll be happy as a lark."

"Not much for crowds, eh?" Cookie pursed her lips. "I'll admit, the chaos that comes with such a large influx of people can be a bit overwhelming."

"To say the least." Neville reached for his fork and tapped his egg's shell.

"Not sure any of the locals were prepared for the crowd, either," Cookie said. "Imagine throwing a party and inviting twenty guests. Twenty-five thousand show up."

"Gracious." Abby picked up a piece of her bacon and took a nibble. Mmm.

"From what I understand, that's what it's been like in the San Francisco area and beyond. The influx overwhelmed all the locals the first few years after gold was discovered. There weren't enough beds, enough tools for panning. There wasn't even enough food, which is why they put me to work."

"You didn't come to open a restaurant?" Neville asked.

"Me?" Cookie laughed. "I came to feed Mr. Harris and young Sammy. That's all. I pictured myself in a fine two-story house, much like the one in Independence. I'd spend my days tending to the two of them, not hundreds more, to boot."

"What a shock that must have been." Abby set down her slice of bacon and wiped her greasy fingers on her napkin.

"Let's just say I never like to see a man go hungry, and leave it at that. The first month I was here I saw fellas who'd give their right arm for a homemade biscuit. I didn't know much, but I knew how to make biscuits." Her lips curled up in a smile. "I don't mind saying, I made quite a killing on those biscuits, enough to sock away some funds for a rainy day."

Abby wasn't sure which stunned her more, the idea that Cookie had been willing to come all this way just to tend to Sam and Mr. Harris's needs or that she'd found a way to earn a lucrative career doing something she loved.

"Fellas came from all over town to buy." Her face lit in a delightful smile. "One offered me ten dollars for two biscuits with homemade gravy."

"Ten dollars?" Neville almost choked on his egg.

Cookie's eyes sparkled. "I turned him down, of course. But these poor fellas had empty bellies, and I certainly knew what to do about that. So, I filled 'em. Started with biscuits and gravy, then I added flapjacks. Before long, Mr. Harris decided I should open the restaurant. After six months or so, he built on rooms and turned the place into the Gold Rush Inn."

"So, that's how this place came to be." Abby grabbed her fork and speared her egg. "All started with a biscuit."

"Yes'm. Started with a small dining hall and kitchen. Now look where we are." Cookie swung her arms wide to show off the place. "I've got a full-service kitchen and hundreds of hungry men who flood this place, day and night. And I'm doing my best to keep up with 'em, but I'm no spring chicken. Some days I long for simpler times." She paused. "Then I think of the potential to reach some of these fellas for the Lord, and all the aches and pains are worth it."

"I'm rather flabbergasted by the sheer number of men in this town, if you want the truth of it."

"I was too, at first. In fact, I think everyone in the territory was floored to see such a rapid influx of fellas, and from all over the world too."

"No doubt."

"Have you ever heard the expression 'too big for yer britches'?" Cookie asked.

"It's not a phrase we use in England, but I am familiar, yes." Abby dabbed her lips with her napkin. "Why do you ask?"

"San Francisco is too big for her britches. And you know what happens when things grow too fast."

"What's that?"

"Seams start popping. Threads burst. It's awkward and uncomfortable. That's what's happened here. Too many people, not enough places to put them. Too much gold, not enough places to invest or spend. Too many single men, not enough wives to calm them down. I believe you can see the dilemma. San Francisco's pants are popping at the seams."

"Fascinating picture, indeed."

"Yes, and I've barely scratched the surface of how tough it's been, if you want the truth of it. Half these fellas lived in tents the first year or two. Now that banker fella's put up shanties to house them. Terrible places." Cookie's nose wrinkled. "Wouldn't put my dog in one of 'em."

"Gracious."

"I suppose it was to be expected. Just four years ago San Francisco was a sleepy town of five hundred. Look at us now! Over twenty-five thousand folks. We're about to bust a gut." She paused. "I'm trying to get to a point here." Cookie stretched her back and her brows grew together in an agonized expression. "This is all too much for me, even with Jin's help. I can't go on like this or my poor old body will break down." She gave Abby a pleading look. "I need help from someone young. Strong. Capable."

Abby's heart quickened. "Why are you looking at me?"

"Because you're young. Strong. Capable."

"In the kitchen? Truly you don't know me, or you would know that I could never—"

"Not just the kitchen, but the dining hall as well. Waiting tables. I need all the help I can get. Wouldn't turn down a soul who offered." Cookie's gaze shifted to Neville, who flinched. "Room and board, of course, and a small salary to boot. I would make sure you were both comfortable, well-fed, and taken care of. I'll even throw in free laundry, if you're interested. Maggie O'Callahan is our washerwoman. She's a peach."

"There's not enough clean laundry in the state of California to entice me." Neville shook his head. "Waiting tables? Have things come to that? We've only been here a few days, after all, and I feel sure, Miss Abigail, that your father would frown on the idea."

"Did Sam put this notion into your head?" Abby asked.

A hint of mischief played in Cookie's twinkling eyes. "He might have mentioned it, yes, but I'm in agreement. It just makes sense, if you plan to stick around, I mean." Her lips curled up in an impish smile. "And I sure do hope you're gonna stick around. I've gotten rather used to you two." Her gaze turned to Neville. "Even if you refuse to drink my coffee."

"We do plan to stay awhile." Abby paused before saying more. After thinking it through, she looked Neville's way. "There may be some sense to her request, Neville. We can't go on sitting in an expensive hotel, waiting on Mother to arrive. It's a ridiculous waste of funds when we could be sleeping here, at the Gold Rush Inn, for free."

Neville nodded. "I wholeheartedly agree. Being in San Francisco is a ridiculous waste of funds, which is exactly why I feel we should book the coach to return to St. Louis. Just say the word and I'm on my way to the depot."

Strong feelings arose inside of Abby. She shook her head, determined. "I'm waiting for Mother. I won't go back without her. She will come, as soon as the roads are clear. I know she will. And, as you said, Father will likely join us too. This is an adventure, Neville, remember?"

Neville's downcast expression conveyed his feelings.

From outside a shout rang out, followed by gunfire. Horse's hooves pounded the street and more shots filled the air.

Sam jumped up from his spot at Reverend Linden's table and raced to the door. He spared a glance their way as he passed by. "Abby, get under the table. Cookie, you too." His voice carried a frantic edge to it.

"What?" Abby's heart skipped a beat. "Why?"

He gave her a "Don't question me" look, and she dove under the table. Cookie took a bit longer, her wider girth a bit harder to maneuver to the ground. She somehow managed to hold onto the tray all the while.

"Never pictured myself having breakfast under a table," Neville said as he eased into the spot next to Cookie. "What kind of foolishness is this?"

" 'For where envying and strife is, there is confusion and every evil work.' " Cookie set the tray down. "Third chapter of James, verse sixteen."

"You can say that twice and mean it," Neville countered.

Abby half-expected Cookie to repeat the scripture, but she did not. As more shots rang out, Abby began to perspire. Neville looked as if he might be ill. Cookie, on the other hand, didn't look any the worse for wear. In fact, she looked downright relaxed.

"I'm making vegetable soup for lunch. Already got it on the stove, simmering. Homemade cornbread too."

"Haven't had a good vegetable soup in ages," Neville observed, and then took a bite of the bacon he'd somehow managed to hang onto. "And cornbread will be a novelty."

"You'll never settle for less once you've tasted mine. Man shall not live by bread alone, unless it's Cookie's cornbread." She gave Neville a wink and his cheeks flushed.

This led to a detailed discussion about the seasonings she used in her cooking, which almost served to distract Abby from the brawl going on in the street.

After some time, the noise subsided. Sam lifted the tablecloth and peered down at them. "All right, the danger has passed. You can come out now."

Abby stared up into his concerned face, not quite convinced. "Are you sure?"

"Very. Those fellas headed on down the road with the sheriff on their tail. Don't think they'll have the courage to turn around."

Abby crawled out and accepted Sam's assistance to stand. "Gracious." She smoothed her skirt and contended with the shiver that wriggled its way down her spine. "That was certainly unexpected."

"Not around here." His gaze swept over her. "Are you all right?"

"I suppose so." She glanced at Neville, stunned to see his disheveled appearance as he rose in one fluid motion from his spot under the table. "Neville?"

"Hmm?" He raked his fingers through his thinning hair.

"You look as if you've seen a ghost."

"We don't get a lot of shootings in Philadelphia, Miss Abigail. It will take me some time to acclimate." He helped Cookie to her feet, even wrestling the tray out of her hands.

After she reached a standing position, Cookie slapped him on the back. "Acclimate. Now that's a two-dollar word if I ever heard one. Ain't a lot of acclimating round here. We mostly just get used to things and don't let 'em affect us anymore."

"As I said. . .acclimate."

"Is that the same thing as learning to be content, Neville?" Abby asked.

" 'Not that I speak in respect of want: for I have learned, in whatsoever state I am, therewith to be content.' " Cookie clasped her hands together. "One of my favorites. Philippians four, verse eleven."

Neville grunted. "Take me into that kitchen of yours, Miss Cookie-Plain-and-Simple, and let me see what you've got simmering in there."

From the look on his face, something was simmering inside of Neville too. Abby felt sure of it. Perhaps the family butler was—what was the word he'd used, again? Ah yes, acclimating.

Chapter Six

*Y*ou all right, Sammy?" Cookie's words roused Sam from his thoughts as he stared out the restaurant's large glass-paned window to watch the sun dip in the sky to the west.

"Yes." He glanced her way. "Just thinking about how fascinating it is that we used to watch this very same sunset from our porch in Independence."

"We did, indeed. Some things never change, honey."

"And some things change so much you don't know if your heart can take it."

"Meaning?"

Sam shook his head and didn't respond until the right words came to him. "I don't know, Cookie. I've been battling a serious longing for home, if you want the truth of it. Don't know how much longer I can take it here."

"Really? Ready to pack your bag and head back to Independence?" Cookie looked surprised by this notion.

"That's just it. . ." He stared at the sun as his truest thoughts ushered forth. "I never sought to be free of that place. I know Father did, but not me. I would have been content to stay put all of my days."

"And yet, here you are, a world away, feeling discontent. Seems there's a lot of that going around."

"Yes, here I am." Sam did his best not to groan aloud. "In a town filled with men who've been given all the independence they could ever want, and they've run too far with it. God brought me here, for some reason unbeknownst to me."

"He will show you, in time."

"For now, I feel. . ."

"Trapped?"

"That's one way to put it."

She rested her palms on the table and looked at him with such intensity that he started to sweat a bit. "So, why not leave and go back home? You don't have to stay. Your father could manage, and you could have your life back."

"I would spend every day worrying about him, wondering how he's doing. Suffice it to say, prying him away from San Francisco will be next to impossible, so I'm here for good. Or at least until the Lord speaks in an audible voice."

"He's done that before, you know. Spoke through a donkey."

"Humph."

Cookie gestured for him to sit at a nearby table. "If I say what's really on my mind, you might misunderstand."

"Try me." He took a seat, curious to hear her thoughts.

For a moment, she said nothing. When she did speak, she caught him off guard. "Sammy, you were the perfect little boy."

"Hardly." He laughed. "Far from it, in fact."

"You know what I mean." Concern flooded Cookie's eyes. "While other little boys were splashing in mud puddles and pulling classmates' pigtails, you were seated with a book or puzzle. Content to stay put in quiet fashion."

"I see your point. But that hardly makes me perfect."

"You were always so. . .good." Her eyebrow arched a bit. "Do you get my point?"

"Not really. Are you advocating a more sinful lifestyle? Should I have climbed out of my bedroom window and pranced around town in my skivvies?"

"Yes, exactly!"

"Cookie, I was joking."

"Oh." Her smile faded. "Sam, I'm not saying you should've been particularly naughty, but you always seemed to live well within the boundaries of society, safe inside the tidy framework your mother created for you. She kept a perfect home in a perfect town and had a perfect child. It was all so. . .perfect. And safe."

"Nothing wrong with safe. Boundaries are a good thing."

"Mostly. But sometimes they squelch our courage. They convince us we're not strong enough to do what our heart tells us in secret that it wants to do. And now, here you are, in San Francisco, startled by the fact that other little boys grew up to be rowdy, whiskey-drinking fools."

"Surely you're not suggesting I join them."

"Not at all. You're missing my point. I'm just saying that your mother's quiet restrictions on your life have made you less than courageous when it comes to standing up to your father, that's all." She released a slow breath, as if speaking those words had taken a lot out of her. "If you really want to strike out on your own, don't let your worries and fears keep you bound. Your father will survive without you. And it's time you learned that you can survive without him as well."

Sam paused, her words striking a heavy chord. "Oh." It was the only word he could manage. So, Cookie thought he was a coward?

The look of concern that followed on her end made him nervous. "Think about what I've said here, Sam." She patted his hand. "That's all I ask. Your father might've yanked you by the arm and pulled you to California, but that doesn't mean his grip on you has to remain tight. Courage says this is one boundary worth crossing."

She marched out of the room, shoulders squared. Sam released a sigh. If only he had as much courage as Cookie, he'd be halfway back to Independence already.

❤

Over the next few days, Abby couldn't stop thinking about Cookie's insistence that she come to work at the inn. It might be fun to have a job, and the idea of sleeping in her own room at no cost held great appeal, especially with finances dwindling.

Neville didn't seem convinced, but then again, Neville had been a hard sell on San Francisco as a whole. The more Abby thought about it, the more convinced she became. She would take on the job and would do so with excitement in her heart. The thought of spending more time with Cookie felt comfortable, and it didn't bother her one bit that she would see more of Sam too.

On Monday morning, after a hearty breakfast at the Gold Rush Inn, she gave the news to Cookie, who seemed delighted.

"Marvelous!" The older woman's eyes sparkled. "Let me show you to your room. Neville can bring your things over from the Ivory Tower any time you like."

Though he grumbled a bit about this decision, Neville headed off to the hotel to fetch their bags. Cookie led the way up the stairs to the rooms above, chattering all the way. Abby ran her hand along the wooden railing, and when they reached the landing at the top, turned to look down on the dining room. Funny, seeing it from this perspective. It seemed larger, somehow.

She followed Cookie down the narrow hallway, past several doors leading to guests' rooms, to a door at the end of the hall.

When Cookie opened the door, Abby tried not to gasp aloud. The room was small in size and in need of cleaning. Immediate cleaning.

"Now, I know what you're thinking." Cookie pulled back the curtains and a rush of dust filled the small area. "This room has been used for storage, but never you mind all of that. We'll get 'er cleaned up before nightfall, I promise."

"This isn't really much of a bed, is it?" Abby stared down at the dirty cot and tried to imagine what it would be like, to rest there.

"Afraid not." Cookie looked concerned for a moment. Just as quickly, her lips curled up in a playful smile. "I know you're terribly impressed. We've given you the best room in the place. But you're worth it, Miss Abby."

"Funny." Abby glanced around, noticing the cobwebs in the corner, the sticky glass of something-or-other on the rickety table next to the bed, and the filthy quilt tossed on the floor nearby.

"I. . .well, I hardly know where to begin."

Cookie patted her on the back. "All jokes aside, this is the only space we have left. I could move you into my room with me, but we'd have to share a bed, and mine isn't much larger than this. And I know how young women are—they need their own space. Privacy."

"Right."

"Not to worry. I'll send Jin to tidy up the room. He can take care of it after breakfast. Would you like to leave your bag?"

"Is it safe?"

Cookie dangled a key in her hand. "We'll lock 'er up nice and tight. No one will bother your stuff. Trust me when I say that most of the folks who venture through this place don't lack for funds. If they want to steal something, it's usually another fellow's panning dish or something along those lines. I doubt seriously anyone will rummage through your things. But just in case, you can keep the room locked up."

"I appreciate that." Abby gave another look around and tried to envision what the room would look like after being cleaned up. "Maybe I can stop by the mercantile and pick up a fresh quilt or some new sheets."

"Good luck finding those. They're in short supply around here, what with all the folks coming through town. But don't you fret, Miss Abigail. Jin will turn this place over in a hurry. He's a miracle worker, that one."

"All right." Abby walked to the tiny wardrobe. When she opened it, something flew out. She let out a scream and jolted backward.

This seemed to get Cookie tickled. She doubled over in laughter. "Just a little bat, honey. You disturbed his nest."

"His nest?" Abby's heart thumped a mile a minute. "Are you saying there are *more* bats in there?"

"Well, sure, but don't fret. You'll get used to them after a while."

"Get used to them?" She watched as the little bat flew out the door into the hallway. "I don't think so."

"Trust me, there are a great many things you will have to choose to ignore. But you will adapt, I assure you. Haven't you already grown used to the men?"

"I suppose." Abby took her bag and set it on the cot. She placed her reticule inside the bag and then shoved it under the bed.

"Not going to put it in the wardrobe?"

"To be used as a nest for who-knows-what?" Abby shook her head, the idea making her stomach churn. "I think not."

"As you like. But don't be surprised if you come back to discover the mice have eaten a hole in your bag."

"M–mice?"

"Well sure. Don't they have mice in England?"

"Outdoors, of course. And occasionally in the cellar. But not inside our bedrooms, as a rule." She pulled the bag out from under the bed and walked over to the musty wardrobe. After shoving the bag inside she closed the door. Well, she tried to close it at any rate. One of the hinges came loose and it swung wildly, nearly clipping her in the arm.

"For pity's sake. Is everything around here falling apart?" She didn't mean for the words to come out as an accusation, but couldn't take them back.

Cookie laughed and rubbed her hips. "Yep, including the help. These old joints ain't what they used to be, that's sure and certain."

Abby followed her new friend out into the hallway. The boisterous sound of men's voices greeted her as they made their way to the open stairway leading down to the dining hall. Then came the whistles and jeers from the fellows as she and Cookie walked down the steps.

"Woo-hoo!" a fellow with a thick gray mustache called out. "Look what's on the dessert menu, fellas."

Abby felt her cheeks grow hot. She wanted to bolt back up to her room and slam the door, but images of mice running under the bed changed her mind.

Just when she was hoping she could rest her thoughts, the tiny bat flew by her and made its way into the dining hall. She swatted at it and let out a scream, then lost her grip on the stair railing. Just as she felt herself starting to tumble downward, a strong hand gripped her arm.

"Careful, there."

She turned to discover Sam was standing behind her. Had he been there all along?

"I'll quiet the fellas down," he said, his voice low. "But I can't promise to get rid of the bats. They come and go as they please."

"I. . .I see."

"Though, to be fair, they tend to be more active at night, so this morning display is probably just for your benefit, to get you stirred up."

"It's working." She tried to act brave.

"You two gonna gab all morning?" Cookie turned back to face her. "I've got work to do and could use a hand. There's a pot of stew simmering for lunch and dough rising for bread, but I need to get it in the oven. There's not much the fellas like better than hot bread with fresh, creamy butter."

"Unless it's your cherry pie," Abby observed.

"You've a fascination with that, haven't you?" Cookie slipped an arm over Abby's shoulder.

"That, and your coffee." Abby suddenly felt quite content. "Cookie, you make the best cup of coffee in the world."

"Really? You think so?"

"Oh, I know so. I've had coffees of every kind, and from so many places around the world. But I can truly say that yours is the finest. What's your secret?"

"Just the beans, I suppose. We use Pioneer Steam coffee. Ever heard of it?"

Abby shook her head. "No, but it's delicious."

"Made its way out west with the gold prospectors. What did you drink in England?"

"Trust me, people are more of a mind to drink tea in Nottingham. I'm a rare bird, in that I always preferred a cup of coffee. Brings a particular kind of happiness, I guess you'd say."

"And perks a body up too. I couldn't get half the work done around here without my morning cup. Now, let's get to the kitchen, shall we?"

"Yes, but as I said, I'm at a loss to know what to do."

"Don't fret. Before long you'll be making the cherry pies. And the bread. I might even let you cream the butter. And if you're really coming along, I'll show you how to make a good cup of coffee."

Abby swallowed hard and worked up the courage to speak her thoughts aloud. "Cookie, I didn't want to say anything earlier, but I have very little—if any—experience in the kitchen. Are you sure you want to take me on?"

"Watch and learn, honey. I dare say you'll be at home in no time. And until then, I will do my best to be patient."

Abby followed her into the kitchen, which was filled top to bottom, side to side, with food products in various stages of production. Jin worked diligently to peel potatoes, which he dropped into the big pot of stew on the wood stove. Abby looked on in fascination, enjoying the sights and the smells.

In all her days, she'd never given thought to what went on in a kitchen. The family's cook simply brought delicious food to the table and then removed the dirty dishes afterward, to a kitchen Abby rarely wandered through.

"Put on an apron, Abby, and be quick about it. One of the white ones will do." Cookie pointed to the pegs on the wall and Abby grabbed an apron, then tied it on. Her hands trembled with such anxiety that she could barely accomplish the task. Why, oh why, had she agreed to this?

"Don't fret, honey." Cookie rested a hand on her shoulder, perhaps in response to the look of panic on Abby's face. "You'll be a quick learner. I'll have you popping out pies in no time."

"I hope so."

" 'Study to shew thyself approved unto God, a workman that needeth not to be ashamed, rightly dividing the word of truth.' Second Timothy, chapter two. Can't seem to remember the verse."

"Right. I will pay close attention and be a ready student."

"And as far as Neville goes. . ."

"Don't fret over Neville." Abby dismissed any concerns with the wave of a hand. "He's spent his life caring for others, and I know he'll do a fine job waiting tables. I doubt he will do so with a willing heart, is all. I feel I've dragged him into a situation he's not happy about."

"He has just as much opportunity to find joy in the situation as bitterness." A thoughtful look came over Cookie. "Give him time. I think he'll come around."

"I hope so." Abby paused to think about the woman's words before responding. "It's going to take time, I think, for him to forgive me for all of this."

"Forgive you? For bringing him to California, you mean?" Cookie looked stunned by this news.

"For all of it—racing off here and there, looking for Mama. It was never his battle to fight, but he has done so admirably."

Cookie clucked her tongue before responding: " 'The Lord shall fight for you, and ye shall hold your peace.' Exodus 14:14."

"My goodness, you do that so well."

"Do what?" Cookie asked.

"Say those verses. You must have many of them set to memory."

"Best way to get through the day," Cookie said with a smile. "And a tremendous source of encouragement when I need it. Nothing like a good Bible verse to soothe troubled waters." She turned back to her work, now humming a familiar hymn.

Abby observed the woman in silence for a few moments, and did her best to figure her out. Cookie stood in stark contrast to the other women in town. While most wore flamboyant dresses and showed off their curves, this sweet gal wore a modest uniform, suitable to her work in the kitchen. She paid no mind to her salt-and-pepper hair, which she'd pulled into a bun. And Cookie certainly wouldn't win any awards for polish and shine. Her shoes were chipped and her apron stained. Still, there was something about the woman that struck Abby as beautiful. The words that came out of her mouth were different too. Kinder. More thoughtful.

Cookie continued to hum as she worked, then glanced Abby's way. "Need any help over there, kid?"

"I, um, no." Abby stirred the pot of stew, nearly burning herself in the process.

"I'm guessing you didn't spend many hours over the stove at home."

A loud snort from across the room caught Abby off guard. Neville had entered the room. He leaned against the wall and crossed his arms, as if to say, "I won't be working anytime soon."

"While I was afforded many opportunities to learn, cooking was not on the list." Abby offered what she hoped would look like a brave smile. "Though I'm always open to trying."

"You might want to try pulling that pot off the heat, then." Cookie bolted toward her and yanked the pot away from the fire. "I can smell the beef burning from here. And if there's one thing we can't afford around here, it's wasted food."

"Because it's so hard to come by?" Neville asked, though he never shifted his position from the wall.

"Because *good* food is so hard to come by." Cookie turned to face Neville, then swiped the back of her hand across her perspiring forehead. She rested her balled fists against her hips and gave him a pensive look. "Though I can see why someone as thin as you are would require a good meal. Didn't they feed you, back where you came from?"

Abby stifled a laugh. For as long as she'd known Neville, he'd been as thin as a rail. No amount of good cooking seemed to fatten him up.

"Begging your pardon, Madame, but I require no such nutritional supplementation. I am in tip-top health, according to my doctor."

"He might need to go back to medical school, then. To me, you look like something the wind could blow over. 'Course, it'd have to make its way through those..." She pointed at his sideburns. "Whatever you call those."

Neville's eyes widened, but he said nothing in response.

"At any rate, we'll fatten you up. A skinny waiter is no walking advertisement for good cooking."

"From what I've gathered, you don't need advertisement." Neville walked over to the pegs on the wall and grabbed an apron, which he tied around his waist. "I've never seen so many hungry patrons in my life."

"Patrons? Is that what we call 'em now?" She released a long, hearty laugh, then slapped her thigh. "I call 'em hoodlums, and that's on a good day." She used her apron to wipe her hands. " 'Course, even a hoodlum needs a fitting meal, so I treat 'em same as I would the banker or that snooty mercantile owner." Her brow furrowed.

"The mercantile owner was perfectly friendly to me," Abby objected.

"Humph." Cookie increased her stirring. "If I didn't already know you were new to town, that statement would be a dead giveaway. But let's talk about the locals after lunch, shall we? Won't be long before this place is filled to the brim with. . .what did you call them again?" She looked Neville's way. "Ah, yes. Patrons."

"I don't recall ever seeing so many different types of people in one place before," Abby observed.

"Even in this room, if you stop to think about it," Cookie said. "I'm from good German stock. You're English. Sammy's. . .what are you, Sammy?"

"Technically, I'm Welsh, but the family has been in America for some time now, so let's just settle on American."

"Sammy's American. Jin is Chinese. Neville is. . ." She paused and her gaze lingered on him.

"Do you even have to ask?" He squared his shoulders.

"British. He got a double-dose, I think." Cookie slapped him on the back. "Point is, we're all from different places and yet somehow—miraculously—the Lord managed to bring all of us together to this place. Right here. Right now. For such a time as this."

"Like Esther," Abby observed.

"You can be our Esther, honey. I'm too old."

"Just don't try to marry me off to the king, please," Abby said with mock seriousness. "Might turn out badly."

"Well, I promise not to marry you off to a king, but I don't promise not to try to marry you off." Cookie's lips curled up in mischievous fashion. "I have a special gifting, you see. Matchmaker."

"Time for me to get to work on that stew." Abby dove into her task, stirring until her hand ached, and then—just as Sam rang the lunch bell—heaped bowls with the yummy smelling stew. Beads of perspiration soaked through her dress, but she didn't mind. Not until Sam came through the kitchen to check on the pie situation. She swiped her brow with the back of her hand and started cutting slices, willy-nilly.

"Best let me do that, Miss Abigail." Neville took her job, and she filled a tray with plates then delivered them to the men in the dining room, who took to whistling as she entered.

"Lookie here!" Jedediah Tucker called out. "If Cookie's pie wasn't already sugary enough, I'd have a big dose of sweetness right here."

"You ever gonna give up and marry me, Abby?" another fella hollered out.

"Too busy learning to cook," she countered.

"Soon as you learn, I'll be waiting." The man gave her a wink. "Good things are worth waiting for."

"Humph." She continued to serve pie until the lunch hour ended. When the fellas dispersed, Abby was finally able to swallow down a few bites of the stew, but still felt queasy. Probably a combination of the heat and all her hard work.

Just when she thought she might be able to take a break, Cookie's voice rang out. "Time to pluck the chickens."

"Pluck the chickens?" Abby grabbed her apron and lifted it to wipe the perspiration from her brow. "What?" She pushed back a wayward strand of hair.

"Well, sure. Gotta start getting things ready for supper. Monday nights I serve fried chicken, remember."

"Well, yes, but..." Abby didn't have the energy to finish the sentence.

"You didn't think they waltzed into the skillet already plucked, did you?" Cookie laughed.

"I don't suppose I ever gave it a second's thought. The only chicken I've ever confronted was the one on my plate, fried to a lovely golden color. Are you saying they come with feathers?"

This brought a raucous laugh from Cookie, Jin, and Neville.

"That's priceless, Abby." Cookie wiped her hands on her apron. "Yes, they come with feathers. Feathers which have to be plucked. Jin usually takes care of that for me, but he's got to get busy on your room, remember?" Tiny wrinkles formed on Cookie's brow. "We'll take some time to pluck while he's away so we're ready to start the evening meal promptly at five."

"But we just finished lunch."

"Hardly finished." Cookie pointed to the sink full of dishes. "We'll tackle those first and then deal with the feathers."

"I'll do the washing." Neville rose and stretched his back. "You ladies pluck to your hearts' content." He walked to the sink, muttering under his breath that no proper English butler should be subjected to dirty dishes.

"I heard that, Neville," Cookie called out as she grabbed a large box and set it on the chopping board. "Around here, if folks care to eat, they have to pitch in." She pulled the lid off the box, and Abby suddenly found herself staring down at a slew of headless chickens.

Chapter Seven

A wave of nausea hit Abby all at once. "I...I...." The room began to spin. Neville bolted her way and slid a chair underneath her. She landed with a plop and leaned her forehead on the chopping table. Her stomach continued to roil.

"It's just too much for you, Miss Abigail." Neville's voice brought some degree of comfort as he fanned her with an empty plate. "I'll help Cookie with the plucking. Can you tackle the dishes?"

She lifted her head and nodded, though she honestly didn't feel she could stand at the moment, all things considered.

"You can't go on swapping out tasks with her forever, you know." Cookie clucked her tongue. "She's got to learn."

"I will learn. I promise." Abby placed her hands on the chopping table and eased herself to a standing position. "Today I'll learn to wash dishes. Tomorrow I'll pluck chickens." She offered what she hoped would look like a convincing smile.

"Are you telling me you've never washed dishes before, child?" The worry lines deepened along Cookie's brows and under her eyes.

Abby shook her head. "Never. But I'm sure it's a mite easier than what you're proposing."

Cookie began to rant about how all young women—particularly those of a marrying age—should know how to wash a dish. Abby only heard half of it. She found herself distracted by the headless chickens once again as she passed by them on her way to the sink.

Minutes later, hands deep in a sudsy sink, she went to work scraping and scrubbing messy stew bowls. She began to mutter under her breath, recounting some of what Cookie had said.

"I'll learn to wash dishes. And sleep with bats. And pluck chickens too, if that's what it takes to bring Mama back home again." Yes, she would do anything it took, even if the process killed her.

❤

After listening in to the conversation in the kitchen, Sam cleared his throat to make his presence known. "Am I to understand that women of marrying age should know how to pluck chickens?"

Abby turned his way, her cheeks as red as the tomatoes in Cookie's stew. "How long have you been standing there?"

"Long enough to know that you're of a marrying age. Oh, and long enough to discover that chickens have feathers. Who knew? This has been quite the revelation."

Cookie reached for a dishtowel and used it to swat his arm. "Enough, Sammy. Don't you dare make fun of her."

"Make fun of her?" He bit back a laugh. "On the contrary. This is better than one of those dinner shows Father proposed a while back."

"Very funny." Abby rolled her eyes. "But never you mind. I'll learn how to pluck a chicken, and how to fry it in a pan too. Just you wait and see."

"Since you're of a marrying age and all, that'll be handy. I'm sure your husband—whoever he is—will be very grateful not to have to pick feathers off his plate."

Abby groaned and turned toward the sink, submerging her arms in the soapy water.

Cookie swatted him again. "Get on out of here before we pluck and fry you."

"And miss all this? Not on your life. Besides, I just came in to remind you about the apple pie. It's Monday."

"Apple pie?" Neville turned to face him, looking a bit ashen. "Didn't we just serve cherry at lunch? Are we really baking again, so soon in this heat?"

"Sure," Cookie responded. "We always have apple pie on Monday nights. That's the day Les goes to the farmers' market for fruit."

"Les?" Abby turned back to face Cookie. "Who's Les?"

"Everyone around here needs to get to know Les. Talk about an inspiration."

"What does he look like? I'll be on the lookout for him."

"He?" Cookie slapped her knee and laughed out loud. "I guess I forgot to mention that Les is a woman. A prospector, to boot. One of the few female 49ers."

"A female prospector?" Abby looked genuinely stunned by this news.

"Yep. Lesley Jenkins," Sam explained. "We've been friends from the get-go." He smiled, just thinking about her.

"Les, for short," Cookie explained. "Owns the biggest house in town. Well, on the outskirts of town, anyway. She happens to love the farmers' market and makes a trip every Monday for me. She'll be along any minute with some apples for the pies, and you'll meet her face to face."

"So, we're to meet this. . .Les. . .soon and start baking apple pies," Neville said, as he pluck, pluck, plucked the chicken in his hands. "Because God forbid we should have cherry twice in one day."

"We don't break with tradition," Cookie said. "The men would have my head. It's apple pie on Monday; carrot cake on Tuesday—on account of the carrots we don't use in Monday's stew; lemon pie on Wednesday—Mr. Harris says you should give 'em something tart midweek so they'll come back craving sweet the next day; buttermilk pie on Thursday, and on Friday I make the most luscious chocolate cake you've ever laid eyes on." She gave him a little wink. "With my own secret ingredient."

"Cookie and her secret ingredients." Sam laughed, remembering how she'd made these same claims back in Missouri. Of course, her audience was smaller back then.

"Secret ingredient?" Neville lifted a now-featherless bird in triumphant fashion. "Chicken feathers, perhaps?"

This got a laugh out of everyone in the room, including Sam.

"Not even close," Cookie countered. "But stick around and you will see."

"I've never been a fan of chocolate, thank you very much," Neville added. "So, I will have to forgo that one."

"You've never had Cookie's chocolate cake or you'd be singing a different tune altogether," Sam added.

"You don't drink coffee and you don't eat chocolate?" Cookie put her hands on her hips and clucked her tongue. "You are not a man to be trusted."

Neville's brows elevated. "I will be happy to not be trusted from a private suite at the Ivory Tower, thank you very much."

Cookie slugged him on the arm.

Poor fellow flinched.

Sam did his best not to laugh at their exchange. "Now, if you folks don't mind, I've got some work to do upstairs."

He spent several hours helping Jin clean and organize Abby's new room. He coughed and sneezed at the dust they stirred up along the way. As they worked, he thought about what Abigail's life must be like, back in Philadelphia. No doubt her room was a far cry from this. Well, no worries. He would spiff up this place, make it as womanly as possible.

And he knew just where to start.

Sam made his way to his room and dismantled the bed, then carried it into Abby's room, swapping it out with the cot, which he brought back to his room. Sacrifices had to be made, but there was no point in Abby making them, not when he could do the deed.

With the bed now set up, the room was starting to take shape. Sam went back to his room and opened his storage chest, a flood of memories washing over him. Inside he found most of his mother's keepsakes, including a quilt she'd made just a few years before her passing. He lifted the beautiful hand-stitched beauty from the chest and gave it a shake.

In that moment, as his gaze landed on the perfectly pieced squares, Sam found himself awash with emotion. How diligent his mother had been. How godly. How kindhearted. And oh, how he missed her.

Jin put fresh sheets on the bed and Sam covered it with the quilt. A perfect fit. Hopefully Abby would like it. If she knew the story behind it, she would certainly try, anyway.

♥

"Les is here with the apples." Cookie's words roused Abby from her near-slumber at the sink.

"Hmm?" Abby turned and almost gasped aloud at the sight of the woman in Levis and button-up shirt. "Oh, my goodness."

"Not every day you see a gal lookin' like me, I s'pose."

Les extended her hand and Abby shook it, getting greasy wash-water all over the poor woman. "Oh, sorry." She quickly wiped her hands on a towel.

"Never you mind that, honey. A little grease never hurt Les Jenkins." The stranger swiped her hand on her pants. "Now, you must be Abby. I've heard all about you."

"Yes, nice to meet you. I'm guessing you're from. . ." Abby paused to think it through. "California, born and raised. You've rarely, if ever, traveled elsewhere."

"Remarkable guess." Les nodded. "Grew up with seven brothers, all miners. Come from Sacramento way."

"Rich western tone in your voice," Abby observed. "Strong. I like it." She had to wonder at the attire, but couldn't fault the woman on her speech.

"Aw, thanks." Les turned to face Neville. "And you, I'm guessin' you're the butler?" She gave a little bow, as if he was royalty, then spoke in prim and proper fashion with a rich, "How do you do?"

"I do just fine, thank you. But I am no longer a butler. You may refer to me as Chief Feather Plucker."

This got a laugh out of Les. "Got a crate full of apples in my wagon. Who's gonna help me haul 'em in?" Her gaze went straight to Neville, who dropped the chicken he'd been plucking back into the box. He brushed his palms against his apron and he and Les disappeared out the kitchen door, deep in conversation.

"That Neville's got a witty sense of humor, albeit a bit on the dry side." Cookie laughed. She turned to look Abby's way. "You doin' all right over there, honey?"

"Yes, I'm sorry if I didn't greet her as I should have. I'm just. . .surprised, is all. Don't often see women dressed like that."

" 'Specially considerin' she's the richest gal in town."

"Fascinating. Certainly couldn't tell it from the way she's dressed," Abby observed. "If you hadn't told me she was a woman, I might've thought otherwise."

"Oh, she's a woman, all right." Sam's voice sounded from the doorway. "Wait'll she pulls that Stetson off and you see that long mane of dark-brown hair tumble out. And she plays cards like a girl too. She can't win a hand to save her life."

This led to a lengthy discussion about women and cards, another topic Abby knew absolutely nothing about.

A couple of minutes later Neville entered the kitchen carrying a large crate of apples.

Les followed behind him but stopped to greet Sam as she came through the door, her face lighting in a smile. "Well howdy, Sam. Thought maybe you'd gone missing."

"Nope. Upstairs working on Abby's room."

Abby swung around to thank him, but his gaze was on Les.

"What's a gal gotta do to get a cup of coffee and a couple of biscuits around here?" Les asked. "Put on a show? Song and dance number?"

"Nope." Sam jumped to attention and fixed a cup of coffee right away.

Abby found herself completely distracted by Sam's gentlemanly ways when Les entered the room. So, this was the sort of woman to catch his eye? Fascinating. Not that Abby minded one bit what sort of woman a guy like Sam was interested in, of course.

Not much, anyway.

Chapter Eight

At the end of a very long day, Abby dragged herself up to her room, worn out. As she climbed the stairs, she did her best not to think about the sad condition of her new living quarters. She also tried not to think about mice. Or bats. Instead, she focused on how good it would feel to finally sleep after such a lengthy and exhausting day.

"You'll hear the wake-up bell at five fifteen," Cookie called out from below. "I'll put on the coffeepot and you can help me with the flapjacks and ham steaks. Fellas start arriving at six."

"When do you rest?" Abby muttered under her breath, then called out a cheerful but forced, "Goodnight!"

She barely made it to the top of the stairs, her feet and ankles caused her such grief. As she reached the landing, she glanced down at the dining hall, amazed to find Neville and Cookie still working to clean the place and make it tidy for the following day's crowd. Did those two ever stop?

"Have a good night's sleep." Sam's voice sounded from the stairway behind her. "Enjoy your new room."

She turned to face him and offered a smile, along with a quiet, "Thank you." Images of the dirty room flashed across her mind and she shivered. "I appreciate having my own space."

"We're happy to have you, Abby." His words were laced with tenderness. "Hope you feel welcome."

"I do, thank you." She walked down the hallway, every joint in her body complaining. When she reached her room, she found a note pinned to her door, something written in a foreign language. Chinese, maybe? Underneath, in English, one familiar word: Welcome.

With trembling hand, she reached to open the door. What she found inside took her breath away. The worn cot had been replaced with a small feather bed. Atop the bed, a quilt nearly as pretty as the one in her room back home in Philadelphia. The broken hinge on the wardrobe had been reattached, the floor swept, the tiny chest of drawers polished to a shine.

"My goodness."

Someone had even thought to place a couple of colorful rag rugs on the floor.

She turned and called Sam's name. His smile answered the question before she even asked. "You helped Jin with my room, didn't you?"

A nod followed.

Somehow, he'd managed all of this. In the middle of his busy day, he had taken the time to make her feel welcome and secure. Her cheeks warmed as she realized he must have set up the new bed and covered it with the fine, intricate quilt.

"Sammy-boy's a true gentleman," Cookie hollered out from the room below. "Even gave up his bed to make you feel welcome."

This stopped her cold. "Are you really telling me you've given me your bed?" She stared at Sam, not quite believing those words. "Why would you do that?"

"You weren't supposed to know." Sam scolded Cookie and then turned back to face Abby. "Doesn't matter, anyway. I sleep like a rock, no matter what sort of bedding I'm on."

"Are. . .are you sure?"

"Of course. Couldn't abide the idea of a lady sleeping on that old cot."

"And the beautiful quilt?"

The edges of his lips curled up. ". . .was my mother's. She was a fine quilter. That one was always one of my favorites."

"And yet you loaned it to me."

"Of course. We want you to be comfortable here, Abby." He spoke her name with such tenderness that it caught her off guard. "So we've rolled out the welcome mat."

"I'm grateful."

"No trouble. We've mostly used the room for storage, but I got this idea a few months back that it might be nice to have a tithe room."

"A tithe room?" This caught her by surprise.

"Yes. You know. . .tithe."

"I've heard the word in church, but never equated it to inns."

"Just saying that some of the new fellas in town haven't got a penny to their name. They come filled with dreams of grandeur, ready to take on the town, but they have no idea what they're up against. They don't have the kind of funds to pay the price of a room, especially not San Francisco prices. So, I've kept a cot in this room. . ."

". . .to give away to men who can't afford to pay for a place to sleep." Abby's heart swelled as she understood his story. "I see."

"Yes."

"But now I'm in that room." She pursed her lips and thought about how that must be affecting things. Some poor fellow would have to go without a place to sleep tonight.

"Never you fear, Miss Abigail. We've got a storage shed out back that Jin took a broom to. It's not fancy, but if anyone comes calling without a nickel in his pocket, that's what we'll offer him."

"Still. . ." Waves of guilt washed over her at the very idea that she'd taken away a perfectly good room. "You could put me in with Cookie."

"I have it on good authority the woman snores." He lowered his voice. "Guests in the room next to hers often complain they can't sleep due to the noise. You'd never get any rest."

"I'm pretty sure I could sleep through a hurricane." An unladylike yawn escaped before she could stop it. "But thanks for the warning."

"We always manage, Abby. God gives us what we need. And we give back to the community, as we're able. It's a wonderful cycle—we offer God what we can and He blesses it and multiplies it. Like the loaves and fishes."

"Ugh. Fish." She shivered. "That reminds me, Cookie says I have to debone fish eventually."

"Don't look at the task." His eyes twinkled with mischief. "Just think about the outcome: golden fried pieces of fish, ready to be put onto plates. Potatoes already peeled and mashed, then placed in a heap with gravy on top. I find it helps to think about the end result, not the work to get you there."

"Good point." She yawned again. "Fried fish. I'll think about that, then. After I've slept a little. Thanks again for your hard work on my behalf."

"Happy to have you with us." He gave her a smile so warm it almost woke her up. Almost. A faint light twinkled in the depths of his beautiful eyes and he added, "G'night."

He headed down the hall in the opposite direction. Abby walked into her room and closed the door, then dressed for bed. The moment her head hit that soft pillow, she found herself dwelling on what Sam had said. Peeling potatoes was no fun, but mashed potatoes sure tasted good, especially with gravy atop. Plucking feathers from chickens had proven to be too big a challenge to tackle, but she loved crispy fried chicken, especially the way Cookie prepared it. Slicing apples was a lot of work, but the smell of apple pie wafting through the air was enough to make her drool.

Yes, there was a lot to be said about focusing on the end goal.

In that moment, her thoughts shifted to Mother and Father. Hadn't she spent most of her teen years focused on the end result there? Didn't she imagine them living happily together in the same home, Mama content to wander no longer? The idea of chasing after her mother, writing letters, scheduling trips out west, didn't feel like work when she focused on the ultimate goal: bringing Mama back home for good.

Abby's heart grew heavy as she pondered just how much she missed her precious mother. Truth be told, she could hardly wait to see her again. As she drifted off to sleep, she whispered a prayer that Mama would come to her. . .and soon.

It seemed just moments later that a bell rang out, startling her.

"You must be joking." She pulled the pillow over her head and groaned. "Please tell me I'm dreaming this."

She wasn't.

The bell continued to ring and she roused herself, took care of morning necessities, pondered the need for a hot bath, but dressed in her plainest dress instead. She pulled her hair up in a bun then peeked out the window down onto the street below. Only a handful of men were out and about at this time, but she took note of Mr. Denueve unlocking the door of the mercantile. He glanced her way and nodded. She closed the curtain, embarrassed to have been seen looking so disheveled.

When Abby walked out into the hallway, she glanced over the railing and saw Neville fussing with the tables, just as she'd left him a few short hours before.

"Have you slept at all?" she called down.

Neville looked up. "Of course. But Cookie's already hard at work in the kitchen, so I came down early."

Abby yawned as she walked to the top of the stairs. She gripped the railing, her aching feet probing for the steps downward toward another long day of work.

Cookie popped out of the kitchen and glanced her way. "There you are. I was about to come looking for you."

"Am I late?" Another yawn followed on Abby's end.

"Nope, but the fellas are early. I hear a couple of 'em at the door. Don't think they'll wait till six." Cookie turned her attention to Neville. "Go ahead and let 'em in, hon. I've got coffee brewing and ham steaks frying. That'll tide 'em over until Abby gets busy on the flapjacks."

"Flapjacks." Abigail released a slow breath. "Right. Flapjacks." And, had Cookie really just called Neville 'hon'?

Neville headed to the door and let the men inside. He glanced Abby's way as she passed by. "I trust you slept well, Miss Abigal."

"Like a rock. And you?"

"As well as could be expected on a cot in Jin's room."

"Oh dear." She wanted to cry at this news. Her decision to work at the inn had landed her good friend and mentor in a terrible position, hadn't it? But what could she do about it now?

"Not to worry, miss. I will be fine." He waved his hand in a gesture of dismissal. "Once the kinks in my back work themselves out, anyway. And, in happier news, I'm well on my way to learning several new phrases in Chinese."

"That's good, I suppose. Might come in handy." Abby walked into the kitchen and turned her attention to helping Cookie, who handled the ham steaks with ease.

"Apron, Abby," Cookie called out. "And let's get to work on those flapjacks. Quick, if you please."

"All right." She reached for an apron and tied it on, then walked to the stove, awaiting further instructions.

"Didn't have time to write down the recipe for you, hon," Cookie said. "So, let me call it out and you throw the ingredients into the mixing bowl as we go along."

"A–all right."

As Cookie hollered out the various ingredients, flour, baking soda, eggs, pinch of salt, milk, Abby did her best to keep up. Was that three cups of flour, or four? She couldn't remember. And what did a pinch of salt amount to? A teaspoon? Two? Three?

She scrambled to sift the dry ingredients as instructed and then she added the milk, stirring just as Cookie instructed.

"Now, heat up that griddle and get 'em cookin', girl." Cookie nodded her head toward the stove. "A minute or two on each side, then flip."

"Yes. Right." Only, how did one get the batter—especially one this lumpy—onto the griddle? Seemed an impossible task.

As if reading her mind, Cookie said, "Fill that large pitcher with batter and pour out flapjacks the size of a fist. Make sure they're all the same size."

"Hmm."

Getting the batter from the bowl to the pitcher proved to be a bit more problematic than Abby expected. She then tipped the pitcher over the griddle, and a large quantity of the messy stuff poured out in chunky clumps. It sat there, doing nothing.

"You've got to heat it up first, Miss Abigail." Neville rushed to her side, stoked the fire, and before long the edges of her lopsided flapjack were sizzling. He handed her a spatula and she gripped it as if her life depended on it.

"Time for a flip," Cookie said, as she passed by with a platter loaded with ham. "But don't just cook one at a time. Cover the whole griddle with blobs of batter. I usually do five or six pancakes at once, not one or two. We've got a lot of mouths to feed."

"Right."

Abby took the spatula and slipped it under the half-cooked flapjack then gingerly tried to lift it. Unfortunately, it split down the middle. She managed to get half of it turned over. The other half landed on the floor. This proved to be a bigger mess than she'd bargained for as Jin happened by and stepped in the gooey blob, then took to slipping and sliding across the floor. He managed to right himself before going down, but spit out a phrase in Chinese that only Neville might've been able to interpret.

"Oh dear, I'm so sorry." Abby knelt down to clean the mess, and while doing so burned a round of pancakes. Wonderful. Wasn't she off to a terrific start?

❤

Sam stuck his head in the door of the kitchen, more than a little worried. "How long till the flapjacks are done, ladies? The men are asking, and asking is putting it mildly."

"Just a few minutes," Cookie called back, then muttered, "I hope."

"You hope?" He took a few steps into the kitchen and stopped at the stove, where Abigail stood, spatula in hand. He'd seen more than his fair share of messes over the years, but nothing like this. She had batter on her apron, batter on her cheek, and scorched pancakes covering the griddle. Poor girl. She looked about as confident as a farmer performing an appendectomy on one of his cows.

"Let's start again." He took the spatula from her hand and stuck it under the flapjack closest to the front and flipped it with ease. Then he turned the second, and the third. All of them came straight off the griddle and into the trash bin. He poured batter once again, this time manning the process himself.

"Watch where you're standing, Sammy." Cookie gestured to the floor and he glanced down to find a blob of batter under his boot.

"What happened here?"

"I happened." Abigail reached for a broom. She nudged him with it and he stepped aside, all the while keeping a watchful eye on the flapjacks.

She managed to get the floor cleaned just as he flipped them with ease.

"Your turn." He filled several plates with flapjacks and ham and then handed her the spatula.

She stood at the edge of the stove, a terrified look on her face.

"Never you mind, Miss Abigail." Neville took the spatula from her. "I'll take over the flapjacks. You just help Sam with the serving."

Serve those rowdy fellows breakfast? She'd rather be incarcerated in the local jail. Still, the idea of standing in front of the stove flipping flapjacks left her feeling wobbly in the knees.

She made her way out to the dining hall and greeted the fellows with a forced smile. Before long, however, they had her laughing. By the time the breakfast crowd thinned, Abby had to admit, the process of waiting tables had been a far sight easier than cooking. Or flipping.

The rest of the day went by in a blur. Maggie O'Callahan stopped by at noon to pick up their dirty clothes. The fiery redhead had a lively sense of humor, just as the coach driver had said. She and Cookie appeared to be good friends, and why not? The two women had much in common—they were both single, in their fifties, and ran successful businesses.

Abby couldn't believe it when the dinner hour rolled around. It seemed they'd just cleaned up the dishes from lunch. Not that she had time to think about it. No, she was far too busy scooping up servings of chicken and rice casserole and serving up healthy portions to the men. And Les, who arrived fashionably late reading a book. She took the table nearest the kitchen and spent much of her meal nose to the page.

Abby approached to refill her coffee cup. "Good book?"

Les shrugged. "I've read it before, but don't have much to pick from out here."

"I'm a reader too. In fact, I read an interesting book on the train."

"Oh?" Les leaned forward and put her elbows on the table. "I love to read, but we have to wait months to get books. By the time I get around to reading novels, they've run their course back east."

"I'll be happy to loan it to you. It's called *Wuthering Heights*."

"*Wuthering Heights*. What a mysterious name."

"For a somewhat mysterious story. And my, the relationships in this novel are complicated."

"As they are in real life, I have discovered." Lesley appeared downcast as she spoke these words.

"You can let me know what you think after you've read it. I'll bring the book down after lunch."

"Wonderful. Thank you."

"The author, Miss Emily Bronte, died just after the novel released. Her sister edited the story and it was rereleased posthumously." She sighed. "I find it rather sad that a young authoress didn't become famous until after her death."

"For pity's sake, me too. If heads are gonna turn my way, let it be while I'm alive and kickin'." Les leaned back in her chair and kicked up her legs in rowdy fashion, then just as quickly put them down again. "Oops. Did I look like one of them gals over at the saloon?"

"Not if you tried all day." Abby patted her new friend on the shoulder. "I better get back to work. Maybe we can visit later."

"I'd love that."

Abby dove back in but after some time, she began to feel dizzy. Probably the heat from the stove. Or maybe it had more to do with the swelling in her feet.

When the meal ended, she and Jin went to work on the dishes. With that task finally ended, she sat at one of the tables in the dining hall, so weary she could hardly move.

Neville took the seat across from her, his face glistening with sweat.

"Miss Abigail, it's too much. We must return to Philadelphia as soon as possible."

She leaned her head on the table and groaned. "Mama will come to us as soon as the roads clear."

"We don't know that."

"I know Mama." Abby looked up from the table. "She will see this as another one of her adventures. She will come, I assure you."

"But will you last until then?" Neville gave her such a compassionate look that she almost burst into tears. Crying, however, would take energy that she simply didn't have right now.

"I will last." She did her best to stand, but uncooperative knees threatened to buckle beneath her.

"Here, Miss Abigail." Neville lent a hand and she managed to stand. Abby didn't mean to groan aloud, but the pain in her back made it impossible to remain silent. She shifted from foot to foot to shift the pain.

Cookie entered the dining hall, wiping her hands on her apron. "You okay over there, girlie?" she called out.

"I suppose." Abby glanced across the room, her gaze landing on Sam and Les, who stood at the front door of the restaurant, deep in conversation.

"Cookie, can I ask a question?"

"Sure, hon."

"I couldn't help but notice that Sam is. . .drawn. . .to Miss Lesley."

"Les? And Sam?" Cookie paused and appeared to be thinking. "Never gave it a moment's thought, to be honest, and certainly never saw them as a couple, if that's what you mean."

"She's older though, right?"

"Older?" Cookie shrugged. "Maybe by a couple of years, but out here folks don't pay any attention to such things. If a fella happens to fall for a woman a few years older—or younger—no one blinks an eye. Guess that's what happens when the pickin's are slim."

"How come no one's grabbed you up, Cookie?" Abby asked. "You're quite the catch."

Cookie's cheeks flamed crimson. "Me? No one could live with a

bossy old thing like me. First of all, I'm not half the gal I used to be."
She ran her hands over her plump backside. "Actually, now that I think
of it, I'm twice the gal I used to be." Raucous laughter followed. "But I'm
not the sort men give a second glance. Never have been."

"You're one of the finest ladies I've ever met." Abby rested her hand
on Cookie's arm. "And any man would be a fool not to notice."

"Well, pooh." With the wave of her dishcloth Cookie dismissed that
idea. "What fun would it be, marrying a woman who spends three quarters of her life behind a hot stove?"

"He'd never go hungry."

"True, but why feed one man when I can fill the stomachs of hundreds?" She shrugged.

"You're a peach, Cookie. Always remember that." Abby gave her a
little kiss on the cheek. "And just for the record, fellas love a woman who
knows how to cook, which just goes to show you that I'll be a spinster
for the rest of my life."

Her gaze shifted to Sam and Les once again. If a gal like Les
could find a fella, then maybe someone like Abby—a woman with no
prospects—could find one too.

Chapter Nine

*O*n Saturday morning, Abby could barely pull herself from the bed. Only when Cookie rapped on her door did she finally stir. Doing so caused every square inch of her body to cry out in pain.

She somehow managed to get dressed and hobble down the stairs. Each step made her wince in agony, the aching in her hip joints and knees excruciating. On top of all of this, her head pounded and her stomach felt queasy.

Abby eased her way across the dining hall, then into the kitchen, where she reached for an apron.

"You all right, kid?" Cookie looked her way, concern etched on her brow.

Abby shook her head, which only served to aggravate the headache. "I think I might be ill."

"Really?" Cookie rested her palm against Abby's forehead then pulled it away. "You don't feel feverish. Is your stomach upset?"

"A little. Right here." Abby put her hand on her side. "I ache all over."

"Mm-hmm. I see." Cookie's lips curled up in a hint of a smile. "Does your back hurt?"

"Oh, yes. Terribly."

"And your feet?"

Abby tried to wiggle her toes but found the task too painful. "I've never felt anything like it. They're swollen too. I could barely lace up my boots. That's what took so long. Almost came down to the kitchen in my bare feet."

"Headache?"

"Something awful." Abby groaned. "Do you think I should see the doctor?"

"No, child. No doctor necessary. But I do know what's ailing you."

"You do?" A wave of relief swept over Abby. "What is it?"

"I believe the expression is 'bone tired.'"

"What?"

"You're bone tired. Your body is exhausted from all the work you've done over the past several days. And I would venture a guess that you've never worked this many hours in a row before."

Abby felt her cheeks grow warm. "I, well. . ."

Behind her, Neville coughed. He slipped on his apron and got to work.

Before Abby could stop it, a groan slipped out. "All right, all right. I've never worked like this. . .ever. The most physical labor I've ever done was when we volunteered at the mission house and I swept the floors. But even then, someone else came along behind me and picked up what I'd left." She plopped down into a chair. "So, you don't think I'm dying?"

"We're all dying, honey. No one lives forever, this side of heaven, anyway." Cookie laughed. "But as for your aches and pains, I'd say your body just needs time to adjust to the new routine. Before long you'll be fit as a fiddle. Those muscles will stop aching eventually and you'll toughen up. In the meantime, I'll give you some liniment to rub on the achy parts."

Abby gestured from her head to her toes. "I hope you have a lot of liniment. I'm going to need it by the bucketload."

Cookie laughed and slapped her arm over Abby's shoulders. Abby let out a cry of pain.

"Oh, sorry." Cookie pulled her arm away. "Shoulders aching too, eh?"

"I told you, everything hurts. Even my eyes hurt when I blink them. And my fingers, when I bend them." She extended a hand and offered an example, wincing when the pain became unbearable as she closed it to a fist. "I'm useless, Cookie. Totally and completely useless."

"Pooh on that. Your body will catch up in short order."

"If I don't die first."

"No one ever died from hard work."

"Not true, not true," Jin said. "I once saw man collapse carrying barrel of water. Too heavy. He die fast. See with my own eyes!"

"Except for that one instance, no one ever died from hard work." Cookie shot Jin a warning look. "Put on your apron, Abby. We've got hungry men coming through in thirty minutes, and we haven't even started cracking eggs yet or slicing bacon. Oh, and we need to peel potatoes. I'm fryin' 'em up with some onions this morning. The fellas like that with their bacon."

"Yes, Cookie." Abby attempted to stand but felt like crying as the pain in the back of her calves made doing so impossible.

"Here, Miss Abigail, allow me." Neville offered her a hand. She braced herself and finally managed to stand aright. "You use that liniment and you'll feel better in no time."

"I hope so." Abby hobbled back to her room and Cookie arrived a short time later, liniment in hand. Abby managed to coat the sore spots, all the while fighting the temptation to climb back into bed. Then she rejoined Cookie and the men in the kitchen.

Sam took one look at her and his eyes grew wide. "You all right?"

She shook her head, but went straight to the stove to lay out strips of bacon and then started peeling potatoes. Before long she was in a steady rhythm, going back and forth between the stove and the sink.

"How did you fill your days back in England?" Cookie asked. "Not by peeling potatoes, I would imagine."

"Or plucking chickens," Sam added with a crooked grin.

"Never peeled a potato in my life, I'm ashamed to admit." Abby paused and her thoughts shifted back to what life had been like in Effingham. "I did take lessons on the pianoforte. And I visited the sick at the infirmary, took baskets of goodies and what-not."

"Things you baked?"

"No." Abby shook her head. "Our family had the most wonderful cook." She clamped a hand over her mouth as she glanced Cookie's way then pulled her hand down and said, "She couldn't compare to you, Cookie, of course."

"Compliment unnecessary, but thank you very much." Cookie nodded. "But you're saying the cook did all the baking and you delivered the goods?"

"Yes." Abby paused, her thoughts shifting. "Guess I hadn't pictured it that way. Always felt like I was the one doing the work, but I suppose she carried the heavier load."

"We all do our part, honey." Cookie rested a hand on Abby's arm. "That's what makes teamwork so precious. All hands on deck, as it were. When we work together, we accomplish much." She gave Abby a compassionate look. "And for the record, I now see that you and Sammy have more in common than I'd first thought."

"We do?" Abby and Sam spoke in unison.

"Well, sure. He's always trying to think of ways to help the down and out. Sounds like you were busy doing the same thing, back in England and here."

"Here?" Abby cast Cookie a sideways glance.

"Don't think I didn't see you giving Jedediah Tucker an extra ham steak the other morning."

"Ah." Abby's nose wrinkled. "Sorry about that."

"Don't be. We've no shortage of food, and he's got a limited supply of funds. I've slipped him several meals myself. So has Sam. And he's stayed up there in Sam's tithe room more than a few times. Which brings me back to my point. The two of you are both focused on others, not yourselves."

"Which is precisely why I've been so concerned." Neville's voice sounded from beside her.

Abby glanced his way, intrigued by his comment. "What do you mean?"

"You've been so busy looking out for the well-being of your parents that you've sacrificed your own personal comfort and safety. That's what I mean." He put his hands on his hips and released a breath. "There. I've said it. Said what I've been thinking for a year and a half now. I dare say, it feels rather good to get that off my chest." Neville turned on his heel and reached for a tray. "Back to work."

"Oh, my." Cookie looked genuinely astounded. "The man speaks. More than a word or two at a time, I mean."

"I suppose he does." Abby marveled at Neville's words. "Though I've never heard anything like that come out of his mouth before."

"San Francisco emboldens folks." Cookie laughed. "Trust me when I say that many a fellow has dared to speak his mind here. Women, too. All inhibitions are thrown aside in California."

A few minutes later, food prepared, Cookie rang the breakfast bell and then opened the door to a waiting public. Abby stood with coffeepot in hand, ready to fill men's cups with the tantalizing brew. The first man through the door was Marcus Denueve. His eyes widened in surprise when he saw her standing there.

"Well, I guess it's true." He shook his head and his eyes narrowed to slits.

"What's true?" She gestured for him to take a seat and then she filled his cup.

"That you'd gone to work for the Harrises. Had to come see for myself. Couldn't picture it, to be honest with you."

"It's true." She brushed a loose strand of hair behind her ear and did her best not to flinch as a pain in her hip nearly caused her to fall.

Marcus gave her a tender look. "Miss Effingham, I hope you don't mind my mentioning this, but you look. . ."

"Like something the cat dragged in?"

"Well, I was going to say exhausted."

She felt like releasing a groan but it would have taken too much energy. "I believe I met and passed exhausted several days ago. I thought, perhaps, I might have influenza. Every joint rebelled at the slightest attempt to put one foot in front of the other. But Cookie assures me I will live. I'm just—as she says—bone tired."

He gave her a look so gentle it almost melted her. "Aren't you tired of living this way? Don't you wish you could go back to an easy, carefree life?"

"I will admit, the idea holds some appeal." She stepped to the next table and filled cups with coffee before rejoining Mr. Denueve in conversation. "But there is value in hard work that I never appreciated before."

"Of course. But perhaps somewhere in the middle would be nice?" He gestured for her to join him at his table, but she had far too much work to do for that.

"Meaning?"

"Meaning, a bit of work, something to bring fulfillment. But not so much that it causes you distress or pain. A young woman of your position should be enjoying life, not wearing herself to a thread."

"I keep reminding myself it's only for a season. I will be going home to Philadelphia by late summer, and must plow forward until then."

"Won't your father send funds to help you until then?"

"He would. . .if I asked."

"Are you saying he doesn't know about your situation?" Mr. Denueve looked aghast.

Abby managed the groan. "He knows we arrived safely. And, from what I've been told, Neville sent word that things are difficult, though I haven't heard back from Father yet. But how was I to know that everything in San Francisco would be triple the price? Or ten times, in some cases? It's highway robbery."

"Folks around here are accustomed to the prices, ridiculous as they might be." He lifted his coffee cup and took a sip. "They toss pieces of gold at shop owners like they were candy."

"I don't have pieces of gold."

"Though you are a fine prospect." His brows elevated mischievously.

"Beg your pardon?" Was the man really flirting with her. . .again? In her current state, no less?

"Sorry." He removed his hat and set it on the table. "Just making a pun. You're worth more than all the gold in that river, Miss Effingham. That's all I'm saying. So take care of yourself. Please."

"Trust me, I'm. . ." What was the word Neville used, again? Ah yes. "Acclimating."

"So, what was it like. . .before?"

"Before what?" Abby asked.

"Before coming here. What sort of life did you lead? Judging from the gown you were wearing the day we met, I'd say you were some sort of socialite."

She brushed damp hair from her face. "I suppose some would say that. I spent my days on charity work and the like. I learned the things that all girls learned."

"Like what?"

"Pianoforte."

"Pianoforte?" His eyes lit up. "Are you telling me you play the piano?"

"Of course. All of the young women in society do."

"You play the piano and you didn't tell us?" He seemed genuinely interested in this notion but she couldn't imagine why.

"Likely, not the sort of music you're accustomed to hearing, but I do play."

"Anything restaurant customers would fancy?"

"Chopin. Mozart."

"Hmm." A pause followed on his end. "What if I paid you a nice wage—a really nice wage—to come and play in a restaurant for a couple of hours each night? You wouldn't have to be on your feet, and I know the fellows would love it."

"Play piano in a restaurant?" She shivered. "I'm trying to picture the look on my father's face. He would be mortified. But why are you asking anyway? You don't own a restaurant, do you?"

"I do now." A mischievous smile tipped the edges of his lips. "I have purchased the Watering Hole and have grandiose plans to convert it into a fine dining establishment. As for your father, he would be equally as mortified, I dare say, to see you in your current condition. Any father with half a heart would." He paused. "Think about it, Miss Effingham. I feel sure your piano pieces could be adapted to a dining atmosphere. Can you play 'Vive La Compagnie'? Things like that?"

She offered a shrug in response. "I suppose I could pick it out, though I do better with written music. But I hear the Watering Hole's pianist playing all of the time. Can't he play for your restaurant too?"

"Yep, but he's headed back to Illinois. Dying mother, or some such thing. So, think about it, Miss Effingham. I'm sure you'll enjoy the money it will bring in."

Earning an income without having to stand on her feet all day over a hot stove almost sounded too good to be true. On the other hand, things that sounded too good to be true. . .usually turned out to be just that.

♥

Sam didn't mean to listen in on the conversation between Marcus and Abby, but couldn't help himself.

"What's all this about Abby playing the piano?" he asked.

Abby turned to face him, her smile strained. "Yes, Marcus has purchased the saloon and is turning it into a restaurant. He's asked me to play some classical pieces for the patrons."

"Did he, now." Sam set a plate of food down in front of Marcus and bit back the temptation to say more.

"Sure did." The fellow reached for his fork. "I'll be changing the name shortly to the Lucky Penny."

"What about the mercantile?" Sam asked.

"Still running the mercantile. But Herb Madison offered me a deal I couldn't pass up on the saloon, so I'll be stepping in as proprietor." Marcus took a bite of his eggs and leaned back in the chair, a satisfied expression on his face.

"Not gonna call it the Watering Hole anymore?"

"That's right." Marcus dabbed his lips with his napkin. "Bringing the place up to higher standards. Grand opening on the last Friday in June. Hope you can join us."

Sam's blood began to boil at this news. Marcus Denueve was a scoundrel, at best. He tripled or even quadrupled the prices on everyday items at the mercantile. What would he do to prices at the saloon? And what was next? Would he buy out Maggie O'Callahan? Then the bathhouse? Before long, every place in town would be owned by the scoundrel, who would raise rates all over the place.

On the other hand, maybe the higher prices at the local saloon would nudge the heavy drinkers toward sobriety. Sam wasn't stupid. He knew the saloon wasn't going away anytime soon, no matter what pretty words Marcus used to entice Abby to work for him.

"We'll be serving food now too. Not just liquor." Marcus took another bite and leaned back in his chair. "Mmm."

"A full menu?" This news took Samuel by surprise.

"Don't fret, Sammy." Marcus gave him a nod but the sour expression that followed seemed more than a little condescending. "There are plenty of hungry men in town. I won't be cutting in on your business. Much. But wait until you meet my new chef." He chuckled. "Fine fellow, by the way. Just arrived from France. Trained as a chef in Paris. He's been a friend of the Denueve family for years." Marcus's gaze narrowed. "I have it on good authority he's wonderful with American fare, though I dare say his cooking won't hold a candle to Cookie's, of course." A strained smile followed.

"Trained in Paris?" Sam did his best not to snort aloud. Who did this fellow think he was trying to impress? Folks round here loved good home cooking, not fancy stuff.

"Yep. Don't let that fool you, though. He's a master at cuisines from around the world, which should appeal to the men in San Francisco, seeing as how they come from the four corners of the globe. I'm sure many of them have been aching for the foods from home, and now they can have that."

A sinking feeling landed in the pit of Sam's stomach. Instead of showing his dismay, he forced a smile. "Well, I wish you the best, Marcus."

"Thanks, friend."

Ugh. Friend?

"See?" Abby glanced Sam's way with a smile that reflected her delight. "This will be so good for business, to have two full-service restaurants in town. So don't worry, Sammy."

"Sam." He didn't mean to spit out the word, but there it was.

"Sammy." She laughed. "I've been spending entirely too much time with Cookie. She's rubbing off on me."

Marcus looked up from his plate. "If her cooking skills are rubbing off, then I might just have to hire you to bake for the restaurant too. Did I mention we're going to offer desserts?"

Now Sam wanted to throttle the man. How dare he try to steal Abby away from the Gold Rush Inn?

"I'm no baker." Abby put her hands up, as if admitting defeat. "Trust me when I say that I won't ever be. I'm doing well just to peel a few potatoes and wait tables."

"All good things come with time," Marcus said, his gaze never leaving Abby's pretty face. "All good things come with time."

Sam went back and forth between wanting to say something he might regret to Marcus and wondering if he should warn Abby about the potential for disaster, if she actually followed through with Marcus's plan.

He pulled her aside and lowered his voice, ready to share his thoughts. "Miss Abigail, I do hope you will forgive me if I've overstepped, but taking care of yourself in San Francisco is a far sight harder than in Nottingham or even Philadelphia. These fellas around here are. . ." His words trailed off. "Different. We'll leave it at that. And, as for Marcus, I find it difficult to believe he's turning the saloon into a restaurant. Believe me, it won't be the kind of establishment you need to frequent."

Abby put her hands on her hips, perturbed by his intrusion. "And what's it to you?"

"Nothing. Just saying the risk is too great."

"I can take care of myself, Sam. Besides, it's just a restaurant. Nothing more." She pulled away from him and turned back toward Mr. Denueve, who flashed a contrived smile before diving back into his eggs.

Sam knew better, but this conversation was clearly over. Abby turned on her heels and headed toward the kitchen, clearly aggravated. Oh well. He'd rather have her upset at him than hurt by the likes of Marcus Denueve any day.

Chapter Ten

"Trained in Paris?" Cookie put her hands on her hips and paced the kitchen. "Is that what he said? He's hired a chef who trained in Paris?"

Sam nodded. "Yep."

Abby looked on as Cookie's face contorted. She couldn't understand why everyone was so upset at this news. Didn't they see that competition would be good for business, not the other way around?

"I heard the whole thing, Miss Cookie," Jin added. "Fancy man cook fancy food."

With the wave of a hand, Cookie appeared to dismiss that idea. The tense lines on her forehead relaxed. "He'll be gone in a week. Men round here won't abide that fancy-schmancy stuff. They like hearty down-home cooking."

"He says this fella knows how to cook foods from around the world, stuff some of the guys have missed out on since coming here."

"He cook Chinese food?" Jin's face lit up and he clasped his hands together. "I go eat. When he come?"

Cookie glared at him. "Jin, in all the time I've known you, you've never asked me to cook Chinese food for you."

"You no offer." He shrugged. "That why."

A groan escaped Cookie's lips and she reached for a dishcloth to wipe the sweat from her brow. "So this is the thanks I get. My own workers, turning on me for a plate of food they haven't even tasted yet."

Abby listened in until her mind took to wandering. What fun, to think about a classically trained chef coming to town. San Francisco could use a bit of culture, after all. She missed fine dining. Why, this new chef might be just the ticket to bring a bit of class to an otherwise chaotic town.

Sam disagreed, if such a thing could be judged from the way he huffed around. He muttered under his breath, but she made out enough of it to realize he was truly upset by this.

After some time, she could take it no longer. "Why are you so worried about Mr. Denueve turning the saloon into a restaurant? I would imagine it to be a good business venture for him, and you've been moaning about that saloon since I met you."

"Oh, he's quite the businessman, all right. I have no doubt he'll turn a profit." Sam seemed to stop short of saying more, which intrigued her.

"Then what does it matter? To my way of thinking, turning the saloon into a restaurant is a good thing. Maybe the menfolk will sober up a bit and eat foods from their homelands instead of ordering whiskey and such."

"I sincerely doubt that."

"You're worried he'll cut into your profits?"

"No." Sam shook his head. "I'm worried he'll undercut me altogether."

"How so?"

Judging from the look on Sam's face, this was not a good thing. "That's how business works, Abby. Competition. He'll start with lower prices, finer foods."

"Hey, now." Cookie put her hands on her hips.

"I'm not saying it'll really be finer, just saying that's how he'll advertise: lower prices, finer foods. Then, after he gets the fellas in his pocket, he'll nudge those prices up."

"Just keep your prices low," Abby argued. "The men will keep coming here." She felt sure of it, in fact.

"While he's raising prices on our supplies? We'll be forced to keep elevating costs on our food too. This plan of his has the potential to end up putting us all out of business—and don't think that's not in his plan. He knows exactly what he's doing."

"Posh. You're overreacting."

From the expression on his face, she'd struck a nerve. Sam looked downright miffed as he muttered, "Am I?"

"Yes." She squared her shoulders. "As you are prone to do."

Oh dear. She'd crossed a line, and a pretty big one, at that. Oh well. Sam would get used to this idea in time.

♥

Sam faced Abby, stunned by her words. "You think I overreact?"

A little shrug followed on her end and her cheeks flamed pink. "Just feels like you're turning a little thing into a big thing." Her brow wrinkled and she appeared to lose herself to her thoughts. "What's that expression you Americans use? Something about mountains and molehills?"

"You honestly think I make too much of things? How is it possible that you've come to this conclusion in the little amount of time you've known me?"

She crossed her arms. "I'm just saying, in this particular situation, that you are already seeing the worst before it even arrives. Try to look on the hopeful side, Sammy."

"Sam. And there's no hopeful side where Marcus Denueve is concerned. Trust me, Abby. I've known him a lot longer than you have. I know what he's capable of." That was the real problem here, of course. Abby didn't know Marcus's history. She didn't realize that his ultimate plan included taking over the town and picking the flesh off the bones of every citizen on his way to the top.

Abby appeared to dismiss his concerns. "Right now, he's simply capable of opening a restaurant, and that has you in a dither. A bit of class might be a good thing, Sam. Can't you see that? And healthy businesses thrive when others give them a run for their money. I've always found that to be true, whether in England, Philadelphia, or San Francisco. Competition is a good thing."

"For the one who has the upper hand, maybe. And trust me, he'll give me a run for my money, all right." Sam couldn't take much more of this conversation. Either Abby was blind or simply naive. He did his best to sound fatherly as the words, "Eyes wide open, Miss Abigail," spilled out. "Some things—and people—require keener vision."

"I've never been accused of sleepwalking."

"I understand. Just be aware that some men are not what they appear to be."

"I'm a big girl, Mr. Harris. And, as for Marcus Denueve, why he seems a perfectly decent chap. Well dressed. Nicely groomed." She looked Sam over from head to toe, as if comparing him to Marcus.

"A clean body is no indication of a clean heart. Don't be fooled by the exterior, or his enticements to pay you a better salary."

Cookie gasped. "He wants to steal Abby away from us?"

"Yep. Wants to put her to work at the saloon."

"What?" Cookie looked as if she might faint.

Actually, Neville looked a bit pale too. Not that Sam had time to pay them much mind at the moment.

"He's sly, that one," Cookie said.

Now Abby looked downright mad. "It won't be a saloon, it'll be a restaurant by then. And just for the record, he's asked me to play a few piano pieces, nothing more. Besides, who are we to judge another man's heart?" She turned to face Cookie. "Aren't you the one who's always spouting off scriptures? How about this one: 'Judge not, that ye be not judged.'"

The words were spoken to Cookie, but Sam had a feeling they were meant for him.

"It's hardly a judgement call on my part to warn you of a man with a reputation," he said. "But don't take my word for it. Ask anyone around here what they think of Marcus Denueve. Ask Cookie. Ask Jedediah Tucker. How do you think he came to lose all of his money?"

Abby shook her head and reached for a dishcloth. "Why would I engage in gossip? Isn't that a sin?"

He released an exaggerated sigh. "I can't win here. So, do as you wish. I can only hope and pray you don't find out the hard way that not every man is what he claims to be."

"I'm not naive, Mr. Harris."

Perhaps she wasn't. This was a woman who had traveled the world, after all. What life skills had he obtained to compare? A trek from St. Louis to San Francisco was hardly the same. Still, staring at her right now, standing in Cookie's kitchen, she looked like a woman in need of protecting. And he would like to be the first to sign up for that job.

♥

Abby fussed and fumed all day over Sam's words. Did he think she was a baby in need of coddling? If so, then shame on him. She didn't need another father figure in her life. She already had one of her own. Actually, two, if you counted Neville. And you certainly had to count Neville, as he was ever-present. What was it with men, to think she couldn't take care of herself? Did she really come across as a pampered child?

The anger that rose up inside of her caused Abby to forget about the pain in her joints. In fact, by early afternoon, after the lunch crowd left, she felt absolutely energized. So much so, that when Les entered the kitchen with a large bucket of cherries, she grabbed it without thinking twice. Of course, she almost dropped it in the process, and Les rushed in to help.

"Whoa, Nellie. That bucket's full-up."

"I can see that." Abby hefted it onto the counter top. "Looks like we'll be having cherry pie again soon."

"I can't resist. I'd pick cherries all day, just for a slice of Cookie's pie." Les glanced around the kitchen. "Where is everyone?"

"Cookie's gone to the mercantile for flour. She ran short."

"I see. And Jin?"

"Don't tell Cookie, but I think he's taking a nap."

"Wouldn't be the first time. And Sam?"

Abby flinched at the mention of his name, but tried not to let it show. "In some sort of business meeting with his father. I don't know. I think they're dreaming up a plan for a bakery next door."

"Yes, I've heard all about that from Cookie." Les took a seat on one of the wooden stools and gave Abby a thoughtful look. "I've been reading the book you loaned me."

"*Wuthering Heights*? What do you think?"

"Well, it's rather dark and dreary, I must say, but I've stumbled across a line that has captivated me."

"Oh?"

"Yes, and it suits my situation perfectly."

"Tell me." Abby took a seat.

Les cleared her throat and then spoke in an exaggerated theatrical voice. " 'He shall never know I love him: and that, not because he's handsome, but because he's more myself than I am. Whatever our souls are made out of, his and mine are the same.' " She paused and dropped her head down onto the table.

"Are you all right?" Abby asked.

"Yes, it's just so beautiful. How wonderful would it be, to have someone feel that way about you? To know that your souls were firmly linked and that he loved the real you, the one and only you."

Abby grew silent at the very thought of this. If all the fellas in the world were like Sam—determined to make her feel like a child—she would never know that kind of love.

Fine wrinkles formed between Les's brows. "You okay, Abby? Seem a bit out of sorts. Was it something I said?"

"Just tired. And wondering how I landed in a town filled with stubborn, pigheaded men."

Les guffawed and slapped her knee. "Welcome to my world. And here I thought I was the only one who felt that way. Go figure."

"Not sure I like your world, to be perfectly honest. These men are of the opinion that we women can't take care of ourselves."

"I've spent my whole life trying to prove otherwise." Les squared her shoulders. "Then again, maybe I've done too good a job."

"What do you mean?"

"I've pushed most of the fellas away with my forward thinking, I guess. They don't look twice at me. Not like they'd look at you, anyway."

For a moment, she looked sad. This caught Abby by surprise.

"You have your eye on anyone in particular?" she asked.

"Mm-hmm." Les nodded and the edges of her lips curled up in a delightful smile, giving her a girlish appearance. "Like I said, I doubt he'd give me more than a glance, seeing as how I dress like one of the fellas most of the time."

Fascinating news. "Ever give thought to changing that?"

Les shrugged. "Gave up on panning ages ago, but these old Levis are worn and comfortable now. Can't picture myself going back to a corset and laces. Too confining."

"I'm not saying you'd have to take it that far, though you've certainly got a slim waistline to accentuate. But if you're ever inclined to dress up, let me know. I've got some gowns you could try, just for fun."

"You think I should?" Les's brow wrinkled.

"That depends on how badly you want to catch the eye of that fella of yours." And by fella, Abby meant Sam. She couldn't argue the notion that Sam and Les had eyes for each other.

"Hmm." Les seemed to lose herself in her thoughts. "I'll keep that in mind, Miss Abigail."

"Please, call me Abby."

"I'll keep that in mind, Miss Abby. But don't think I'm going to end up looking like you—a picture postcard."

"I'm no picture postcard."

The expression on Les's face showed her thoughts on the matter. Clearly, she disagreed. "Compared to the few women in this town, you certainly are. So, hold your head up high and carry on. Folks'll live vicariously through you. I know I do." For a moment, Les seemed to lose herself in her ponderings. Just as quickly, she snapped to attention.

"Interesting," Abby countered, "because that's just what I'd say about you. I admire you very much, Les. You're so independent and strong. I wish the fellas around here saw me like that instead of a baby to be coddled."

"Sounds like we could give each other lessons."

"Lessons? Funny idea." Abby shook her head. "If you want the truth, half the men in this town could stand to take a few lessons in manners.

Then they would know how to treat a lady—gently, but with respect. There's a balance to it, I think, one that eludes most men."

Les's eyes sparkled with excitement. "Well, there you go, Abby." She slapped her knee. "You should teach classes. I know I'd come."

"Teach classes?"

"Sure. Manners 'n' such. For the men and the ladies. Folks would pay for a class like that, I dare say."

"Would they now?" Abby paused to think it through. Maybe there was something to Les's suggestion. She would have to give it more thought. Right now, though, she simply had to don her apron and get busy plucking more chickens.

Chapter Eleven

*S*unday morning dawned clear and bright. Abby could hardly believe she had the luxury of sleeping in. With the restaurant closed on Sundays, she was free to lounge in bed until time for church. And, upon rising, she was finally able to wear one of her nicest dresses. All of this, in preparation for her first visit to church with Cookie. The smell of bacon tempted her, as always. By the time she made the descent down the stairs, the others had already eaten.

"Oh, am I too late?"

Cookie shook her head and pointed toward the kitchen. "I saved you a plate, honey. But eat quick. It's quite a walk to the church, and we'll need to leave in about twenty minutes."

Abby ate her food and helped with the dishes, then they set off on their way, Cookie leading the pack out the door.

"I'm so glad the restaurant is closed on Sundays," Abby observed as Sam put the CLOSED sign in place on the restaurant's door.

"Wouldn't have it any other way." Cookie's appearance conveyed her peacefulness. "We're closed so that folks can rest and recuperate. I keep some baked goods on the table out front. Don't know if you noticed, but they're leftovers from the week, so that the men can always find food. Most just go to the saloon, though."

"On Sunday?" Abby cringed. "Really?"

"Folks don't pay any mind to religious customs around here, I'm afraid," Sam interjected from behind her. "Not for lack of trying on our part."

"Yes, as for me and mine. . .we'll rest and worship on Sundays. Nothing less." Cookie took off at a faster clip toward the church.

"Could you slow down a bit?" Neville called out. "These aching joints of mine can't keep up with you."

"If you'd shave off those sideburns you'd move a lot faster." Cookie slowed her pace and lit into a monologue about the weather. After a while, she grew silent.

"I love how quiet and peaceful the town is on Sunday mornings," Abby observed as she looked around the various places of business, all closed up tight. "I'm glad most places opt to stay closed today."

"Most of the fellas are still asleep, after a night of brawling and gambling," Sam said. "I heard music coming from the saloon until two in the morning. It was all I could do to sleep."

"They don't go to church. . .at all?" Abby asked.

"Most of 'em don't. A few will come and go from time to time. I notice that Chet Jamison came last Sunday. That was a pleasant surprise."

"Who's Chet Jamison?"

"I feel sure you'd recognize him if I pointed him out. Comes to the restaurant nearly every day. Kind of a tall, lanky fellow with thinning hair."

"Oh, yes. I know him. He's a happy-go-lucky sort of person?"

"He covers the pain with laughter, I think. Chet came to town back in '49 with his brother, Adam. They formed a mining company. Did well for a season, but he blew through most of the money within a year."

"Sad."

"It's happened to far too many. I've seen fellows come to town with stars in their eyes, only to leave with their pockets emptier than ever. There's nothing more sobering than watching a man lose hope. That's what happened to Chet. So I'm happy to see him in church. Maybe God will grab hold of his heart and turn things around."

"I hope so."

"I've done my best to remind him that hope isn't found in possessions or in money. The only lasting hope is found in the Lord."

"Amen to that." Abby nodded. "Though I would imagine he didn't care for your sermon's message?"

"Didn't present it as a sermon; just a friendly conversation. I do understand what he's going through, to some extent. It's in the heart of every man, to find his destiny, to seek and conquer new places, new lands."

"The heart of every man?" Abby questioned.

"And some women too," Cookie countered. "Those with a daring sense of adventure." She slipped her hand through the crook of Abby's arm. "Like you. . .and me."

"And Mama. She's always had the wanderlust." Abby spoke the words aloud, but realized her mother's desire to travel probably had more to do with running away from Papa than discovering new lands.

"I don't suppose we've had it as hard as the miners, that's a fact."

"Oh?"

"Their working conditions are deplorable. Can you imagine being in water coming off of the glaciers for ten or twelve hours a day?" Cookie shivered, as if experiencing it firsthand. "The sun beats down on these poor fellas, so they're scalding hot from the waist up. But the water is as cold as ice, so they're freezing from the waist down. And most of them don't have a clue what they're doing. They've never mined before. Then they finally strike it rich, only to have someone take advantage of them. The whole thing is a fiasco, I tell you."

"My goodness, what a mess."

"Yes. Sorry to carry on so, but it's a long answer to a short question about why these men don't go to church. Lots of folks end up in California, but not as many end up in the Lord's house on Sundays, and that's a pity."

"I dare say most of the men around here wouldn't even know how to direct you to the local churches," Sam added.

"All of these souls and none of them attend to the Lord's work?" This notion broke Abby's heart.

"Half these men came from small towns where they sat in

hard-backed church pews every Sunday," Cookie explained. "They followed the dos and don'ts they learned in Sunday school. Out here, there's no one to monitor their comings and goings, so most have chosen different Sunday activities."

"Such as?"

Cookie pursed her lips. When she spoke, her words were edged with frustration. "I guess you could say that many have run amuck. They're like wild animals at times, as you have observed. Tempting, I'm sure, for those accustomed to rules and regulations."

"I've never assumed my faith to be based on rules and regulations. Quite the opposite, in fact."

"Then you've had a different upbringing than many of the men here."

"So how do they spend their Sundays?" Abby asked again.

Cookie slowed her pace. The color of her cheeks deepened to a dark red. "In the brothels, honey. And gambling halls."

"On the Lord's Day?" Abby's hand flew to cover her mouth. She couldn't imagine such a flagrant disrespect for God's holy day.

"Miners don't work on Sunday, but they do find other ways to, um. . ." Cookie cleared her throat. "Occupy their time. Let's just leave it at that."

Abby pulled down her hand and busied herself as she thought through her friend's words. "I see."

"I dare say you're getting quite the education here, Miss Abigail. Not sure your father would approve of any of it." Concern laced Neville's words.

Abby didn't blame him after what she'd just heard. Father would, indeed, be mortified by all this.

"Stay put in the restaurant as much as possible." Sam rested his hand on her arm. "That's my suggestion. Eyes wide open."

There he went, coddling her again.

"Yes, and keep your head down whenever you have to serve food too," Cookie added. "Now that the men are getting more familiar and comfortable with you. . ."

"Guard myself? In the dining room?"

Cookie nodded. "The menfolk here think nothing of slapping a woman on the backside or pulling her out to the dance floor for a spin, even if she's got a serving tray in hand. Best to ignore it and not over-react. I learned the hard way that putting up a fight will just make them try harder."

"Goodness." Abby wondered if perhaps getting on a stage back to St. Louis might be in order after this sort of warning.

"I'm hard pressed to figure out why these men seem to let go of their morals once they arrive in San Francisco." Sam slowed his pace, as if talking about this wearied him.

"Too much liquor," Neville observed, breaking his silence.

"And gambling is too common as well," Cookie threw in.

"Point is, they're bored." Sam shrugged. "That's my take on it any-way. They get bored and do things they wouldn't otherwise do. Then those things become habits."

"Bad habits." Cookie paused to look both ways before leading them across the street. With so few people out, they had little to worry about this morning. " 'Let all bitterness, and wrath, and anger, and clamour, and evil speaking, be put away from you, with all malice.' That's from the book of Ephesians, one of my favorites."

Abby thought through her friend's words. It boggled her mind to think about sweet, simple farm boys from across this great country turn-ing their souls over to the devil. How did a man transition from clean living to spending time with prostitutes and the like? She shivered, just thinking about it.

"I believe I need to make a dedicated effort to pray for the people of San Francisco while I'm at church," Abby said at last.

"While you're at church, at the restaurant, and in your bed at night. They need all the prayer you can offer, honey." Cookie picked up her pace and the church came into view. "These poor fellas are as lost as lost can be. It breaks my heart when I think of how the Lord must grieve over them."

"It's the story of the prodigal son all over again," Sam said. "Only, few return home to the Father, asking for forgiveness."

"Heartbreaking." Abby felt the weight of this conversation and it wearied her.

"Speaking of fathers, I haven't seen mine this morning." Sam's eyes narrowed and he paused. "Anyone catch a glimpse of him?"

Abby shook her head. "No, but I slept in, remember?"

"I didn't see him, either," Cookie added. "Guess he needed the rest?"

"I saw Mr. Harris early this morning." Neville kept walking as he spoke. "He left before dawn."

"Left before dawn?" Sam looked genuinely perplexed by this. "How odd."

They drew near the church and Abby stared at the building, simple in structure, a far cry from the elaborate cathedral she frequented in Philadelphia. Still, something about this sweet building drew her in. She accepted Sam's outstretched hand as they reached the steps.

"I had a thought, related to what we were talking about before."

"Oh?"

He continued to hold her hand as he spoke. "Remember when you were a child, how you despised your parents' rules?"

Abby nodded. "Sure."

"Well, picture all these young men, coming to a place where rules no longer apply. Many must feel like they've been set free to do as they choose. To them, it's a free-for-all."

"But I find myself here, in this same town, like all of them. Yet I cling to what I've always known to be true—my morals, my faith…everything. Nothing has changed inside of me."

Sam opened the door leading to the sanctuary. "Same here."

"That's how you could pray for these men, Abby." Cookie took a few steps into the sanctuary. "Pray that they return to their roots, that the work the Lord began in them back in their hometowns—be it Topeka, New York, Philadelphia or elsewhere—will be completed here."

"Is that even possible?" Abby asked.

Cookie paused and turned to face her. "With God all things are possible. He's bigger than these hoodlums. And we've got a biblical promise that if He started a work in the lives of these fellas, He'll be faithful to complete it. That's what my Bible says, anyway."

"Mine too," Abby agreed.

"And remember, 'Moreover the law entered, that the offence might abound. But where sin abounded, grace did much more abound.' That's from the book of Romans, fifth chapter."

"So, grace is the answer?" Abby asked.

"If a black eye doesn't work, then yes." Cookie chuckled, then offered a thoughtful pause. "Just joking about the black eye, of course." She waved at Reverend Linden, who approached with a smile.

"I don't believe these men give the Lord much to work with," Neville piped up after a long silent spell. "The black eye sounds like the better option, if you're asking my opinion." He stepped inside the church and walked up the aisle to a pew near the front.

Cookie shook her head. "Don't really agree with that, to be honest. These men give the Lord plenty to work with. I daresay the Almighty is hard at work right now, even now, tugging at hearts and drawing folks to Him."

"Amen to that!" the reverend said, and then extended his hand in Abby's direction. "Good to see you here. Welcome to our little congregation, Miss Abigail. We're happy to have you."

"I'm happy to be here," she countered.

Sam led the way to the pew Neville had chosen, where he gestured for Abby to take a seat. She scooted into place and soon found herself wedged between Cookie and Sam, with Neville on the other side of Cookie.

"It's going to take a miracle to turn things around in San Francisco." Sam spoke quietly, his words carrying the weight of his concern.

"I heard that, honey," Cookie piped up. "But remember, we happen to serve a God who specializes in the miraculous, and folks respond to miracles." She adjusted her position in the pew and looked directly at Abby. " 'And a great multitude followed him, because they saw his miracles which he did on them that were diseased.' That's what John chapter six says. And I'm of the firm opinion that God hasn't changed one iota. If He cared enough to perform a miracle on behalf of those folks in Bible days, then He cares enough to perform one now."

"Perhaps, but I've read my Bible cover to cover and don't recall any barroom brawl scenes," Neville countered, his words curt.

"True, but I do believe the Lord can tackle just about any challenge." Abby looked around to see if others were entering the church behind them. Marcus Denueve, perhaps? Surely she would see him this fine morning.

A couple of men stepped inside, along with the reverend and his wife, who greeted the men with a smile.

"The key here is to stay out of God's way while He's working." Cookie brushed her palms against her skirt. "More than once I've whopped a fella upside the head with a frying pan instead of listening to the voice of the Holy Spirit."

"Maybe it was the Holy Spirit telling you to knock some sense into them," Neville suggested. "Did you ever think of that? Some of these fellas need a comeuppance."

"I might just agree with you this time, Neville," Abby said.

"I'm pretty sure the Lord wasn't the one instructing me to leave a bruise on Ed Braynard's shoulder a couple months back." Cookie paused and a thoughtful look came over her. "The Bible says we should turn the other cheek."

"Do that around here and you get walloped on the other." Neville shrugged. "That's just my take on it, and I'm not sure what I—or anyone else—can do to fix that."

In that moment, Abby remembered her conversation with Les. It grabbed ahold of her and she couldn't wait to share. "I believe I can be of some service to the gentlemen while we're here."

"Gentlemen?" Neville's brows elevated. "What gentlemen?"

"The ones who frequent the restaurant, of course. The idea came from Les, actually. She suggested I offer my services to the fellas."

"Plenty of women in town doing that already," Sam whispered. "Not your best idea."

Abby slapped him on the arm. "You know that's not what I meant. I'm simply talking about courses in etiquette. Social graces. Diction. The things you once asked me to teach you. Remember? It wouldn't do you any harm to learn, either."

"I was joking," he said. "In case you couldn't tell. Just trying to make a newcomer feel welcome."

"That doesn't cheapen the idea," she countered.

Cookie snorted. "And just what, pray tell, are those ruffians going to do, once you've transformed them into butterflies?"

"Why, become husbands and fathers, of course." Abby smiled as the reverend's wife passed by. She gave Mrs. Linden a little wave.

"And where will you find the women?" Sam asked. "In order to be husbands, you have to locate a few wives."

She released a lingering sigh. "I haven't worked out that part yet. But first, we need to get the men looking more like the fellows back home."

Neville looked perplexed by this notion. "Home in England, Miss Abigail, or home in Philadelphia?"

"Philadelphia. I wouldn't presume to turn them into British gentlemen. My skills are good, but not that good." She tried to think through a plan, but nothing came to her.

"Are you serious about this, Abby?" Cookie asked. "If so, where will these classes be held?"

Abby paused and then looked around the quaint little room surrounding them. "Why not right here, at the church?"

Sam's expression soured. "Half the fellas will turn and run the other way. They won't grace the doors of the church."

"Even for something like this?" she asked.

Sam gave her a knowing look. "Especially for something like this."

"Well then, why not the restaurant? Tuesday evenings, perhaps? We could hold class. Neville will help me, won't you, Neville?"

The older man flinched. "Me? Teach lessons? Certainly not. Do I look like a schoolmarm to you?"

"But you would be perfect to teach a fellow how to speak to a lady, how to hold himself, how to dress."

"How to shave his sideburns," Cookie added.

"And Cookie. . ." Abby turned to face her. "You could teach table manners."

"Table manners?" Cookie laughed so hard she almost fell out of the pew. "That's priceless." After a moment, she looked Abby's way and said, "You're serious?"

"More so than I've ever been in my life."

Sam crossed his arms at his chest and gave her a knowing look. "I can tell you right now, Abby, that the men in this town aren't going to take to this lightly. No one will show up, wait and see."

Abby countered with the words, "They will if the grand prize is a lovely wife."

Sam shook his head. "Still don't know how the wives factor in, unless you plan to bring some from other parts of the country."

"I might." Abby paused to think it through. "Or, while we're converting the fellas, maybe I'll set my sights to work on the women over at the saloon too."

"So now we're converting the whole town?" Sam chuckled. "Might as well pray for the Red Sea to part, while you're at it."

"It happened once before," Cookie said.

"We've got our work cut out for us," Abby said. "But by the time my parents arrive, they will see that San Francisco isn't the godforsaken place they've read about in the papers. They'll find cultured, refined citizens at every turn." She paused, then snapped her fingers. "Citizens like Marcus Denueve. We can ask for his help too. He's respected by the men in town."

"Those he hasn't robbed blind," Sam muttered.

Abby shook her head, saddened by Sam's response. "I don't know why all of you are so hard on poor Mr. Denueve. He's truly one of the finest men in town. I've found him to be nothing but a gentleman. Why, if anyone could set a good example, he could."

Yes, she made up her mind then and there to involve Mr. Denueve in her plan to educate the townspeople. He would be just what the doctor ordered.

❤

Nothing but a gentleman? Sam wanted to slap himself on the forehead, just thinking about it. Abby found Marcus Denueve to be a gentleman? Why, the woman barely knew him. If she took the time to figure him out, she would see what a manipulative rapscallion he truly was. His hours behind closed doors with the local women would horrify Abby, if she knew.

Should he tell her? Marcus never so much as ventured through the doors of the church, except to give the reverend his bill from the mercantile or to toss Maggie a bundle of dirty clothes to wash. Why, he was anything but a gentleman.

Abby went on about her plan to educate the men in the social graces, but he didn't hear half of it. Instead, he found himself strangely focused on the dimple in her cheek whenever she smiled. How had he not noticed it before? And the lustrous color of that upswept hair under the glow of sunlight streaming in through the church windows. . .how had he not taken note of the flecks of gold in it, lovelier than any nuggets in the American River?

"Snap out of it, Sam."

Had he really spoken those words aloud?

"I'm sorry, Sam. What did you say?" Abby glanced his way just as the reverend passed by, headed to the front of the room.

"Oh." He shook off his ponderings and fought for an answer. "I need to snap some. . .peas."

"Snap peas?" Cookie gave him an incredulous look. "Since when do you snap peas?"

"It's the least I can do. You ladies work so hard in the kitchen." He turned his attention to the reverend, who now approached the podium.

"But I don't have any peas to snap." Cookie looked genuinely perplexed.

"Oh, I see." He shifted his position in the uncomfortable pew. "Well then, let me know when you do. I'll be happy to help."

He faced the front of the sanctuary, embarrassment washing over him. What in the world was all that nonsense about snapping peas? Had he lost his mind? Something about Abigail Effingham had that effect on him, and he wasn't sure he liked it one little bit.

Chapter Twelve

*A*bby enjoyed the church service immensely. Every word the reverend spoke seemed to confirm the fact that she should teach lessons to the men in town. Yes, this was certainly God's reason for bringing her here, not just to wait for Mama.

The service ended just before noon. Before they even made it down the steps of the church, an unfamiliar fellow approached her. The man was old enough to be her father, but with far less gray in his hair. He extended his hand and spoke, his voice smooth and clear. "Charles Daring, Miss Effingham. Editor at the *Gazette*."

She shook his hand, but took note of the concern in Sam's eyes as he passed by.

"I wonder if you would be so kind as to do me a favor." Mr. Daring continued to hold onto her hand, even giving it a squeeze, as if they were familiar friends.

"A favor? Of what sort?" She hardly owed this stranger a favor of any kind.

"A story for the paper. It's not often we get young women brave enough to travel all the way to San Francisco on their own. Not women of your ilk, I mean."

"My ilk?" She withdrew her hand, unsure of what to think about his word choice.

"You get my drift, Miss Effingham. We've got older ladies like

Cookie. And Maggie O'Callahan over at the laundry, of course. But younger women like you in the San Francisco area are few and far between—outside of the saloon, anyway—and it's a unique story, you traveling all this way on your own."

This man only had part of the story right, so she corrected him at once. "I came with Neville, our butler."

He patted her hand, as a father would do to a small child. "Yes, but alone in every other regard. Mr. Denueve told me all about your journey. Remarkable thing you've done, very brave."

"Oh? You're a friend of Mr. Denueve's?" A wave of relief passed over her. "I see."

Still, she couldn't help but notice Sam's wrinkled brow as he watched from across the churchyard.

Mr. Daring's expression brightened as she mentioned Mr. Denueve's name. "Business partners, I guess you would say. He's been instrumental in getting the *Gazette* up and running."

"Gracious. Is there a business in town he's not involved in? What an impressive fellow."

"As of yet, the restaurant and the barbershop." Mr. Daring grinned. "But he suggested that, perhaps, you would be kind enough to grant me an interview for the paper. I think it's a wonderful idea. This article will be of interest to men and women alike."

"Why would anyone be interested in me?" Abby shook her head. "There's nothing remarkable in my story, after all."

His eyes lit with excitement. "I dare say, your story—heading to the Oregon Territory alone to find a family member, then being diverted to San Francisco—is the stuff dime novels are made of."

"Ah. I wish my father saw it that way."

"No doubt he's sick with worry." Mr. Daring patted her arm. "That's another angle altogether. Consider the fact that most of the men who've come to California looking for their fortunes have left daughters—not unlike yourself—back home. They fret over those daughters, and sons too. Perhaps it will bring peace of mind to many, knowing that young women can take care of themselves and even find a sense of normalcy in the city of San Francisco."

Gracious. This fellow was really pushing the angle of his story, wasn't he? Abby squared her shoulders. "Again, I did not come alone. Neville has been helpful in more ways than I can count. And I would never have survived this long in San Francisco if not for Cookie and Sam."

"Sam Harris. Yes." He scribbled something onto his notepad. "I understand he's got you working round the clock, doing manual labor?"

What an odd question. It caught Abby completely off guard. "Not at all. He's offered me a position in exchange for a small bit of pay, along with room and board."

"How small, if you don't mind my asking?"

"I. . .I do mind you asking. I'm afraid that's my business, and mine alone."

"Always trying to root out corruption, Miss Effingham. It seems to me that a man like Harris could afford to pay you a decent wage, that's all."

"But I never said he didn't. I'm not even sure why you have concerns along these lines. He's given me all I need."

"And not a penny more."

Her temper flared. "My, how you've turned this story on its ear already. And we've barely begun."

Those cool gray eyes of his sparkled. "So you're agreeing to the interview, then?"

Now she found herself completely flustered. "I. . .I never said that."

"Think about it, Miss Effingham." He gave her a thoughtful look. "Everyone in town will admire your tenacity, your kindness, your bravery, once they read the story of how you crossed the miles to search for a lost loved one."

"My mother's not lost. She's simply traveling."

"Ah." He scribbled something else down. "Good to know. As you've said, it's all about the angle."

An idea struck her at once. Yes, this would be the perfect angle to pitch. "If you want something to write about, do a piece about the lessons I plan to teach at the restaurant."

"Lessons?"

"Yes, in etiquette and social graces. Any time you want to talk about that, I'll be happy to oblige." She gave him a curt nod. "Now, good day, Mr. Daring. I've got to get back to the restaurant to spend the day resting and relaxing with my friends."

"I see." He closed his notepad and nodded.

"Take that and chew on it," she wanted to add. . .but didn't.

♥

Sam couldn't stop thinking about Charles Daring's conversation with Abby. Why it irked him so much, he couldn't say, except that Denueve had Daring in his pocket. The two of them were clearly trying to woo Abby, to pull her into some sort of a web. And she seemed a willing candidate, if not oblivious. He would have to keep an eye on this situation, for sure.

When they arrived back at the restaurant, Sam headed upstairs to look for his father while Cookie, Abby, and Neville went to work preparing leftovers for their lunch. Strange, he found his father's room empty.

After pulling off his coat and tie, Sam made his way back downstairs to the dining room, where he found Cookie hard at work, loading platters of leftovers onto one of the tables.

"Where are the others?" He kept his voice low, so as not to be overheard.

"Abby and Neville are in the kitchen, slicing pie. Jin is around here somewhere. I think he slept in this morning. He wasn't feeling well." Cookie's gaze narrowed. "You're still worked up over that Daring fellow talking to Abby, aren't you?"

"Sometimes I think you can read my mind, Cookie."

"Just sometimes?" She grinned. "Trust me, I'm worried too. Did you hear? Charles did a big write-up in the *Gazette* about the new menu Marcus plans to offer at the saloon."

"Haven't read the *Gazette* in ages." Sam tried to appear nonchalant. "Don't care to. But I'm not surprised he's supporting the saloon with an article like that. They'll want to give the whole idea a big plug to draw in patrons."

"That food might look good in print, but taste is another thing. Hope so, anyway. Don't need the competition." She continued to organize the platters on the table.

Sam turned to face Cookie, his heart stirred to action. "I'm surprised he hasn't tried to steal you away from me, Cookie, if you want the truth of it."

"Mm-hmm."

Sam wondered, based on the lengthy pause that followed if, perhaps, Marcus had made her some sort of an offer.

"Don't worry. I wouldn't go for all the gold in the American River." Cookie gave him a pat on the arm. "You're stuck with me, Sammy. I'm like a bad itch that won't go away."

"A lovable itch." He reached over and gave her a kiss on the forehead.

"Still worried about Abby, though." Cookie plopped down into a chair. "How do we get her to steer clear of the likes of Marcus Denueve and Charles Daring? I worry for her safety."

Sam shook his head. "I'm more worried about these lessons she's planning to teach. Abby's lost her ever-lovin' mind if she thinks that's a good idea."

"You think?" Cookie glanced his way.

"Oh, I don't think. I know. The men in this town are never going to take manners lessons. I was just joking when I asked her to teach me how to speak correctly and all that, by the way. Didn't think she'd take me seriously. It was just a joke on the day we first met."

"I'm guessing the fellas would love to take a few lessons from a pretty girl like that."

"I sign up, Mr. Sam. First thing." Jin's voice sounded as he entered the room with a pitcher of tea in hand.

"I hope you're not serious." He gave his good friend a "You wouldn't dare" look.

Jin proceeded to fill glasses with tea.

After a moment of careful reflection, Sam added his thoughts. "If you want the truth, I'm worried the men in town will see this as an opportunity to get too close to Abby. I'm afraid they'll hurt her."

"I see." Cookie smiled. "So, it's Abby you're worried about."

"Yes." He sighed. "I don't like the way the men look at her."

Cookie tilted her head at him. "They look at all the women in town that same way."

"But she's not like the other women in town."

Cookie's brows elevated as she responded. "True, but I didn't realize you'd spent enough time with her to notice the difference. I'm proud of you, Sammy-boy."

"A man would have to be blind not to notice. She's well-bred, sophisticated, and. . ."

"Innocent."

"Yes." He felt his cheeks grow warm. "A far cry from the womenfolk around us, and that's no exaggeration. I'm afraid the men will notice that and work overtime to try to woo her or to flatter her, and she will fall into their trap."

"You're not giving her much credit, Sam. We could look at this little idea of hers as a potential investment in the inn. Marcus Denueve is over there raking in the dough at the mercantile, trying to outwit us at every turn. Now he's taking over the saloon too. And the paper. What's next? This restaurant?"

"Over my dead body." Sam's blood boiled at the very idea.

"Well, maybe Abby's lessons will offer us a new and fresh way to get the fellas to stick around the restaurant. Don't you think? One more thing to endear them to us."

"They don't need anything but your good food, Cookie." Sam took a seat at the table, his thoughts in a whirl. "These lessons of hers are just as likely to turn them against us and send 'em running for the hills. What if she ends up offending them with some of this highfalutin hogwash? Ever think of that?"

"No." Cookie shook her head. "I'm more inclined to think they'll start off taking her lessons as a joke, but eventually learn a thing or two about how to behave in gentlemanly fashion. It'll be great fun, I would imagine, and something to divert their attention away from the saloon."

"We make good friends," Jin added as he filled the last glass. "Bring more customers. Good for all."

Sam gave him a warning look.

Cookie glanced Sam's way again. "It did occur to me that this might be a terrific way to advertise for that new bakery."

"How so?"

"Well, we could serve sweets. Samples of the goods I'll be selling once the bakery opens in the fall."

He shrugged. "An expensive form of advertising."

"I'll cover the cost myself. I've been saving up, Sammy-boy. I don't mind."

He gave her an admiring look. "Cookie, I don't say this often enough, but you're a marvel. Truly. I don't know what we'd ever do without you."

"Hopefully you'll never have to find out. So, can I tell her my plan? I think the men will come for free desserts and such."

"Okay, tell her. But don't let your generosity get out of hand. Don't want you to end up overextending yourself."

"I'll do my best. But I'm not just thinking about the bakery, or the men. I'm thinking about the women over there at the saloon, and the few other women—like Les, for example—who find themselves in San Francisco. Surely these gals will eventually want to marry. To have children. To settle down."

"I doubt the women at the saloon want to marry any time soon." He reached over to fill his plate.

"Not to contradict you, Sammy, but I disagree. They are women, same as the rest of us. Yes, they're lost right now. And yes, they're caught up in sin. But every woman, in her heart of hearts, just wants to be loved for who she is, even those gals over at the saloon. And God sees them through that lens."

"Hmm."

" 'For by grace are ye saved through faith; and that not of yourselves: it is the gift of God: Not of works, lest any man should boast.' " She paused and gave him a thoughtful look. "Don't you see? In so many ways they're just like me. And Abby. Women in need of rescuing."

"Never thought about it that way." Sam paused to think through

Cookie's passionate speech. The woman always seemed to bring him around to her way of thinking. How did she manage that?

Abby crossed the room with slices of cherry pie in hand. "Amen to every word you said, Cookie. Amen! I wholeheartedly agree."

"Glad to see someone sees clean through to my heart." Cookie gave Abby a little wink. "Just set that pie down here, girlie." She pointed to a spot on the table.

"I agree with your words, Cookie," Abby said as she put the plates down. "But I see a problem too. What if these men and women do turn their lives around and marry. Then what? If there are no schools to educate their children, no politics to guide them, no new churches to settle them, then what? Will the city of San Francisco be passed to future generations with no structure at all?"

Sam rubbed his chin and wondered how the conversation had led to this. Did these women really think the local men and women would eventually settle down? It would take an act of God to accomplish such a drastic change.

"It's only fair to future generations if we begin to bring about order now, don't you see?" Abby took the seat next to Sam and brushed a strand of loose hair out of her face. "All the more reason why I need to offer lessons on social graces. Why, the whole community could be transformed."

"You speak as if you plan to stay, Abby. Do you?" Sam turned her way, surprised by the odd look of homesickness that flickered in her eyes.

"We are here for a short season only." Neville entered the room with a coffeepot in hand. "No time for such foolishness, Miss Abigail."

"I. . ." She paused. "I hadn't given it any thought until now. But it breaks my heart to think a place as beautiful as this might be given over into the enemy's hands."

"Enemy's hands?" Neville asked.

"Yes. The enemy of our souls. He loves chaos, anything to pull God's children away from their heavenly Father. What a field day he must be having over the current state of affairs. How joyous he must be."

Sam listened as Abby poured out her heart. She didn't know much about San Francisco, but she clearly knew quite a bit about the Lord and His plan for His children.

He didn't have long to think about it, though. At that moment, Sam's father entered the restaurant, dressed in his finest suit.

"Father?" Sam called out. "Where have you been? We missed you at church."

"Oh, I. . ." A pause followed. "Had an appointment, son."

"An appointment? On Sunday morning?" A thousand questions ran through Sam's mind at once. No one—short of Charles Daring or Marcus Denueve—did business on Sunday morning. But, where had his father gone. . .really?

From the suspicious look on his face and the hint of a twinkle in his eye, the man was up to no good. Sam cringed, just thinking about the possibilities.

Chapter Thirteen

On the day after Abby attended church for the first time, her thoughts remained firmly affixed to her new idea to teach etiquette lessons. Working out the details would take some doing, but the more she pondered the notion, the more realistic it became. Hopefully she would hear from her parents soon, to know their travel plans. That would give her an end date, a time frame for shaping up the fellas in town. Yes, this would be just the ticket.

After serving lunch, Abby happened to catch Cookie alone in the kitchen, drinking a cup of coffee. She decided to join her.

"Neville and I have an ongoing feud about which is better, coffee or tea," Abby said as she filled her cup with her favorite hot brew. "He says tea, of course."

"Well, I love a good cup of tea," Cookie said, "but there's something about freshly brewed coffee that sways me even more. Perhaps it has something to do with the smell. It permeates the room, awakens the senses."

"You should write advertisements for Pioneer Steam coffee, Cookie," Abby said. "You said that so beautifully. If I didn't already love coffee with undying passion, you would have swayed me with those words."

"Funny you should say I'm good with words. I always felt my truest calling was teaching. Never dreamed I'd end up in a kitchen. And certainly never dreamed Mr. Harris would drag us all the way to California.

I came kicking and screaming, but I'm awfully glad I came." She took a sip, a relaxed expression on her face.

"I'm glad too. Otherwise we would never have met."

Abby paused. She'd been wanting to ask a question for days now, but hadn't had the chance.

"What can you tell me about Mr. Harris?" she said at last.

"Sam's father? Honey, some folks are harder to figure out than others. They're like onions."

"They make you cry?"

"No, they have layers. Lots and lots of layers. Now, if you'd asked me back in Independence what Mr. Harris was like, I would've given him glowing reviews. When the missus was alive he was a fine, upstanding citizen, first in church when the doors opened. But the man you see right now isn't the same fellow he once was. He changed after she passed. I hardly recognize him anymore."

"Sad."

"Very. But that's all I've got to say about that. No point in tipping this cart with gossip or other foolish jabbering." She paused. With the back of her hand she swiped loose hair off her brow. "Just saying, when you throw something in a pot of boiling water, it'll bring about a change—like a potato cooking down soft-like, or like an egg, firming up." A reflective look came over her. "Let's just say he used to be mashed potatoes and now he's something else."

"I see."

"Not that I'm one to talk about others, mind you. I don't care for that, not in the slightest."

"Of course."

"Only, when you see such a marked change in a person, you can't help but wonder what sort of deep hurt has happened in his heart to bring about such a shift. You know what I mean?"

Unfortunately, Abby did know. "I don't suppose Mama was ever mashed potatoes," she said. "Guess she started out like a boiled egg. Father's spent years trying to turn her into something—or someone—she isn't."

"Can't unboil an egg, now can you?" Cookie laughed. "Oh, but God can. He can soften even the hardest heart. He can turn a person back toward home again, in the process."

"Do you really think so, Cookie?"

"Think so?" She grinned. "Honey, I know so. Oh, the stories I could tell you about where I was headed before God got ahold of my heart."

"I've tried my whole life to change her, but haven't won her over."

"Only God can change a heart, honey, whether it's the heart of a rowdy gambler or a woman on the run from Him." She paused. "And I'm not judging your mama. For all I know, she's not on the run from the Lord. Maybe she's just adventurous, in need of a break from her home life. That happens, you know. Nothing's too big for the Lord, though."

Cookie began to sing a hymn at the top of her voice. Abby listened, mesmerized. She'd never heard such a vocal display of a person's faith before.

When the song came to a close, Cookie placed her hand on Abby's arm. "Walking with the Lord has placed a joy in my heart and I just can't help it. I have to sing. Can you feel it, honey? That's the joy of the Lord, filling this very room."

The sound of Cookie's singing filled the place, even as Abby worked hard to clean the dining room minutes later. Most of the patrons had long since headed out, but one person remained, Jedediah Tucker. He appeared to be about the same age as her father—but the dear soul had been beaten down by his life here in San Francisco. That much, she could not deny from his haggard appearance. Abby couldn't help but notice the sad expression on his face as he read what appeared to be a letter.

"Mr. Tucker, is everything alright?"

"Hmm?" He glanced up at her and then folded the letter and shoved it back into its envelope. "Just a note from home."

"From your wife?"

He nodded and tucked the envelope into a pocket inside his coat. "My oldest daughter is to be married the first Sunday in September."

"What lovely news. Will you be making the trip back home, then?"

"Back to Illinois?" His shoulders slumped forward. "Not sure I could go back now, miss."

This took her by surprise. "Why ever not?"

"I'm a different man from the one who left there three years back. They wouldn't even recognize me." He scratched his bushy beard. "Maddy would make me shave this off, first thing. That'd be a pity, seeing as how it's just now growing back in."

"Would that be so awful?"

He paused and appeared to be thinking through an answer. "Guess not, but I've grown to like it. And the longer hair too, which she would also frown on."

"Those are small things, Mr. Tucker. You can grow to like a clean-shaven face again, as well as cropped hair. That's the beauty of change. We adapt as we go." She took the seat next to him. "Tell me about your family. I'm dying to hear about your daughter."

For the first time in all the weeks she'd known him, the man's eyes lit up. "I've got three daughters, actually. It's the oldest who's getting married. The other two are fifteen and twelve."

"And you haven't seen them in three years?"

"Only seen glimpses through their letters. They've grown up without me, I'm afraid. Though I dare say they're living a far better life on the monies I've sent than they did as little kids."

"If I had to choose between fine things and time with my father, I would choose time with my father." As soon as Abby spoke the words, she doubted them. Would she really choose time with her father? If so, why had she come all this way, leaving him behind?

Mr. Tucker grunted. "Don't know if they would want to spend time with me now. They hardly know me."

"It's not too late." Abby placed her hand on his. "I'll be praying that God shows you what to do."

"God." He spoke the word and then appeared to lose himself to his thoughts.

"He's still here, you know. You might've wandered from Him, but

He hasn't gone anywhere."

"Doubt He'd have much use for me now." Mr. Tucker pushed back his chair and rose.

"On the contrary. I dare say He could use you now as never before, not only to bless your family, but everyone who hears the story of all He's brought you through. Pray about it, Mr. Tucker. And while you're at it, read the story of the prodigal son. Great things happened when he returned home."

"The prodigal son?" He pushed his chair in. "That some sort of dime novel or something?"

"No, it's a story from the Bible. There's a Bible in the foyer of the church, should you need one. I think you will find the story in Luke familiar. Best of all, it has a joyous ending."

"I could use a joyous ending. After all the money I've squandered—er, lost—here. Trying to picture what it would be like to return home with nothing in my pockets. Maddy would be so ashamed—of me and for me."

She placed her hand on his arm. "Your story will end well, if you let the Lord pen the next chapter. And if you're wanting to prepare yourself for the journey home, then come to one or two of the classes I plan to teach."

"Classes?"

"In social graces. I plan to start next Tuesday night." She spoke her plan aloud and couldn't take it back now. "I'll get you ready to go back home, Mr. Tucker, I promise. You'll return to your wife and daughters a perfect gentleman, if you let me work my magic."

"It would take magic, indeed. That, or a miracle." He tipped his hat and gave her a quiet "Good day" before leaving the restaurant.

Abby took a seat, deep in thought. She'd gone and done it now, hadn't she? Now she'd have to come up with proper lessons, and in just a little over a week's time too.

The more she thought about it, the more excited she got.

To her right, someone cleared his throat. She turned to discover Sam standing next to her.

"What was all that about?" he asked, and then took a seat next to her.

The sting of tears caught Abby by surprise. "Jedediah Tucker's daughter is getting married."

"And you've encouraged him to go back home?"

"Yes. I hope he will take my advice." She felt a smile tug at the corners of her lips. "I promised to help him prepare for the journey."

"With lessons in social graces, starting next Tuesday night." Sam's wrinkled brow shared his concerns. "I hope you know what you're doing, Abby."

Tender feelings for Mr. Tucker were now replaced with angst. "Sam, I wish you wouldn't treat me like a child."

"What?"

"You do it frequently. I might not be worldly, but I'm not a fool, either."

"Why, I never said you were."

"But you've implied it. You're always treating me like a youngster. Don't you see?"

"I. . .I hadn't realized, Abby. I'm just looking out for you because, well. . ." He paused, and concern flashed in his eyes. "I care about you."

Her anger dissipated as she gazed into his handsome face. "I appreciate the caring. I really do. But some things I just need to try on my own, to see if they work. These little classes of mine could prove to be a big flop. But I'd rather learn on my own. If I fail, I will be the first to admit the idea was foolish. But if I succeed, then men like Mr. Tucker will be better off for it." She paused to think through her next words before speaking. "And I seem to recall you wanted my help as well, so I will expect you to attend, of course, to set an example for the others."

"Oh, no." He put his hand up. "Not my cup of tea."

"We'll see about that."

She would talk him into taking etiquette lessons. Then the other men would follow his lead. Yes, she could almost see it now—the room filled with gentlemen ready to learn social graces. What a wonderful plan this was turning out to be.

♥

After his conversation with Abby, Sam headed into the kitchen to talk to Cookie. He found her standing in the open door, gazing out onto the back alley.

"Everything all right?" he asked as he approached.

She turned to face him. "Oh, sure. Just got a little overheated."

"It's hotter out there than in here," he observed.

"Hardly. This kitchen is like an oven. Or maybe I've just been on my feet too long. Feeling a mite exhausted."

He pulled a chair over to the open doorway and encouraged her to sit. She eased her ample frame downward, beads of sweat trickling down her brow in the process.

"You work too hard, Cookie," Sam said. "I've got to remedy that."

"I was born for hard work. And these fellas are worth it." She pointed out to the alley, where several of the local men sat on wooden crates, gabbing.

"They're a piece of work, in and of themselves."

"They are, but like I said, they're worth every minute of work on my part. Sometimes I stand here and pray for them—pray for the whole town, actually. I lift up their names to the Almighty and ask Him to turn their hearts toward home."

"Funny you should say that. Abby just told me that Jedediah is giving thought to going back to Illinois."

"Is he, now?" Cookie looked pleased to hear this. "Well, there's another prayer answered, then."

"If they all go home, you won't have any customers left," Sam teased. "What then?"

"Well, I don't mean home in the literal sense. I've been praying that God tugs on the hearts of these men, to turn them back to Him."

"I see. Just what we were talking about on Sunday morning. You take this task seriously."

"More seriously than you know." She turned back to look out the door. "Sammy, I know what everyone thinks about San Francisco. It's nothing but a bunch of philandering hoodlums throwing money this way and that. Men filled with greed. Lust."

"Can't argue any of that."

"Right." She paused and appeared to lose herself to her thoughts. "But I see something completely different, Sammy-boy. Every time I walk these streets I try to imagine what this place will look like a hundred years from now."

"Can't even imagine. Thank goodness, we won't be around to see it."

"No, but those who come after us will be, and we have an obligation to set things a'right for their sake. If we stay the course, if we pray, if we take a stand for what's right, then this city can rise from the proverbial ashes and become a place folks will be proud of in years to come. Think on that, honey. We have the power to change things, right here and now, and those changes will have long-lasting effects."

"When you put it like that, I can almost see it myself." And he could. He could almost picture a city filled with godly folks, normal folks, tending to their daily business with sensible heads on their shoulders.

"Even in the biblical cities of old, God honored the faith of the people in a place," Cookie said. "He spared folks because of a few who were diligent to pray."

"True."

She turned to face him, her shoulders squared. "So I've made up my mind to be one of the ones who never gives up on this city. I'll keep on praying until God moves in a mighty way." Her words increased in passion. "And who knows, Sammy. There may come a day when the mud has dried up, and beautiful houses are filled with happy, laughing families—husbands, wives, children. We simply have to believe that God is capable of using us as a springboard for all of that."

"Where did this amazing faith come from, Cookie?" he asked. "Seems to me like you must've been born with it."

A dark cloud seemed to pass over his friend for a moment. When Cookie did speak, her words carried a hint of pain. "My life hasn't been easy, honey. Before I ever came to work for your mama, my husband passed away. I was just a young thing, not much older than yourself."

Sympathy gripped his heart. "Oh, Cookie, I'm so sorry. I had no idea."

"Not something I talk about, to be honest. All I ever wanted was a happy marriage and a houseful of kids to cook for."

"There were no children?" These words came from Abby, who must've entered the room without his notice.

"There was one." The edges of Cookie's lips curled up in a gentle smile. "Evie. We named her after my mother, Evelyn."

This news caught Sam completely off guard. He didn't remember Cookie having a child. "Where is she now?"

"With her daddy. In heaven."

Sam's heart plummeted to his belly. How was it possible he hadn't known this about a woman who'd cared for him all of her life? Sweet Cookie had poured out her love on him, never once thinking of herself. His admiration for her grew, nearly at the same rate as the lump in his throat.

♥

"Oh, Cookie!" Abby's heart was so heavy, she couldn't help but weep. She drew near and slung her arms around her friend's shoulders. "It's too much to bear." She bowed her head, the tears now coming with abandon.

Cookie patted her on the shoulder and let her cry.

"I thought so at the time. My husband had only been gone a few months when Evie got sick with scarlet fever. I'd walked the valley of the shadow so recently I felt I knew its crevices too well." She fell silent. When she did speak, her words were laced with pain. "Of course, this all happened years ago, but it still feels fresh when I speak her name."

"Evie." Abby whispered.

"Yes. Evie." Cookie's eyes misted over as she looked into Abby's tearful face. "Can I tell you a little secret, honey?"

"Of course." Abby stepped back and swiped at her eyes with the back of her hand.

"Evie would be the age you are now. At least, I'm guessing she would be. How old are you?"

"Twenty-three."

Cookie brought her hand to her heart. "To the year. And when I look at you with your glorious honey-colored hair and pale complexion, I can almost see what she would have looked like. My Abe had light hair and fair skin. I feel sure she would have turned out to be very much like you."

"With more sense, I would hope," Abby said.

"Probably not, considering her lineage. But a girl with a joyous expression on her face, and a song in her heart, always thinking of others."

"Oh, Cookie, is that what you think of me? You think I put others first?" A lump rose in Abby's throat. "I wish I could say that, but I'm more selfish, I fear."

"Selfish?" These words came from Sam. "Abby, you're anything but. You're the first—maybe second, after Cookie—to think of those around you."

"Perhaps it looks that way, but I know my heart better than anyone else." She tried to swallow the lump in her throat. "The truth is, I came all the way to San Francisco to prove a point to my parents. To hurt my father for driving Mother away. I didn't do this for them. . .I did it to them. Don't you see?"

Cookie slipped her arm around Abby's shoulder and leaned in close. "Perhaps, sweet girl, but even with that, I have good news. What the enemy meant for evil. . ."

"God will use for good." Abby nodded. "I pray that is the case here. It was a long road to travel, just to let the enemy win."

"He never does, unless you let him." These words came from Sam. "And just for the record, you two have convinced me that we must work harder to assure he never does."

"Does that mean you're putting your stamp of approval on my classes?" Abby's heart lit with the prospect of what that would mean for the others.

"If I have to don my finest suit and walk around the dining hall balancing books on my head to show my gracefulness, then yes. I'll do it." He gave her a look so tender it almost melted her heart. "But not so much for the menfolk, Abby, as for you."

My goodness, it suddenly felt very, very warm in here, didn't it? Still, judging from the playful expression on Sam's face, things weren't going to cool off anytime soon.

Chapter Fourteen

*A*bby didn't have to advertise for her etiquette classes, after all. Turned out, Charles Daring did a fine job of that for her in his article about her trek to San Francisco. It was the only thing in the article she found palatable. The fellow had made her journey to California a far bigger story and had even gone so far as to accuse Sam and his father of withholding her pay. It took several days of assuring their patrons before the men finally understood the story had been fabricated. All but the etiquette lessons, of course.

She somehow managed to talk several of the fellas into attending her first session. Les also agreed. In fact, the woman couldn't seem to wait. Abby had her suspicions that Les wanted to develop her ladylike skills to draw Sam's eye. Why that troubled her, she couldn't say, but she agreed to teach Les to walk, talk, and act like a lady, nonetheless. She invited her new friend to come to the restaurant early the night of the first session, and had a special surprise in mind. She led Les to her room, where she presented her with one of her finest dresses.

"What?" Les looked flabbergasted. "For me?"

"Just for this evening's class. If you like getting dolled up, we'll take it from there."

She spent the better part of the next hour getting Les into the corset, gown, and shoes. Things went so well—and she looked so beautiful—that Abby decided to fix Les's hair as well. She started by unfastening the clip that held the long, dark mane in place and was stunned to see the gorgeous locks hanging in graceful curves over Les's shoulders.

"Why don't you ever wear your hair down?" Abby asked.

"Too much trouble, I guess. Just easier to pin it in a twist and leave it alone."

"You've been blessed with so much beauty here." Abby could hardly contain herself as she fashioned Les's hair into a gorgeous bun.

Finally, when she'd put the finishing touches on her friend's attire, she stood back and proclaimed Les a work of art.

Les examined herself in the mirror. "I. . .I have no words." She stared at her reflection, her eyes wide. "I don't even know who I'm looking at."

"You're looking at a lovely woman named Lesley, who deserves to be the belle of the ball."

Indeed, the young woman's figure was curving and regal, quite a contrast from before. And the dusty rose of her cheeks spoke of a woman quite content with the results of Abby's efforts.

Abby swallowed hard and then added, "And I dare say, you'll catch the eye of that fella your heart's been pining for. How could he look away, when you're such a vision of loveliness?"

"What?" Les's eyes widened. "You know who I'm sweet on?"

"Mm-hmm. It's written all over your face whenever you're around him."

"Oh, Abby, I haven't told a soul. Not a soul." Lesley's face flamed red. "I can't believe you guessed when I've worked so hard to hide my feelings."

"You know what they say about women's intuition."

"I don't, actually." Les shrugged. "Too much time acting like one of the guys, I guess."

"Well, we women have a sixth sense about such things. It's easier for a woman to tell when someone is smitten. That's how I guessed."

"I see." Lesley paused and appeared to be thinking this notion through. "I'll keep that in mind." She turned her gaze back to the mirror and continued to stare at her reflection.

Abby left the room and walked out onto the landing, where she hollered down, "Cookie. Neville. Sam. Come quick!"

"What is it?" Cookie's voice sounded from the kitchen. "I'm in the middle of baking cookies for the fellas."

"Come anyway."

Cookie barreled into the dining hall and looked up at Abby. "What's so all-fired important that you have to pull me away from my work?"

Sam entered on Cookie's heels, paperwork in hand. "Building on fire?"

"Nope."

"Are you injured, Miss Abigail?" Neville asked as he came into the dining room from the kitchen, mixing bowl in hand.

"Not at all. I just wanted to show you something."

"You pulled me away from my cooking to show me something?" Cookie put her hands on her hips. "Better be important."

"Oh, it is."

Abby gestured for Les to take a few steps out into the hallway.

The minute the young woman came into view, Cookie let out a gasp. She practically raced up the stairs to have a closer look. "Les! You're a dream."

Apparently, Sam found her to be a dream too. He couldn't take his eyes off her. Not that Abby blamed him. No, with her dark tresses upswept and pinned with a silver comb, her figure beautifully framed with that dark-green dress, her face lustrous after a facial treatment, the woman looked like a picture from a catalog.

"For pity's sake." Cookie continued to stare. "Remarkable. You're beautiful, Les."

"Lesley," Abby corrected. "Let's try that on for size, shall we?"

"Lesley." This time Sam was the one who spoke her name. He put his paperwork down and bounded up the stairs. "Let me help you, Lesley. You're going to trip and fall in those ridiculous shoes."

"Perhaps." Lesley's cheeks flushed pink as she took Sam's hand. "They're a mite too small, but I squeezed my feet into them, just to see if I could manage it."

Sam looked back and forth between Abby and Les and asked, "What's all this about?"

"Oh, just trying to see what it would feel like to get prettied up." Lesley's smile lit her face, which further emphasized her beauty, at least to Abby's way of thinking. "Feels nice, actually."

From below, Neville gave her an approving nod.

Sam guided her down the stairs, then led her to the closest table. "I don't know what to say."

"Say you'll be a gentleman and pull out that chair for me." Lesley's pained expression let Abby know something was amiss. "With this corset tied so tight I can't even bend over to attempt it."

"Sure." He pulled out the chair and she eased herself down, though Abby could tell it took some doing to accomplish the feat.

"Before long you'll get used to it, Lesley," she said as she rested her hand on her friend's shoulder. "And just wait till the fellas see you."

"Not sure I want to. But it's fun to playact, I suppose."

"Playact, my eye. You were born for this." Cookie let out a little whistle and leaned down to examine Lesley's face. "Are you wearing blush?"

"No. Just warm in this gown, I guess. It's cutting off my air. Ever heard of a woman fainting 'cause of corset string?"

"Yep. You might want to loosen the corset a little then, because you look flushed to me."

"Embarrassed is more like it."

At that moment Jin entered the dining room. He took one look at Lesley and his eyes grew wide. The poor fellow could hardly speak, though he tried several times to formulate words.

Abby laughed as she watched his reaction. "If the other men respond half as well, then we're off to a good start," she observed.

Yes, she felt really good about the transformation. . .until Sam drew near and whispered the words, "Why are you doing this to her, Abby?" into her ear.

She turned to face him, her heart in her throat. "Do this *to* her? Don't you mean *for* her?"

"She's been perfectly comfortable for years, just as she was." His words sounded more like an accusation than a compliment.

"You think I put her up to this? For the record, she was ready for the transformation. I didn't thrust it upon her."

"All right." He hung his head and then glanced up with a sheepish expression. "Forgive me?"

"Hmm. I suppose. But there is one thing you can do for me—and her—to make it up to me."

"What's that?"

"Make sure the fellas don't cause Lesley any discomfort tonight. Be her chaperone."

"I'll do my best." He gave a deep bow then headed to Lesley's side. Minutes later men started flooding through the door. Abby could hardly believe the turnout. Maybe she owed Charles Daring a note of thanks, instead of a dressing down for misquoting her. The men took one look at Lesley and the whistling began. Sam managed to hold them at bay, thank goodness.

After a few moments, Abby was ready to begin. She called the room to order.

"Hey, where's them sweets we was promised?" Jedediah Tucker called out. "Ain't gonna sit still for no sissy lessons lest I get what I was promised."

Ah, so that's why they had come, to sample Cookie's bakery goods.

"Sit still and you'll get them," Cookie hollered from the kitchen door. "Got cinnamon rolls in the oven now, fellas. They'll be ready at the halfway point in the lesson."

"Cinnamon rolls?" Mr. Braynard licked his lips. "Ain't had a good cinnamon roll in ages."

"And Snickerdoodles too," Cookie hollered out.

"What's a Snickerdoodle?" Jin called out from his spot at the front table.

"A cookie," she explained.

Abby needed to get control of this crowd, and fast. Still, she couldn't stop fretting over the fact that Mr. Denueve hadn't accepted her invitation to attend. Didn't he realize his presence would serve as a help to her? Thank goodness Sam had agreed. Better forge ahead.

"Now, fellas, I want you to rise, please, and face me."

The scuffling of chairs followed and the men all rose.

"When a lady enters the room..." Abby sashayed across the room in front of them and several whistled. "You give a little bow."

"Bow?" Mr. Braynard snorted. "You the queen of Sheba or sumpthin'?"

"No, but I'm a proper lady, and a gentleman would always acknowledge my presence with a slight bend at the waist. And if he happened to be sitting, he would stand, naturally."

Mr. Braynard bowed in a grand gesture. He leaned over so far that he almost toppled to the floor.

Abby gestured for Lesley to join her at the front of the room. "Now, fellas, imagine you've asked a lady to tea."

Chet Jamison let out a long whistle. "She's quite a lady."

Lesley's face turned pink and she gave a little curtsy.

Abby repeated herself. "Say you invited her to tea."

"Don't drink tea," Jedediah hollered.

"To dinner, then. Picture yourself sitting across the table from her at a fine eating establishment such as the Gold Rush Inn, having a meal. You're wanting to court this lovely lady..." Abby pointed to Lesley. "But she hasn't reciprocated your emotions."

"What's reciprocated?" Jin asked, his nose wrinkled in confusion.

"It means she doesn't feel the same way," Abby explained.

"Oh." His smile tipped downward into a frown.

"So, how then do you win her heart?" Abby asked the men.

"Tip her over and give'r a kiss she won't soon forget," Mr. Braynard called out. "That's my method. Works like a charm at the saloon."

Abby almost lost control of her audience at this point. The men took to laughing and guffawing, which led to noisy conversation from all in attendance.

"Absolutely not." She clapped her hands to bring the room to order. "To win a woman's affections—her admiration—you must treat her like a lady. For example, you should always pull back her chair when she's ready to sit. Who would like to demonstrate?"

Jin raised his hand.

"Perfect. Now, pretend Lesley is your date, Jin."

His face lit up and the men gave a cheer.

"Plant one on her," Jedediah hollered.

Jin looked terrified at this notion and took a giant step backward.

"No, no. Don't do that." Abby shook her head. "If you do, she will slap you across the face and refuse to be seen in public with you again."

Lesley doubled her fists as if ready to box it out with Jin.

"You ain't met the gals over at the Watering Hole, then." Chet laughed, long and loud. "Give one of 'em a kiss and you get sumthin' a lot nicer than a slap."

"Ain't that the truth," Adam, Chet's brother, added. "And them gals don't care if you pull out their chair or what."

"How much nicer would things be if you did treat them in a ladylike fashion, though," Abby said.

"Then they might come to expect it," Chet argued.

"My point exactly." Abby released a slow breath and tried to regain her patience. "Now, pull Les's chair out, please, Jin."

He pulled back the chair, the legs scraping against the wooden floor. Lesley had just started to sit when Jin caught sight of Cookie coming through the door with a tray of Snickerdoodles, hot from the oven. Lesley nearly took a tumble to the floor as he pulled the chair too far in the process.

"Oh, sorry!" Jin pushed the chair in so fast that it caught her behind the knees and nearly caused her to tumble forward into the table.

Lesley flashed a worried look at Abby, who forged ahead, undeterred.

"Now, every man take a partner."

"More men than women," Chet fussed.

"Cookie will help. And those who don't have a partner can just pretend."

This led to a kerfuffle. It took a few minutes to bring the room to order.

"Practice pulling out her seat, gentlemen." Abby watched as they followed her instructions. "Don't forget to gently nudge the chair forward so that she knows it's safe to sit."

All the men did as instructed except Mr. Braynard, who yanked the chair out, leaving Cookie to fall to the floor.

This, of course, led to a ruckus. And a punch to Mr. Braynard's jaw from Jedediah Tucker, who declared the clumsy man a traitor to the sex. Cookie managed to stand with Neville's help, but Abby could tell her backside was tender from the way she flinched when she walked.

"I'll just head back to the kitchen where I belong," Cookie said. "Gotta ice those cinnamon rolls, anyhow."

This led to more chaos. Abby clapped her hands to bring the room to order once again. The men refused to cooperate. By now all of them had joined in the argument and tempers continued to climb.

Until Les pulled out her gun and threatened to shoot the first fella who refused to play nice. For the first time all night, the men in attendance were ready to sit up straight and pay attention. For that, Abby was extremely grateful.

❤

Sam watched as Abby attempted to get control of the room. He had to laugh at the sight of these fellas pretending to be gentlemen.

The laughter stopped once the fistfights began, though. "Enough, fellas!" he called out. "We've got ladies in the room, you know. Don't want any of them hurt."

"Sam, I need your help." Abby said. "Please join me."

He walked to her side and she spoke to him under her breath. "I have no idea where Mr. Denueve is, so please do me the favor of setting a good example. These men need a leader."

So, Marcus had let her down? Good. Perhaps this would serve to rouse her from her slumber where the deceptive fellow was concerned.

"The purpose of this," Abby said to the men after she regained control of the room, "is to teach you to respect the gentler sex."

"Respect?" Chet snorted. "You ever met Lottie and those other gals at the Watering Hole? They don't care nuthin' 'bout no respect."

"Well they will, after they've had a few etiquette lessons from me."

"Aw, don't go spoilin' a good thing, Miss Abigail," Adam fussed. "I like those gals just the way they are."

"But would you marry one of them?" Sam called out. "Take her home to Mama?" He could tell from the looks on the men's faces that he'd struck a nerve.

Chet's face turned beet red. "Ain't never thought'a that before. Mama wouldn't abide no saloon girls in the family."

"Exactly," Sam responded.

"Thank you for pointing that out, Sam." Abby smiled at him.

"Anything I can do to help." He gave her a little wink and then grinned as her cheeks flushed.

For a moment, she stared at him, not moving. Then, just as quickly, she snapped to attention.

"Neither would a proper lady care to introduce any of you fellas to her parents unless you learn to treat her with dignity," she explained. "If you want to win over the parents, start by winning over the woman."

Was she speaking to Sam, specifically, or did he just happen to feel the heat of those words?

This led to a discussion about what folks back home might expect, which only brought chaos to the room once more. Sam let out a loud whistle.

Les put her fingers in her ears and groaned. "Warn a person, will ya?"

She glared at him, and he offered an apologetic shrug. "Sorry."

Abby looked like she was reaching the giving up point. A few moments later, she seemed to gather her wits about her. "All right now, fellas. Let's practice a minuet."

"Minuet? What's that?" Adam took a seat.

"A dance, of course. A lovely, peaceful dance, where you hold the lady in your arms and gently lead her across the floor."

"I danced with Lottie last night and didn't do no men-you-et," Chet grumbled. "Didn't hold her gently, neither, if'n you catch my drift." He laughed long and loud. Until Les punched him on the arm.

"But don't you see? She will respond in kind when you gently sweep her into your arms and prove that you care about treating her with great tenderness," Abby debated. "Women love to be wooed, fellas. I'll turn you into fine gentlemen, if it's the last thing I do."

"If it's the last thing I do." Sam couldn't control the laughter as he repeated her words to himself. If Abby thought she'd convert these men into the kind of fellas a girl could take home to Mama, she had another thing coming. Still, he'd better play along, for the sake of all involved, including Cookie, who'd managed to hide out in the kitchen with Neville for most of this evening's event.

Abby began to sing a familiar melody: "La-de-da-de-da-de-da-de-da, La-de-da, La-de-da." Then she repeated the phrase and clapped her hands together. "Let's dance, folks!" She gestured for Sam to join in.

He took Les as his partner and gave a deep bow in gentlemanly fashion. The other fellas followed suit, some dancing with imaginary partners.

Les took to the idea with ease, even smiling demurely, which almost caused him to stop cold. He'd never seen an expression like that on her face, not once. Still, he'd better get to it, or Abby would have his head.

In spite of his best attempts, Sam moved awkwardly about the room, stepping on Les's toes a few times as he attempted the minuet. She didn't appear to be much smoother on the dance floor, but Sam could see that she was genuinely trying.

Interesting, to see Les like this, so dolled up. She didn't look like one of those porcelain dolls, covered in powder and paint. No, Lesley looked perfectly natural, even lovely.

Lovely.

He would never have used that word to describe Les before. Something about the way she held herself in this beautiful dress caused him to rethink his former opinion of her, though.

On the other side of the room, Jin leaned against the wall, watching. Either he didn't care to participate or couldn't abide the idea of dancing with an imaginary partner. Sam didn't blame him one little bit. In fact, if all of this didn't mean so much to Abby, he would've bolted out the door ages ago. Instead, he circled the room with his partner, determined not to make a fool of himself in the process.

Chapter Fifteen

*O*n the morning after the etiquette lesson, Abby had a letter from her father. She read it quickly, then pressed it into the waistband of her apron.

Neville hovered nearby, a concerned look on his face. "Well?"

"He says we have much to discuss, but he's coming. I'm to look for him the second Saturday in July." She spoke the word "July" again, as if to reassure herself. "Just two and a half weeks."

"When does your mother arrive?"

"I received her letter just the other day. She's arriving that same week, just one day before him, in fact. Should I let him know, or just surprise him?"

Neville apparently had to sit down before giving an answer to that question. After a moment he said, "Perhaps it's more important to let your father know than your mother. If she's aware he will be here, she might not come at all."

Abby took a seat, confused by his words. "Do you really think it would change her mind? Are things that bad with my parents, Neville?"

He released a slow breath. "Things between them are bad, Miss Abigail. Yes. And worse than I've let on. Not that it's any of my business, mind you. I shouldn't be telling you any of this."

"You will tell me. . .this, and all there is to know." The poor fellow looked as if he'd been placed before a firing squad. "Now, talk."

Neville got off to a rough start, but managed to get out enough to clue her in. Mother's trek to the Oregon Territory served a dual purpose, it seemed: to satisfy her wanderlust and to get her away from a marriage she no longer desired, one she had attempted to end on more than one occasion.

"How could I not know this?" Abby asked. "She was unhappy, yes. Unsettled, even. But ready to leave the marriage?"

"Consider her plight, Miss Abigail. Married at a young age to a man many years her senior. Bound together by stern British parents who saw their union as advantageous to both families."

"An arranged marriage? Is that what you're saying?"

"Not in so many words, but I always felt your father got the longer end of the stick. He acquired a wife with excellent credentials and—pardon my saying so—her family's financial backing for his business ventures as well. In many ways, he would not be the man he is today without her connections."

"I see." Abby was unable to comprehend the height and depth of this conversation. It tore at her heart in ways she could not explain. "And Mother got. . .?"

"The finest daughter anyone could ask for." He rested his hand on her arm. "She never minced any words about that."

Why this got Abby rankled, she could not say. Perhaps it had something to do with Father, or maybe it was that Mother never stayed around long enough to get to know her daughter very well.

"She gained a child, yes, but surely her affections for Father grew over time. I saw them together. They were. . .cordial."

"Cordial." Neville nodded. "That would be the correct word, yes. But cordial won't stand the test of time. Only love will do that."

"If she doesn't love him, she won't stay put. And clearly her love for me isn't enough to hold her in one place, either. I fear we've lost her forever." A lump rose in Abby's throat, but she pushed it away.

"I cannot see inside the heart of another human being, so who am I to judge such things? I can only say that, from all outward appearances, she does not appear to be happy. Neither does she seem to want to work toward a common end. So I'm not altogether sure I would let her know that he will be here when she arrives. This is just my humble opinion, Miss Abigail."

"I see."

She did. Clearly. For the first time in forever, she truly saw the situation for what it was, and her heart nearly broke in two.

"Neville, how did you come to work for my father?" she asked after pushing back the lump in her throat.

"Me, miss?" His nose wrinkled, and for a moment she wondered if he would answer the question. When he did speak, his words were quieter than she'd expected. "I wasn't much older than yourself. My parents passed away in a house fire."

"Oh, Neville! I had no idea."

"Not something I talk about much, I suppose, but I was unsettled, to say the least." He paused and gestured with his head toward the window. "Not unlike many of these young rowdies, I guess you'd say. I fell off the narrow path. Couldn't seem to find my way back."

"You, Neville?" Abby could hardly believe it. The straight-laced butler had a shady past? "Truly?"

"It's not something I'm proud of, nor do I recommend it. I spent quite a few years in shady living, and then I happened upon a young man—a rather forthright, hardworking young man—who saw something in me."

"This is a remarkable story. So, Father hired you?"

"After a bit of cleaning up on my end, yes."

"I wish I'd known." Somehow this put the situation with her father in a slightly different light.

Unfortunately, she didn't have much time to think about it. Lesley arrived for breakfast wearing a simple skirt and blouse with her hair pulled up in ladylike fashion. Several of the local men—the ones who had not had the privilege of seeing her the night prior—were beside themselves. An older fellow with a wiry mustache rushed to pull out her chair, but Neville managed to shoo him out of the way and took care of it himself.

"Thank you, kind sir," she said as she took a seat.

Abby looked on with a smile. Well, until Cookie put her back to work waiting tables. Then she rushed from place to place, filling coffee cups, scooping scrambled eggs onto plates, and offering slices of bacon.

Just when she thought she'd scooped her last eggs, Marcus Denueve entered the restaurant, hat in hand. Abby couldn't help but smile when she saw the handsome man. Just as quickly, she remembered that he'd missed out on last night's class. She decided to give him a talking to.

"I know, I know." He sat at a table near the door, a look of chagrin on his face. "I failed to support you last night. I do hope you will forgive me. It simply couldn't be avoided."

"What happened?"

"We've got the big grand opening at the Lucky Penny this Friday night, remember? I've worked hours on end to whip the place into shape. Stayed late into the night last night to make sure the painters did their job."

"Oh, I see." She relaxed and poured coffee into the cup on his table. "Well, you're forgiven, then."

"Thank you. I knew you'd understand. You've got such a sweet heart, Miss Effingham." He spoke her name with such tenderness that flutters skittered across her stomach like butterflies taking flight.

"I've talked our piano player into staying for the first couple weeks, but he's dead set on leaving after that." Marcus gave her a pouting look. "Hoping someone will change her mind and consider the job. Money's good and she wouldn't have to be on her feet all day."

"I just don't know that I could," Abby said. "My skills aren't up to par."

"How will you know unless you try?" He reached to put his hand on hers. "Maybe this is your time to shine, not to wash dishes or serve tables."

"Hmm." She paused to think through his words as she headed back to the kitchen to fetch his plate. While playing piano at the restaurant didn't sound like an ideal setup, she couldn't deny the fact that cooking and waiting tables was taking a toll on her.

She returned to his table and set his plate down. He dove in, then looked up with a smile. "I must admit, your cooking skills are winning me over."

"Cookie made the eggs and bacon today. I'm just serving."

"There's no such thing as *just* serving. You have a servant's heart, Abigail Effingham. I saw it that very first day at the mercantile. You're a beautiful person, inside and out."

She hardly knew what to do with such flattery except offer a hushed, "Thank you."

At the next table over, Les sat with her eyes affixed to Marcus and Abby. Was she trying to give Abby some sort of signal, or simply being nosy? Before Abby could give it much thought, Neville approached and engaged Les in conversation. Abby breathed a sigh of relief.

Mr. Denueve continued on, oblivious to Abby's ponderings. "I believe you've been brought here, to San Francisco, for such a time as this—to tame the wild beasts and to lift weary spirits."

Abby's heart wanted to burst into song. "My goodness, that's a Bible verse, Mr. Denueve. Straight from the book of Esther. She was sent to her people 'for such a time as this,' and her obedience won the heart of the king. She saved her people in the end. Do you know the story?"

"No, but. . ." He eased his chair a little closer to hers. "The Almighty does work in mysterious ways, or so I've been told. Shall I call you Queen Esther?"

She felt her cheeks grow warm at his nearness. He reached to take her hand and gave it a squeeze.

"I'm no queen," she replied.

"A princess, then," he said, his eyes filled with sweetness. "One who deserves to be treated as such."

"I. . .I don't know about that. And trust me, my parents are coming soon—mid-July—and will whisk me off to Philadelphia before you know it."

"Don't go. Please. This town is in need of saving, Miss Esther. Give some thought to making San Francisco your home. I think you will learn to like it here, if you just give us—it—a chance." The smile that followed from Mr. Denueve lit the room and lifted her spirits. In that moment, a world of possibilities swept over her. She could almost picture herself staying in San Francisco, teaching lessons. Why, sure. Instead of waiting tables, she would open a school, an etiquette school. Surely the Lord was preparing her for that, even now.

"I will pray about it."

"Good. And promise you'll come to the grand opening at the Lucky Penny on Friday night?" His words stirred her to attention. "You will be my special dinner guest."

"You're asking me to dine with you at the new restaurant?"

"I am. But not just you. Bring your friends. It will be a night no one will forget. Free food and drink for all to celebrate the grand opening. You will love the cuisine, I promise. C'est magnifique!"

"I. . .I'll think about it."

"I won't pressure you about the piano playing, if that's what you're worried about. Just come and have a good time. You need a night off." He squeezed her hand, and she realized for the first time he must've been holding it for some time.

As she refilled coffee cups around the room, Abby kept a watchful eye on Neville, who hovered close to Lesley. After some time, a thought took root in her mind. She rushed to the kitchen to share it with the only person who could be trusted with such a thing.

She found her friend scraping plates. Abby blurted out her name before she could stop herself. "Cookie!"

The woman turned to face her, eyes widening. "Are you all right, Abby? You're flushed."

"Yes, I've just had a revelation."

"Revelation? Do tell." Cookie continued to scrape and stack plates. "But while you're at it, let's get going on these dishes."

Abby walked to the sink, talking all the while. "I've figured it out, Cookie. I thought Les had a crush on Sam."

"Sam?" Cookie looked astounded. "Our Sam?"

"Yes, but I was wrong. I can see now that it's not Sam that Les is interested in at all."

"No?" Cookie's brow wrinkled. "Then who?"

"I'll show you who. Follow me." Abby brushed her hands on her apron and walked to the door leading to the dining room. Once there, she opened it, and pointed to the table where Neville sat across from Lesley.

Cookie's eyes widened. "Ridiculous." She closed the door with a thud. "I refuse to believe such a thing."

"I know what you're thinking."

"Hardly."

"He's double her age. I'll give you that. But don't they look natural together?"

"They do not." Cookie huffed back to the dirty plates. "She's most certainly not his type, and that's all I have to say on that matter."

"I've never given a moment's thought to Neville having a type," Abby admitted. "In all the years I've known him. But now I can see that he was looking for a strong, confident woman, one who's not afraid to be herself, regardless of what others think."

Cookie's brow knitted. "Well, if he has a type—which I'll give you, most men do—she's not it."

She turned on her heel and stormed out of the kitchen, muttering under her breath.

Abby didn't have time to ponder her friend's strange reaction. She was far too busy thinking about all the things she wanted to say to Lesley, when she got the chance. And, my oh my, did she suddenly have a lot to say.

♥

Sam looked on as Abby made her way into the kitchen. He followed and put on an apron.

"About to bake some pies?" she asked as she glanced his way.

"Nope. About to do some dishes. With everyone else gone, I figured you could use the help."

"Thanks." She stuck her hands in the water and grimaced. "Ugh. It's gone cold. That's what I get for spending so much time gabbing with Lesley."

"Saw you two talking. Everything okay?"

"Mm-hmm."

Funny, she didn't sound okay.

"I'll start the kettle, then." He walked over to the stove and began the process of heating up some water to add to the sink.

"I had a letter from Father. He's coming in a few weeks."

Ah, so that was it. "It will be nice to meet him," Sam said after a moment's pause.

"Mother is coming at the same time."

"Perfect coincidence."

"I doubt it's a coincidence." She spun around to face him. "And trust me, it should prove to be anything but pleasant."

He walked over and put his hand on her arm. "Abby, I hate to see you distraught. How can I help?"

She paused, and tears filled her eyes. "Pray that my mother learns to love again? Pray that broken relationships will be mended?"

"I don't know how to do much," Sam said, his words chosen carefully. "But I do know how to pray. So I will set my mind to doing just that."

And while he was at it, he would pray for the woman standing before him at this very moment. Judging from the somber look on her face, she could certainly use it.

Chapter Sixteen

When their conversation ended, Sam helped Abby tidy up the dining hall. Then he made his way back into the kitchen, where he found her hanging up her apron. He worked up the courage to ask the question on his heart.

"I wondered if you might have some free time between now and lunch. I'm headed to the fish market and thought you might like to come along for the ride. You've hardly had a chance to get out of here and the ride might do you good. Open air, and all that. Might give you a chance to clear your thoughts."

She gave a little shrug. "I guess so, if Cookie's all right with it."

"She seems a little out of sorts this morning, but told me to take my time. She's feeding the fellas sandwiches for lunch and won't need our help for a change. Perfect time to sneak away."

"All right." Abby pulled off her apron and hung it on a peg. "Just give me a minute to fuss with my hair. It's a mess."

"It's perfect." He took her by the hand. "And trust me, it'll get even messier in the wagon."

"So, you're saying it is a mess?" Abby cocked her head as if daring him to respond.

"Not at all." He laughed. "A fella can't win for losing, can he?"

Moments later, he helped her up to the wagon seat. Sam was happy to have Abby to himself for a change. All morning long he'd been thinking of ways to approach her about Marcus Denueve. She needed to be warned about the man. But no point in diving into that conversation just yet. This was one river that needed to be waded into.

He glanced over and caught a glimpse of Abby's profile. That gorgeous golden hair. That cute nose. Her stubborn chin. How they drew him in. If he dared to broach the topic on his mind, she might very well retreat, turn away from him. Then what?

"Keep your eyes on the road," she scolded after the horses threatened to careen into a ditch. "I'd like to live to see the bay, if you please."

He snapped to attention and nodded. "Sorry 'bout that. Have a lot on my mind."

"If you'd like to survive to tell about it, stay focused."

The time passed in quiet reflection before Sam finally thought of a way to engage her in conversation. "What do you think of San Francisco so far, Abby?"

"It's not as I'd pictured, and certainly not quite the painting in my head after the conversation with Jimmy Blodgett on the train. But I'm learning my way."

"Good."

"Of course, I feel like I'm choking on dust half the time."

"And the other half?"

"Is spent in a whirl, trying to ease my way through the ever-present mob of fellas trying to propose to me."

"They're still proposing to you?" This got him rankled, but he tried not to let it show.

She nodded. "But no worries. I'm going to keep my distance."

"Good idea, Abby. Distance is a good thing." Sam didn't trust himself to say more, though he certainly wanted to. Instead, he turned his attention to playing the role of tour guide as they made their way toward the bay. He babbled on about the role French immigrants had played in shaping the town, and even pointed out several jewelry shops, silk merchants, and the like. He made note of the various banks, and lit into a discussion about how robber barons had invaded the town, their mansions gaining fame among the locals.

Finally, when he felt sure he'd bored her to tears, he told her about the latest chocolate shop in town, a new place called Ghirardelli's.

"Sounds marvelous." She released a contented sigh. "Nothing wins my heart like chocolate."

"So, that's the way to your heart then?" he asked as he slowed the horses to a more reasonable gait. He would have to keep that in mind.

"Chocolate is the way to every woman's heart," she countered, flashing him a bright smile.

Moments later, the sparkling waters of the bay came into view.

Abby leaned forward and put her palms to her cheeks. "Oh, Sam, it's glorious." She reached over and grabbed his hand. "To think I came all this way to San Francisco and stopped just short of the water. Who would have known this was just beyond? Thank you, thank you for bringing me."

"You're welcome." He paused, enjoying the feel of her hand in his. "Isn't that often how it is in life? We work so hard, get so close to God's best, but stop short because we think we'll never make it? It's like taking the time to pluck the chicken but not fry it up."

"I hadn't thought of it that way, but I'm sure you're right." She rested her gaze on the water for a moment before pulling her hand back. "I just can't believe how pretty it is. These rolling hills. That water. What a paradise. And to think, it was here all along."

"Hardly a paradise." He laughed. "Never heard anyone call San Francisco that, anyway."

They fell silent and stared at the water for a couple of minutes. Then Sam clucked his tongue and stirred the horses to action. "C'mon, boys. Let's go to market."

Moments later they approached the fishermans' market. Abby's nose wrinkled as the overpowering scent of fish—both fresh and spoiled— filled the air.

"Sorry. Should've warned you, I guess."

"Oh, my." She reached for her reticule and opened it, then pulled out a hankie, which she brought to her nose.

"Guess I'm used to it," Sam said with a shrug. "Hardly bothers me anymore."

"I dare say it might be awhile before I grow acclimated to such an odor." Abby coughed.

"Not as bad as plucking chickens, though, right?" He laughed.

The smile that followed from Abby brought joy to his heart. He pulled the horses to a stop and jumped down, then rounded the wagon to the other side and helped Abby down.

"Time to pick out some fish for dinner."

"I wouldn't know where to start."

"Follow my lead." He crooked his arm and gestured for her to slip her hand through. "Better stay close. Don't want to lose you."

The words struck him directly in the heart. Before long, he would lose her. Her parents would arrive, and they would take her back to Philadelphia. He would never see her again.

The fact that this suddenly brought so much pain caught him completely by surprise.

❤

Abby made her way through the fish market, her arm linked with Sam's. This place was unlike anything she'd ever seen or smelled.

"What do you think of this fellow?" Sam pointed down at a large fish. "It's a bass."

Abby glanced down and the creature's beady eyes stared up at her. She swallowed hard and allowed the wave of nausea to pass over her. "The only fish I've ever seen are filleted and broiled, then placed on my plate."

"Well, they have to come from somewhere. Didn't you ever consider that?"

She turned to face him. "Sam, I must confess, there's a lot I never thought about before. Everything in my very spoiled life has been handed to me, ready to go. Every bite of food. . .prepared. Every article of clothing. . .pressed and ready. Everything. Don't you see? I'm utterly and completely clueless. How you ended up with such a person in your kitchen is confounding, at best. Either God has a delightful sense of humor and is playing a terrible joke on you and Cookie. . ." She glanced back down at the fish. "Or maybe He's trying to teach me a lesson I won't soon forget."

"I suppose that's possible."

"I must confess, I've been one of those girls who grew accustomed to the finer things in life."

"Things?"

"You know, possessions. I used to think they were important. I suppose I learned from my father. He cares a great deal about impressing others with our family's status."

"Ah, I see. 'What shall it profit a man if he shall gain the whole world. . .'"

"Only to lose his soul." She sighed. "Now you sound like Cookie, with a verse for every situation."

"Hardly. I can barely remember my own name, let alone chapter and verse of every scripture." He paused. "And just for the record, I'm not saying your father has lost his soul, so please don't misunderstand. I don't even know the man. That scripture just popped into my head, that's all."

"I don't really know where Father stands with the Lord, if you want the honest truth of it." Her heart quickened. "I'm not really sure about either of my parents. We attended church in Nottingham, of course. Everyone did."

"Unlike here, where almost no one attends church."

"True." She paused and felt her lips curl down into a frown. "I suppose some would say that church attendance is indicative of where one stands with the Lord, but even in that—attendance, I mean—Father was a bit of a showman."

"How so?"

"Let's just say that his demeanor inside the church was a bit different from his actions outside. I used to love to go to church services because it was the only time I ever saw him slip his arm around Mother's waist or speak to her with any sort of affection. At home he was rather . . .cold."

"Sad."

"Yes. And sadder still that I didn't realize how bad things had gotten between them until I asked Neville." Abby startled to attention. "How did we jump from talking about possessions to church attendance?"

"Natural progression, I suppose. The point is, we're not always who we appear to be."

Sam looked nervous as he spoke the words. When he added, "I suppose that could be said of any of us," Abby wondered if, perhaps, he was trying to tell her something.

At that very moment, her gaze landed on something slimy looking. She extended her index finger. "Oh, my goodness! What is that?"

"Squid." Sam laughed. "Would you like to try it?"

Bile rose in her throat and she looked away. "No, thank you."

All around, people called out in a variety of languages. Chinese, she recognized, after spending so much time around Jin. And she felt sure the man to her right was speaking Italian. Or Spanish. But the fellow with the blond hair? She couldn't even begin to place his language.

"That's Bjorn," Sam said, as if reading her mind. "We call him The Swede."

"Ah. Swedish, then. Couldn't make it out to save my life."

"Don't be too impressed with me. I only happen to know because we've met and I know his story." Sam paused and appeared to lose himself in his thoughts. "They've all got a story, just like you and me," he said after a moment.

"Fascinating, to think about it like that."

"Isn't it?" When he glanced her way, she could read the joy in his expression. "I love it when all of the languages overlap. It's like a symphony playing a marvelous piece of music with a multiplicity of parts."

"I've been to the symphony, Sam," she countered. "It didn't sound anything like this."

"Speaking figuratively, of course. Picture each language as a different type of instrument."

"If I could think clearly, I would, but it's so loud here—and the smells are so strong—my senses are completely overwhelmed."

She might be overwhelmed, but Abby could not deny one thing: as she watched Sam interact with the locals, as she saw him bartering over his purchases, she found herself drawn to him in a way she never had before. Sam Harris was a fine man, a respected man. And though she hadn't planned to see him as anything other than her employer, she had to admit that something about him tugged at her heart in a way she simply could not explain.

Chapter Seventeen

*A*bby enjoyed her visit to the fish market, in spite of the smells. Most of all, she enjoyed the fact that she could, for once, completely relax. No urgent matters awaited her. No dishes to wash. No tables to wait. No guests to avoid. Here, with Sam at her side, she could simply. . .be.

"You've gone quiet on me," he observed. "Getting weary?"

"Not at all." She smiled. "I'm enjoying myself so much."

"Glad to hear it. Would you like to make a little stop on the way back? There's an overlook I'd love to show you, one with a beautiful view of the bay."

"Sounds marvelous. Are you sure Cookie won't mind?"

"This is my usual fish market day, so she's accustomed to me being away awhile. Stop fretting, Abby. She won't scold you." He gave her a little wink that set her heart to fluttering. Playfulness sparkled in his eyes as he added, "And if she tries, I'll fire her. How about that?"

"I'm trying to picture the Gold Rush Inn without Cookie. Such a task is impossible."

He laughed. "True. And I could never let her go. She's been like a mother to me, ever since mine passed away."

Abby's heart went out to him in that moment. She'd never thought to ask him about his mother before. "I'm so sorry. When did you lose her?"

"Two and a half years ago, just before we left St. Louis. In fact, I'm convinced her death was what prompted Father to come west. He couldn't abide the idea of living in the same house he had shared with her. His heart was too broken, I think."

"That makes sense. Sometimes a building will carry memories so strong you can't shake them."

"You sound as if you understand."

"I do. My memories of our home in Nottingham are precious to me. I miss that house so much. I've smiled and pretended to like Philadelphia too, but it's not home to me. I've never adjusted, no matter how hard I've tried."

"I'm sorry to hear that."

The most magnificent view appeared in front of them as he turned the wagon to the right. Abby couldn't help but gasp. "Oh, it's wonderful, Sam. Breathtaking."

"This is my favorite place in all of San Francisco." His eyes took on a faraway look as he pulled the horses to a halt. "Sometimes I come here just to think."

"I can see why." Her gaze shifted back to the water—that glorious, magnificent water. "Now, this is a place I could become accustomed to." Her thoughts shifted back to the conversation. "I'm not saying Philadelphia isn't lovely. There are some scenic spots there too. But I just can't seem to get used to it." She allowed her thoughts to still as she took in the waters of the bay, twinkling under the midmorning sunlight. "But this? This might just be enough to win me over."

"Then I will bring you here every day."

His words caught her by surprise. She looked his way, heat creeping to her cheeks.

Just as quickly, her thoughts contorted. She thought of Mother, all the way up in Oregon Territory. How many beautiful sights had her mother seen. . .without her? Without Father? How many breathtaking overlooks? How many fish markets? How many railroad stations?

"Have I lost you again?"

She shivered, a little chill suddenly gripping her.

"It's the breeze off of the bay." He pulled off his jacket and draped it over her shoulders. "This should help."

"Thank you." Thinking about Mama caused tears to cover her lashes.

Sam handed her a handkerchief. "Please tell me those are tears of joy, not sadness."

"Just missing Mama, I guess. I can't tell you how long it's been since she went away. Six months? Seven? I've truly lost count. I honestly don't know how a mother can go away like that and leave her child behind. Do you?"

She turned to face him, but the somber look on his face reminded her at once of his own situation, his personal grief.

"Oh, Sam, please forgive me." She clasped her hands to her chest as full realization set in. "I told you, I'm a spoiled, selfish girl. I'm rambling on about my mama, and you've lost yours. Terribly insensitive of me."

"There's nothing to forgive. And you feel the loss of your mother keenly. I can see that every time you mention her."

"Yes, but my situation in no way compares to yours. I can't even picture what my life would be like if I lost Mother forever. My heart does go out to you. I just want you to know that."

"Thank you. There are some losses you learn to bear, but there are others that leave a hole you realize will never be filled."

"I can't even imagine." She rested her hand on his arm. "Still, my mother's wanderlust hardly compares to a loss like yours."

"Your mama's absent from your life and you are hurting." He gave Abby a compassionate look. "Anyone can see that."

Abby's eyes filled with tears, and she felt free to broach the conversation once again. "I just don't understand her selfishness, Sam. I don't. She puts her personal wants and wishes above, well, everything and everyone. Whenever she feels like flitting off on another adventure, there she goes, with not a care or a thought to how it will affect me." A lone tear slipped down Abby's cheek.

Sam slipped his arm over her shoulder and she leaned into him, feeling more secure.

"I suppose I'm grieving the mother that I wish I had," she said. "Not the one I actually have. The type of mother who would agonize over parting with a child. A mother who would weep and wail at the very idea of such a lengthy separation. That's the kind of mother every child deserves, not one who leaves without so much as a good-bye."

"She didn't even say good-bye?"

"Well, hardly a good-bye, anyway. Her bags were packed and in the foyer before I even knew she planned to leave. That was my first clue. Neville loaded them into the cab and off she went, headed for the train station."

"But surely she writes."

"To tell of her adventures, sure. And to ask Father to send money. And yes, there's occasionally a little note for me, something meant to remind me that she's still alive and well. But nothing of a personal nature. And certainly no emotional apologies for leaving or any letters stained with tears. Nothing along those lines. Maybe I've been a fool to keep expecting those sorts of notes from her."

"Not foolish at all. And her behavior is certainly outside the norm. But God can change her heart. We need to pray that He does so—in His own time and His own way."

"Yes." Abby paused and decided to shift the conversation a bit. "I feel your mother was different from mine." Her eyes sought out Sam's. "Tell me about her. What was your mother like, Sam?"

❤

Sam hated to respond, especially after hearing the painful description of her mother. But Abby looked as if she really wanted to know, so he told her.

"She was. . . .remarkable. Very much the kind of mother you would expect. Doting. Loved to play silly games. We played hide-and-seek in the house when I was a boy." He paused as the sting of tears took him by surprise. "Sometimes I still look for her. I wonder if maybe she's just hiding behind the library door or in the pantry."

"We do have that in common, as well." Abby released a little sigh. "Many times I've thought I heard Mama's voice, only to realize it was someone else. And I can't tell you how many times I thought I recognized her in a crowd—usually from behind—a woman in a hat like hers or something like that."

His heart quickened and he could barely speak above the lump that rose in his throat. "Same here."

Abby's expression shifted to chagrin. "There I go, changing the conversation back to myself again. See how selfish I am?" She sighed, and Sam found himself captivated by the curve of her face, the downward turn of her beautiful lips. Even when sad, Abby Effingham was exquisite.

"I'm looking forward to the day when we're reunited in heaven." Sam turned his attention to the vast waters below. "Everything will be remedied there. In the meantime, it brings a certain degree of comfort to realize she's not suffering. There's no more pain or sorrow for her."

"A lovely thought."

"Father has changed so much, though. I think the grief has turned him into someone folks back home wouldn't even recognize anymore."

"Maybe, but how wonderful, to have loved like that. My parents are cordial, at best. When Mama's home, I mean."

"Cordial is better than angry, I suppose."

She shrugged. "Maybe, but when I marry, I want so much more than that, don't you?"

"Of course. I want what my parents had."

"I want a romance story, one filled with heart-thumping adventures, like in the books I read."

"I see."

"I want to be swept off my feet, romanced, wooed. Is that asking too much?"

"Depends. Do you mean in the beginning or for the duration of the marriage? It would be a tall order for any fella, to keep the adventure going."

"Oh, forever. I don't want the flame to go out." She seemed to lose herself in her thoughts. "Don't you see? I want to be reminded—daily, if you please—that I am loved. That the man who has won my heart would scale the highest mountain just to be with me. That no obstacle he might ever encounter would keep him from me." She faced him. "That's not too much to ask, is it?"

"Not if you're marrying Don Quixote."

She giggled, and her cheeks flamed pink. "Silly. I would never marry a man who spends most of his days on a horse, traveling from place to place, especially not one who drifted from woman to woman. I want a settled man, a peaceful man."

Ah. Now things were looking more hopeful.

"A man who enjoys spending time with a good book."

Hmm. Perhaps not.

"A man who will sit in front of the fireplace at night while I darn his socks, a man who will share his heart with me—his ideas, his ideals, his goals, and ambitions. Don't you see? I want someone who includes me."

"That's how a fella romances a woman, then?" Sam realized his arm was still draped over her shoulders. He took a chance and pulled her a bit closer. "By involving her in the ordinary day-to-day goings on?"

"Sure."

"Might not be as complicated as I'd feared." He didn't mean to speak the words aloud, but there they were.

She didn't seem to notice. "I'm not saying I would object to flowers on occasion or to jewelry, even. But give me a quiet walk by the creek, hand-holding, sweet nothings, quiet conversations about the future, visits to places such as this." Abby grew silent as she focused on the water. "I'd be in heaven," she said after a few moments. "Do you know what I mean?"

"I guess I do." He realized she'd just provided him the perfect segue into a conversation about Marcus. "I suppose you've got your pick of any number of men here in San Francisco."

Her nose wrinkled. "What San Francisco lacks in quality, it makes up for in quantity."

"I'll try not to take offense at that." He pulled his arm away from her shoulders in playful fashion.

She slugged him on the shoulder and laughed. "Silly. I wasn't talking about you, of course. You're different from all the men I've met here."

"I'm not big and tough like Chet and Adam. Is that what you mean? And I'm not handsome like Marcus Denueve." He paused to gauge her reaction, but Abby never so much as glanced his way. "God made me a little. . ." He paused. "Less inclined to dress like a cowboy and more inclined to be an ordinary Joe."

"Really?" She shrugged. "I wouldn't have put it that way. I can imagine you in a cowboy hat and Levis."

"You can?" He shook his head. "I tried the cowboy duds, when we first came here. Felt like a foreigner, as if I was trying too hard to fit in with the others. Finally decided that fitting in wasn't what God wanted from me. He just wanted me to be myself."

"I'm grateful you stood your ground, then." She gave him an admiring look. "It's one thing to change your clothing; another altogether to lose pieces of yourself to a place you barely know."

He rested his hand on her arm. "I'm living proof that you can live in San Francisco without giving up who you truly are. It starts with spending time with the people you trust and not getting pulled into a web that could end in your demise."

There. He'd said it. Hopefully she would take the hint.

"What are you saying?" Confusion registered in her eyes.

"Spending time with Marcus Denueve is dangerous business if you're looking to stay the same." Sam's breath caught in his throat as he released the words to her ears. "That's all."

Abby pulled away from him. "What does my friendship with Marcus Denueve have to do with this conversation?"

"More than you know, Abby. And please don't get angry. I just don't want to see you hurt."

"I'm a big girl. I can take care of myself."

"Not in San Francisco. People think that all the time, but in this place, we have to look out for each other, trust me." He paused. "And you *can* trust me, Abby. That's all I'm saying. I have your best interest at heart."

She kept her gaze on the waters, but the next words were clearly meant for him. "Then let me make my own mistakes. If they are, indeed, mistakes, then I'll fix them."

"I've known many a fella to say that same thing over the past two years, only to reach the point of no return."

"So, now I'm headed toward a rocky cliff?" She swung around and faced him, defiant. "Is that it?" She pointed to the ledge in front of them. "Afraid I'll fall?"

"If you keep on with Marcus, perhaps." Sam fought to find the right words. "You don't know him like I do. He casts a spell over people. Some would call it manipulation. Others call it greed. Whatever name you choose to give it, it's dangerous. He's dangerous. And I care too much about you. . ." Sam's voice cracked. "I care too much about you to let him pull you into some sort of web."

As the words were spoken, the pounding in his heart went to double-time. For, while he'd kept those thoughts to himself, he could no longer deny the truth: his feelings for Abby Effingham were rising faster than the yeast in Cookie's bread dough.

♥

Abby could hardly believe the direction the conversation had turned. Why did Sam continue to see her as a child?

"I thought your lessons went well last night," he managed after a few moments of silence.

"Is this an attempt to change the subject?"

He nodded. "Yes, and I hope it's not too late."

"In response to what you've said, yes, the first lesson went well. The men were more cooperative than I would have imagined."

"Yes, I was pleasantly surprised."

Her angst dissipated as she remembered how he had come to her rescue last night and participated in the class session. She gave him a tender glance. "Thanks for helping, by the way. You're very. . ."

"Reliable?"

She nodded. "That's a good word."

"That's me—good old reliable Sam."

Strange, he sounded pained by his own words.

Off in the distance the church bell chimed three times. Sam startled to attention. "Time to get back to the restaurant. Cookie will be looking for us."

"I suppose she will, though I don't know if I can make it through another round of service today. I'm aching all over from carrying those heavy trays."

"Maybe when your Don Quixote comes along you won't have to work." Sam roused the horses from their rest and nudged the wagon away from the overlook.

"What?" She could scarcely believe he'd said such a thing.

Sam clucked his tongue at the horses, never giving her a look. "I meant Prince Charming, not Don Quixote."

There he went, treating her like a child once again. "You're poking fun at me," she said, her spine stiffening at the very idea.

"I'm not."

She brushed her hands against her skirt. "Go on and ridicule. But one day Prince Charming will come along and my life really will be the thing fairy tales are made of."

"Until then?" he asked, his gaze penetrating to her very soul.

"Until then. . ." She glanced away, her thoughts in a whirl. "I wait."

Chapter Eighteen

Abby spent the next couple of days thinking through a plan for managing her parents' arrival. Hopefully things would go well. She would have spoken to Neville about it once again, but he seemed distracted with Les, who had been spending more time than usual at the restaurant. Every time she found Neville missing, he turned up with Les. Just proved to confirm Abby's suspicions.

On Friday morning, just about the time Neville and Cookie headed off to the mercantile, Abby happened to catch Les alone in the dining hall, playing solitaire.

She took a seat near her friend and rested her palms on the table. "Lesley, can I ask a question?"

"Well, sure." Les looked up from her cards. "Ask me anything. I'm an open book. Speaking of books, I've finished *Wuthering Heights*. Not my favorite. Wasn't fond of the ending."

"I felt the same. Strange, how some stories turn out."

Les sighed. "Why isn't love ever simple?"

Perfect segue. Abby patted Les's hand. "It didn't take much detective work on my part to figure out who you've got your eye on."

"Oh?" Les pursed her lips and her cheeks flamed bright pink. "Guess I'm a little too bold, then, if I'm that obvious. My secret is out?"

"It's out, indeed. And you couldn't have chosen a finer man." Abby's heart quickened at the idea of it. Just as quickly, she thought about how sad it would be, once her parents arrived. Would her father tug Neville back to Philadelphia, away from the woman he so clearly loved?

"I agree." Lesley clasped her hands together at her chest. "Though, for all the tea in China, I can't get him to give me a second look."

This made no sense at all. "What do you mean, give you a second look? Why, it was all he could do not to stare at you all morning long. In fact, I've noticed for days now that he has paid you more attention than ever."

"Really?" Lesley's lips curled up in a smile. "I guess I didn't notice." She reached to grab Abby's hand. "Oh, but he's a handsome devil, isn't he? And such a fine, proper man."

"He is. And I can tell you with all assurance that he's a complete gentleman," Abby assured her.

Lesley sighed. "I know."

"I've known him for years, and can bear witness to the fact that— while he's a bit crusty on the outside—Neville is as sweet as sugar on the inside."

"Neville?" Les paled. "*Your* Neville?"

"Well, of course. I saw him at your table again this morning. Everything about him says he loves you. The look in his eyes as he watched your every move. The kindness in his voice as he spoke to you. My goodness, but he's got it bad."

Les scooted her chair back and her knuckles turned white as she gripped the edge of the table. "Abby, if you saw that as anything other than friendship—and I do mean friendship—then you are sorely mistaken."

"What?" Abby shook her head, her heart beginning to pound against her chest. "Now I'm confused. I'd just adjusted my thinking to the notion that the two of you were. . ." Her words drifted off.

Lesley pushed herself to a standing position and brushed her palms against her skirt to smooth it. "Abby, he's old enough to be my father." The words came out in a hoarse whisper.

"Cookie says no one around these parts pays any mind to age differences."

"Are you saying Cookie thinks this too?"

Abby nodded. "Well, I don't know if she thinks it, exactly, or if she's confused by the whole thing. She didn't exactly take to the idea with ease for some reason."

"No doubt she didn't." Lesley paused. "You know what's really going on here, Abby?"

"Clearly, I do not. I'm as lost as can be."

"Neville knows that Cookie and I are friends. He approached me about, well. . ." Lesley paused and lowered her voice. "Winning her affections."

"What?" Abby didn't mean for the word to come out with such volume, but couldn't control her excitement. "Are you sure?" If so, then Cookie must feel the same way. This certainly accounted for her odd behavior the other day, at any rate.

"Well, of course I'm sure." Les chuckled. "No one knows Cookie like I do. I know her favorite foods, her preferences, the things that make her jump for joy. I've been helping Neville put together a list to woo her."

"Well, you could blow me over."

Les chuckled. "I still can't get over the fact that you thought Neville and I. . ." She slapped herself on the thigh. "Oh, that's priceless. Wait till I tell him."

Abby's cheeks heated at the very idea. "No, please don't. Then he'll know that I know about his feelings for Cookie. That will just make things uncomfortable."

"Won't be long before everyone figures that one out. But in the meantime, Neville has been doing me the most wonderful favor."

Now Abby's curiosity was truly piqued. "What's that?"

"Teaching me to speak like a lady. My speech has been lazy and fraught with poor habits. He's been giving me diction lessons."

"Outside of my etiquette lessons, you mean?"

"Yes." Lesley sat up straight and cleared her throat. "How very kind of you to invite me to this lovely reception," she said with crispness and perfect tone. "See what I mean? I'm getting better already. Before long, Mr. Denueve will see me for who I really am."

"Marcus Denueve?" Abby put a hand over her mouth. "Is that who you're enamored with?"

"You betcha." Les's smile faded into a pout. "He doesn't seem to notice me coming or going, though." She grew more thoughtful and turned Abby's way with a somber expression. "But he sure spends a great deal of time trying to win your heart. At least he did the other morning at breakfast."

"I have no aspirations in that direction," Abby managed over the lump in her throat. At least none she'd voice aloud.

"Thank goodness." Lesley's face brightened. "I've had my eye on him for years."

A tight cord wound itself around Abby's heart as she thought about Les and Marcus Denueve as a couple. Not that it was any of her business, of course, but she couldn't picture the man with someone like Les. No, he needed a woman of refinement, one who would help him with his goals and aspirations. And Les needed to be with someone more. . .well, she couldn't think of anyone at the moment, but someone other than Marcus.

Marcus. Abby sighed as the cord twisted a bit tighter.

"You all right over there?" Lesley asked.

"Hmm?" Abby looked up and snapped to attention. "Oh, of course. I'm just tired, I think. Lots to do. Best get to the kitchen to help Cookie with the dishes."

"She's gone to the mercantile, remember?"

"Oh, right. But I did promise to finish up the dishes and start on tonight's pies."

Lesley laughed. "If I didn't know any better, I'd say you were smitten as well."

"Not at all. I'm just passing through, remember? Why, when Mother and Father arrive, we'll all head back to Philadelphia in a hurry."

"And leave a broken heart behind, no doubt."

"What do you mean?"

"Why, everyone in town has you pegged for Sam."

"They. . .they do?"

"Of course. From the minute he saved you from the fellas that first day. I know you think you're bolting after your parents arrive, but why not give this a go while you're here? Might as well make the whole town happy and start the courting process now to see where things lead. That's what I'd do, anyway. If I wasn't pining for Marcus, I mean."

"Sam. . .has feelings for me?" Abby shook off her ponderings.

"I'm no expert in courting, but I would think so, from the way he looks at you." Lesley chuckled. "Don't tell me you've been blind to that."

"I guess I have."

Suddenly, Abby felt completely out of sorts. She wanted to jump and run from the table, to spend a few quiet minutes in her room, thinking about the condition of her heart. Instead, she headed to the kitchen to wash dishes.

A short while later, Cookie and Neville returned, their arms loaded down with items from the mercantile.

The heightened color in Cookie's cheeks caused Abby a bit of concern. "Is it hot out there?" she asked. "You're flushed, Cookie."

"Am I?" Cookie dropped a crate of produce on the counter. "Hot and bothered, is more like it. You wouldn't believe the prices on these things." She yanked several items out of the crate and set them to the side. "That Marcus Denueve has us painted into a corner. We have to buy the ingredients for the baking from his store—the flour, the baking powder, and so forth. He knows that. So, he's upped his prices, and not just on baking supplies, but other food items we use daily as well. In the meantime—mark my words—he'll charge lower prices at his new restaurant over at the saloon. He'll feed the fellas for half of what they pay here." She slammed a bag of flour on the counter. "It's just like Sam said. The man knows exactly what he's doing."

"He's been so kind to me, though," Abby countered. "Even offered me a good wage to play piano at his establishment."

"Establishment. That's a fine word for it." Cookie muttered something under her breath. "Anyway, I'd like to put the man out of my mind, but it's very difficult with that grand opening happening tonight. Most of the fellas are going." She mumbled something else and then added the word, "Traitors."

Abby garnered the courage to say, "Just call me a traitor too."

"What?" Cookie spun around on her heels.

"I was invited."

"But surely you wouldn't go there, Miss Abigail," Neville said. "It's not a fitting place for a lady."

"It's a restaurant," Abby countered. "How bad could it be?"

"And here you think you know a person. . ." Cookie clucked her tongue. "I'm so stunned I hardly know what to say."

"Mr. Denueve personally invited me to the grand opening. I believe he wants me to look at the piano, to see if I might be able to play on occasion. I have some wonderful classical pieces in mind."

"Surely you wouldn't consider such a proposition." The way she stressed the word proposition, Abby had to wonder if the word had double meaning.

"I don't think I will do it. I don't think my skills are up to par. But what would it hurt to peek inside his new place and see that piano for myself? No harm done."

"Trust me, those aren't the kind of skills Marcus is interested in." Cookie brushed her hands on her skirt. "Anyway, it's none of my business. Go if you like." The flustered woman muttered something under her breath that Abby couldn't quite make out, then turned Neville's way. "Tell me you're going with her. I won't hear of her venturing into that place alone."

Neville blanched. "I cannot imagine going into such a place, but neither would I send her into a den of iniquity without a proper chaperone."

Abby did her best not to roll her eyes as his over-dramatic description of the Lucky Penny. Did everyone around here think she was a child, unable to walk into a restaurant on her own?

"Come if you like, Neville. I won't argue. Mr. Denueve was kind enough to extend the invitation to all of us. It's not as if he singled me out."

"Sure he didn't." Cookie slammed another bag of flour onto the counter.

"I will be like a ghost," Neville said. "You won't even see me. But I will be hovering in the background, ready to pounce, should the man so much as look at you improperly."

Abby doubted mightily that Neville would be discreet about his intentions. But, with her feelings in such a state, she didn't really care what Neville or Cookie thought. She would go to that grand opening tonight and have a wonderful time.

♥

Sam paced the dining room, his heart in his throat. He wanted to rush upstairs, to knock on Abby's door, and tell her not to go. Instead, he spent the time fretting and fuming.

"Trust God, Sammy." Cookie's voice sounded from the open doorway. He swung around to face her. "Don't try to fix this yourself. Isn't that what you always tell me?"

"Under most circumstances, yes. But this isn't an ordinary circumstance."

"Because you've fallen for her, am I right?"

As the words were spoken, all the fight washed right out of Samuel. He slumped down in a chair, his elbows landing on the table in front of him.

"I can't say I blame you, Sammy-boy. She's a wonderful girl. If I got to pick God's finest for you, I would've chosen her myself. And I understand why you want to protect her from the likes of Marcus Denueve. That man is wicked."

"Then why are you dead set against my intervening?"

"You just need to move with caution, or your plan might backfire. If you're not careful, you might drive her straight into his arms. That's all I'm saying."

"I see." He released a slow breath. "So, hang back? Do nothing?"

"Pray. That's all the Lord requires of you at the moment. When He gives the go-ahead, you can race across the great divide and save her from the fire-breathing dragon. In the meantime, take some assurance in the fact that Neville will be with her. He plans to keep a very close eye out."

"I sure hope so."

Sam found himself distracted by a noise at the top of the stairs. He looked up to see Abby descending, dressed in that beautiful blue dress of hers, the one that showed off her gorgeous eyes. He sprang from his seat and headed up the steps to offer her his arm.

"Thank you, kind sir." She released a girlish giggle. "Grateful for the help."

When they landed in the dining room, he reached for her hand. "Abby, you look wonderful. Prettier than a picture."

"Hardly. I've never been a beauty, even in my finest clothes, but I make do with what I've been given."

He stopped cold at her proclamation. "Are you serious?" His eyes came up to study her face. Based on her expression, she genuinely believed those words to be true.

"I've never fancied myself pretty, even. To be honest, the boys back in Nottingham didn't pay me much mind. I drew the conclusion some time ago that I wouldn't even pretend to be something I'm not." She appeared to lose herself in her thoughts.

"You must be joshing me." He stared at her, not quite sure what to make of all this. "What makes you think you're not pretty?"

She brushed a strand of loose hair out of her face. "The mirror?"

"Then the mirror is lying." He fought to control the emotion in his words. "Maybe you need to invest in a new one."

"Really?" She did not look convinced.

"Really. I'm not just saying this to appease you, Abby. You're a very beautiful woman." He cleared his throat, the words causing a lump to rise.

She fussed with her reticule. "In a town with only a handful of women, I suppose I look somewhat appealing."

"In a large city with thousands of women, you would still stand apart. The fact that you don't see that just convinces me all the more of your inner beauty. Abby, I don't know what fool notion has planted itself in your head, but you need to rid yourself of it immediately. You're beautiful, inside and out. It has nothing to do with the number of women in town. If we'd met in St. Louis, if I'd seen you walking down the street in a crowd of women, I would have taken notice of you."

"Because of my bulbous nose, perhaps."

"No." He took her hand. "There's something about you that sets you apart. So accept the compliment. Begin to see yourself as God sees you. As I see you."

"Hmm." She slipped the bag under her arm. "I will try."

"Remember how you dressed Les up in frills and lace, how everyone took notice of her outer beauty?"

"Yes."

"It's not like that with you. There's no transformation necessary. And I'm not saying it was altogether necessary with her, either. Folks around here, at least those who were paying attention, always saw her charm. But in your case, it wouldn't matter if you were wearing a dirty apron over a worn dress, your beauty would always shine through."

"Thank you." When she looked his way, he couldn't help but notice a hint of tears on her lashes.

"I've made up my mind not to keep you from the grand opening, though it's tearing me up inside."

"I'm a grown woman, Sam."

"Clearly." His eyes swept the graceful curve of her waist. "And I'm not the only man who will notice, I assure you. So take care. That's all I'll say. Take care."

She muttered something under her breath that he couldn't quite make out, but Sam found himself distracted by her beautiful upswept hair as she turned toward the door. Oh, how he wanted to run and grab her, to convince her not to leave.

Instead, he planted his feet, whispered a prayer for her well-being, and watched her walk out the door.

Chapter Nineteen

*A*bby did her best to look brave as she made her way down the sidewalk toward the Lucky Penny. Before long, Sam would see that she could fend for herself, even in a place that he and Cookie disapproved of. And what was wrong with attending the grand opening of one of San Francisco's new eating establishments, after all? Surely half the town would be there.

As they approached, she gave the Lucky Penny a closer look, her gaze landing on the rough-hewn facade and wooden boardwalk. The hitching posts were all in use, the horses content to rest while their masters took a meal inside. A watering trough for the horses was dry as a bone. Abby was tempted to stop and tend to the poor animals, but found herself distracted by the goings-on inside the restaurant.

The noise level greeted her long before she walked through the double doors. She decided that half the town had shown up, after all. Judging from the sound of the voices, mostly men.

Neville put his fingers in his ears and she could read the alarm in his eyes. "Sounds like a brawl. I say we turn back, Miss Abigail. Too risky."

"Don't be silly. It's just the crowd, Neville. Everyone is celebrating the grand opening of this fine new eating establishment, that's all." Voices raised in song—and argument—barely edged out the rowdy piano music. She thought about what it would be like, to sit at that piano and entertain the guests. She could never play songs with that much gusto, even if she gave it her all.

She brushed through the swinging doors and was greeted at the door by a couple of the older fellas, who let out a whistle as she came through. "Well, lookee here, Joe!" One of them elbowed the other. "We got us a real lady with us tonight." He pulled off his Stetson and gave a bow. "Purty as a picture."

"A real lady, eh?" One of the saloon girls—a pretty blond—pushed her way past the man and approached Abby. She turned up her nose and then doubled back around to where she'd come from. "She ain't so much."

Abby entered the room and looked around, overwhelmed. She'd never had all of her senses accosted at once like this. The smell of liquor hung thick in the air, as if ready to ease its way into her pores. The fellow at the piano banged out a song—if one could call it that—his forehead dripping with sweat. To her left, several of the men hollered at each other, one of them punching the other in the jaw. That, coupled with the smell of men who hadn't bathed in many days, if not weeks, was almost more than she could bear. Would these folks consider it rude if she pinched her nose?

Abby swayed and thought she might go down. Instead, she managed to lean against the long mahogany bar, where she did her best to catch her breath.

"What's your pleasure, folks?" a man behind the bar called out. "Drinks on the house tonight, thanks to our new proprietor."

"I'm looking for Mr. Denueve, actually," Abby called back to the bartender. "Have you seen him?"

"He's around." The edges of the man's mustache tipped up in a smile. "Now, what can I get you?"

"Nothing at the moment," Neville hollered from behind her.

"Yes, nothing at the moment," Abby echoed. She rested the toe of her boot against the brass foot rail that encircled the base of the bar and her gaze shifted to the row of spittoons spaced along the floor. This place looked nothing like a restaurant. Along the edge of the bar, she noticed towels hanging. No telling what those were for.

The man on the barstool next to her took a swig of his beer and used one of the towels to wipe the suds from his mustache. Ah. So that's what they were for.

Abby found herself completely distracted. She wanted to find Marcus, but was scared to move away from her current spot. Only when several of the men surrounded her, their whistles piercing the air, did she get the urge to bolt.

"Who have we here?" An older woman with bright-red hair stepped into place next to Abby and ran her finger over Abby's blue silk skirt. "Nice dress. Where'd you get it, anyhow?"

Abby shrugged off the woman's forward conversation and glanced around one more time in an attempt to find Marcus. A couple of other ladies—if one could call them that—pushed through the crowd and stepped into the spot in front of her. One of them grabbed Abby by the hand and gave her a spin.

"You the new girl?"

"Oh, well, I . . ." Abby didn't know how to respond to that question.

"Marcus said you was pretty, but he didn't tell us you was a debutante." The brazen woman stretched the word, bringing a laugh from the others. "Highfalutin duds you got there, honey. Not that you'll stay dressed in 'em if you hang around here." A high-pitched laugh followed. "Get it? Clothes don't last long around here, less'n they're on the floor at the foot o' the bed."

Abby gripped the edge of the bar and eased her way down onto a barstool. The pianist changed tunes to something even rowdier than before. The women grabbed men and took to dancing across the floor. One of the women even hopped up on a table and did some sort of a jig, her skirt swinging this way and that. The feathers in her hair bobbed up and down, and her low-cut dress threatened to reveal far more than Abby cared to see.

She found herself torn between wanting to watch the ladies with their satin dresses and wanting to look away.

The blond woman, probably about Abby's age, tapped Neville on the shoulder and hollered, "Dance with me, honey."

The look of panic in his eyes shared his thoughts on her suggestion. She pulled him onto the dance floor and pressed herself against him. On the opposite side of the room, one of the dancers did a cartwheel, showing off her undergarments. This led to a rousing cheer from all the men. Well, all but Neville, who looked as if he might be ill.

Fear and anger knotted inside of Abby at the sight of all this. Surely Marcus hadn't begun the transformation process yet. If he planned to turn this place into a restaurant, he would have to fire these women at once. Then again, maybe all of this was part of his plan. Maybe Sam and Cookie were right about him? Their concerns found root in her heart and she felt like a fool for coming.

What had made her think this place would be acceptable? It didn't look like any restaurant she'd ever seen before. Abby's stomach clenched tight as she glanced around one last time for Marcus. If she didn't find him soon, there would be no choice but to leave. Judging from the daggers coming out of Neville's eyes as he tugged himself away from his dance partner, he was more than ready already.

"Miss Abigail, I insist we leave at once."

"But I'm here to look for Mr. Denueve. He invited me to dine with him."

"I'd just as soon you dine with the devil himself. Any man who would own and operate such a place does not deserve to be sought out by an innocent young woman like yourself."

"Innocent, eh?" The blond sidled up next to Abby. "I remember when I used to be innocent too." She slung her arm over Abby's shoulder and laughed. "Don't worry, honey. I'll teach you my ways in time, and you'll never look back. Welcome to the fold, by the way. I'm Katie. I remember what it was like to be the new girl. Wasn't so long ago, actually."

The forced smile was overshadowed by pain in her eyes, and Abby was suddenly overwhelmed with sadness for the woman.

She slipped out from under Katie's grasp and stepped backward. "No, thank you. I'm not here to work, just to spend the evening with Marcus Denueve."

"Aren't we all?" Katie laughed. Just as quickly, her expression shifted to one that could only be construed as jealousy. "You're not his type, honey."

"I didn't claim to be his type. I'm only here to discuss a business transaction."

"*Business* transaction." The girl laughed and clasped her hands together. "That's one way to put it."

"Where. Is. He?" Abby spoke through clenched teeth, the woman's words grating on her last nerve.

"Upstairs. With Molly." The woman gave her a knowing look. "But I wouldn't interrupt them right now, if I were you. You know how testy he can get when you bother him in the middle of a *business* transaction." She emphasized the words, as if they were laughable.

"I came in response to his invitation to dinner, thank you very much."

"Dinner? Well, why didn't you say so? If Marcus invited you to dine with him, let me show you to a table. I'm sure he won't be long." These words were followed by a sarcastic laugh. "He's quick on his feet, or off of them, if you get my meaning."

She led the way to a table where some men were playing some sort of card game. "Up and at 'em, fellas. This here lady needs a place to sit."

"We ain't even halfway into our poker game, Katie," one of the men responded. "Get 'er another table."

"Nope." Katie grabbed the edge of the table and flipped it over, knocking the cards out of their hands. Instead of responding in anger, one of the men gave her a kiss on the cheek and another swatted her on the behind.

"Gracious." Abby shook her head. She wanted to bolt.

Katie turned the table right side up and slapped it with her palm. She gestured for Abby and Neville to sit. "Now, what's your pleasure? Rotgut?"

"Rotgut?"

"Tanglefoot, honey. Red Eye. Liquor, of course."

She'd like to give the woman a red eye, for insinuating that she was a drinker.

"Our Tequila's the best in the territory," Katie added. "That's my favorite."

Abby nearly gagged, just thinking about it. "Nothing, thank you. Could I see a menu, please?"

"Menu's on the board." Katie gestured to a large slate overhead as she walked away. Someone had scribbled the words *steak* and *oven fried potatoes*.

Abby turned to face Neville. "What was all that business about rotgut?"

"Saloon owners like to stretch their profits by adding turpentine or ammonia to their whiskey."

"What?" She put a hand to her chest. "Are you serious?"

He nodded. "Sometimes they even cut in some gunpowder or cayenne."

"For pity's sake. And no one has died?"

"People die all the time in San Francisco, girl." An older woman's voice sounded from beside her. "Ain't no one blamed it on the Tanglefoot yet. Don't be blamin' the drink for the fellas round these here parts keelin' over. They're more likely to die from brawlin' or from lack of bathin'." She laughed and stuck out her hand. "Name's Lottie. What brings you to the Lucky Penny?"

"Just stopped in to have dinner with Mr. Denueve."

"Oh, I see. Guess you're the new girl, then. Was told you'd be showing up soon. We've been waiting on you. You'll be bunking with Donna Sue."

"Oh, I'm not. . .I mean, I won't be working here. I could never do that."

"Why not?" The woman looked her up and down. "Oh, I get it. Prim and proper sort, eh?"

"I suppose those words would fit, but I. . .I. . ." Abby shook her head and pushed her chair back from the table, convinced this whole thing had been a huge mistake. "I think it's time for me to go."

♥

Sam slammed the door to the restaurant and leaned against it, his head throbbing from the noise outside. "They call that a grand opening? I'm about to go deaf in both ears."

Cookie entered the room from the kitchen and groaned. "I hope they'll pipe down sooner rather than later. My blood pressure's rising."

"I somehow doubt it. This is liable to go on all night."

Cookie swiped at her brow with the back of her hand. "Sounds like quite a party going on over there."

"I can't picture Abby in the throes of it, not at all."

Cookie laughed. "The one I'm having the most trouble picturing is Neville. Poor guy. But he'd do anything to look after that girl." She paused and a reflective look entered her eyes. "That's what you do when you love someone. You travel to the ends of the earth for them, go places you never thought you'd go."

"Like you did for me." Sam took her hand. "You came all the way to San Francisco, just to make sure I was taken care of."

"And to make sure your belly was full." She winked at him. "Some-one had to do it."

"Don't know if I've ever told you how grateful I am, Cookie. San Francisco might not be my idea of the best place on earth, but as long as you're here with me, it's certainly more tolerable." He paused. "Can't imagine how I would've survived without you."

"That's the sweetest thing you've ever said to me, honey." Cookie threw her arms around him and gave him a motherly hug.

The strangest feelings came over Sam in that moment. He remem-bered, if for just a few seconds, what it felt like to be wrapped in his mother's arms. To smell her perfume. To hear the sweet, calming voice of reason.

"You all right?" Cookie pulled back and put both hands on his shoulders.

"Yes. Thinking about Mother tonight. And thinking about what you once said about me."

"What did I say?"

"That I was a perfect little boy."

"Ah. Yes, I remember that conversation." She pulled her hands off his shoulders. "And I remember the boy. He grew into a man who traveled to San Francisco. Wasn't very happy to be there, away from everything he knew and loved."

"True."

"He longed to go back home to Independence, to pick up where he left off."

"Yep."

"But I suspect that same young man is now finding his heart twisted up over a certain girl who's also traveled the miles to land in the same spot. Am I right?"

Sam fought the temptation to laugh. "Cookie, as much as it pains me to admit this, you're always right."

"'And ye shall know the truth, and the truth shall make you free.'" She gave him another wink and added, "John, chapter eight, verse thirty-two."

♥

As Abby tried to bolt from her table, she caught a glimpse of Marcus through the crowd. He walked down the steep wooden stairs with a woman on each arm. The buxom brunette to his right looked rather unkempt, as if she'd just tumbled out of bed. The woman to his left wore her ruffled dress off one shoulder. Something she said must have been funny, because Marcus laughed.

Then he glanced Abby's way and his expression shifted. He shook off the women and finished the flight of steps alone. Moments later, he arrived at her table. "Miss Effingham."

"Mr. Denueve." She hardly managed the two words.

"Glad you could come." He spoke above the music. "What do you think of our opening night celebration?"

She fought to come up with words that wouldn't offend. "I've found it very. . .colorful. And loud."

"Indeed." He gestured for the pianist to lower his volume. "You can see our need for a true musician, no doubt. I know I promised not to talk about it, but I would be honored if you would consider—"

"I am not the right one for the job, I assure you."

"Don't be so hasty, Abigail. I can call you Abigail, yes? Surely by now we're old friends. Let me woo you over a lovely meal."

She could picture just how he would woo her. It would start with enticing her to play the piano. Later, after he'd won her confidence, he would woo her right into the same job the other gals in this place had.

No thank you.

"Our chef is in the kitchen, even now, preparing the most wonderful steaks you've ever seen."

"I don't believe so, Mr. Denueve, thank you. I need to go. It's getting late and Neville is tired."

"Your butler scolds you as if you were a schoolgirl?"

"He's more of a fatherly figure to me, you see."

"Hmm." Marcus looked over his shoulder at Neville. "He needs to find a new pastime. You're a grown woman, Abigail. Every angle shows it off. You certainly don't need a nanny."

Why the words stung, she could not say, but Abby decided she'd had enough conversation for one night.

"I'm tired, Mr. Denueve, and we've got an early morning tomorrow. Breakfast is served at six."

"Ah, yes. Always working." He tried to slip his arm around her waist, but she pulled away. "Well, go get some beauty sleep, though you certainly don't need it."

His flattering words make her sick to her stomach.

He reached over and placed his hand on her backside. She jolted, and yanked away.

"Skittish, eh?" He laughed. "I like a girl who makes it hard on me. Cat and mouse games are fun."

"See if you think this is fun, my friend." Neville reared back, doubled his fist, and delivered an unexpected wallop to Marcus Denueve's jaw.

Abby gasped and her hand flew to her mouth as she saw a trickle of blood rolling down Marcus's chin.

"Let's get while the gettin's good, Miss Abigail." Neville gestured with his head that they should leave.

Abby turned, her hands clenched stiffly at her sides. Before she could think twice, she hiked her skirt and bolted toward the saloon door, ready to put this whole evening behind her.

Chapter Twenty

$\mathcal{G}$unshots split the night air. Sam bolted to the door of the restaurant and peered out onto the sidewalk, trying to make out the direction of the shots. If anyone had hurt Abby...

No, he wouldn't let himself think like that.

Cookie joined him, skirt hiked as she ran. Her words, "Everything all r–right?" came out breathless.

"Just up to no good, as always."

Cookie clucked her tongue. "Their celebrations and temper tantrums are so much alike, I can scarcely tell one from the other anymore."

"They're holy terrors." He walked back inside the restaurant and Cookie followed on his heels. "That's my word for them, anyway."

"Beg pardon?" she asked.

He turned to face her. "That's my name for the fellas in this town. They're holy terrors. Well, the terror part feels correct, anyway, but I'm not so sure about the holy."

Cookie faced him, hands on her hips. "Are we or are we not all created in God's image?"

"Of course."

"Even those men out there?" Cookie pointed to the door.

Sam released a quiet "Humph." He knew, of course, that all men and women were created in God's image. But how could one go about reconciling evil with that notion?

194

"Truth is, we're all His children, clean or dirty, good behavior or bad. Makes no never-mind to the Almighty where we come from or how messy we are. When He looks down at us, He sees His children."

"Some more trouble than others."

"That's just it. Some are more trouble, and some—like you—are pretty close to perfect."

"Hardly."

"Just like I said earlier. You were the ideal little boy and you've grown into a man who walks the straight and narrow. Nothing to be ashamed of there. But if you think about it, walking the straight and narrow isn't what makes us holy."

"It isn't?"

"Nope. We're righteous—made right—because of what He's done, not of our own accord: 'As it is written, There is none righteous, no, not one.' Romans 3:10."

Sam had just about had enough of this conversation. "I understand, but what's your point, Cookie?"

"Just saying that good, clean living doesn't make us holier, now does it? Not saying you should do the opposite. The point is that the only thing that sets us apart from others is that we've come to know and accept what God did for us when He sent His Son to die on the cross. We've accepted that free gift and have given our hearts to Him. But it's still His holiness, not our own, that makes the difference. You see?"

"Never really thought about it from that angle, I suppose." Sam plopped down at one of the tables and went back to work on the stack of bills, including the one from the mercantile.

"Maybe it's time we all did. Perhaps that's how we reach these men. We stop judging them and telling them they're sinners bound for hell. They've heard enough of those sermons back home. Maybe we're just to love them and show them a better way so they can begin to see hope in their own lives. Make sense?"

"Not sure that'll stand up in a pulpit, and I'm not sure I have it in me to be particularly loving to these fellas when they're swinging guns in my face."

She shook her head. "I'm not saying we need to abide sin, so don't misunderstand me. It breaks God's heart to see folks turn their backs on Him or live in degradation. But I'm beginning to think that our just giving these fellas a list of dos and don'ts probably breaks His heart too. They can't follow rules when their hearts haven't been changed."

Her words struck a nerve and Sam mumbled his response. "I suppose."

"When a heart is changed, the desire to please God kicks in and off we go, living better lives. We do the right things out of obedience and love for our heavenly Father, not out of fear. Fear will only cause you to line up and walk straight for so long before you finally give up and do the wrong thing again. It's a vicious circle."

Sam looked up. "You've given me a lot to think about, Cookie."

" 'For as the heavens are higher than the earth, so are my ways higher than your ways, and my thoughts than your thoughts.' "

"Your thoughts are higher than mine, Cookie. Won't argue that point."

She laughed. "Just quoting Isaiah 55:9. Those are the Almighty's words, not my own, thank you very much."

Maybe, but Sam had to admit, Cookie's way of thinking was far superior to his own. Where she mustered such compassion for these fellas, he could not say. But she had a heart as big as the state of California. Sam just prayed it wouldn't get her into trouble anytime soon.

❤

Abby trudged along the sidewalk in the dark, her fists clutching the sides of her skirt, which she lifted a couple of inches to avoid the mud. With so much on her mind, she needed to talk, but Neville wasn't the right person to listen to her thoughts, not the ones tumbling through her brain right now. She wanted to thank him for rushing to her rescue, but couldn't find the words. Maybe tomorrow such a task could be accomplished, but not tonight, not with so much on her mind.

Instead, she plowed through the front door of the Gold Rush Inn, raced past Sam, who sat at the table closest to the door, and headed straight to the kitchen, where she hoped to find Cookie. Thank goodness, Neville didn't follow her. He plopped down next to Sam and put his head in his hands.

As she'd suspected, the older woman was hard at work on the cinnamon rolls for tomorrow morning's breakfast.

Abby greeted her with the words, "I feel like such a fool," and then leaned against the counter, tears springing to her eyes.

"Why?" Cookie looked up from the dough and swiped her forehead with the back of her hand. "Because you fell for a man's sweet nothings?"

"Yes." Abby's cheeks grew warm. "I was warned at every turn, but fell straight into his trap, nonetheless. My judgment is not to be trusted." The last few words came out strained, painful. The truth stung.

"I wouldn't say that, honey. Every woman wants to be courted, and he went out of his way to flatter and woo you to get what he wanted."

"He did, indeed." She paused and thought through the chain of events. "I'm just ashamed of myself, if you want the truth. I've never been the silly schoolgirl sort, falling for men like Marcus Denueve. That's not me."

"You've just learned something else about yourself, that's all. Don't spend too much time fretting over what's happened, girlie. Just take what you've learned and move forward from here. And thank the good Lord above that you didn't get caught in his web. This story could've had a far worse ending, trust me."

"All I've learned is that I'm capable of having the wool pulled over my eyes, just like any other human being."

"I see." Cookie looked amused by this. "So, you're scared to learn you're human?"

"I guess."

"I can't tell you how many times I've had to learn the hard way. But God is gracious. He keeps putting me on my feet again and pointing me toward the next hurdle."

"I guess. But Cookie, the things I saw tonight. . ." She shivered. "Those people. They're so. . ." Her words trailed off.

"Opposite of what you know to be good and right?"

Abby nodded. "That's it, exactly. I was completely out of place. The things they do over there are just plain awful. Ungodly. Shameful."

"True on every count, but isn't it wonderful—and somewhat perplexing—to remember that God loves each and every one of them as much as He loves you and me?"

Abby shook her head, trying to imagine such a thing possible. "He has to brush a lot of dirt off first, I guess."

"No, sweet girl. That's the most amazing thing about God. He loves us, even in our dirtiness. He loved us when we were kids, innocent and free from the cares of this life, and He loves us when we stumble and fall into the mud puddle. Even in the thick of it, His love sweeps over us. And if you think Marcus was good at wooing, just think about what a master the Almighty is. Even now, He's wooing those men and women to Himself."

"It's hard to believe, but I suppose you're right. One of the girls—I think her name was Katie—looked so sad, Cookie. I could see it in her eyes. She didn't really want to be there. It was as if she'd been trapped in a life she didn't plan for herself."

"Like many feel trapped in their lives or situations, I suppose."

"Mother. She felt trapped in a marriage she didn't want. And sometimes I think Sam feels trapped here, in San Francisco."

"He does, but I believe God is working on him, even as we speak."

Abby sighed. "So much pain. So much sorrow. So much. . .sin. Sometimes I think God must look down on us and feel like crying."

"Maybe, but He never gives up, even when we're in the deepest pit."

"I would give up, that's for certain." Abby shook her head.

Cookie brushed her hands on her apron and gestured for Abby to sit on the stool by the counter. "Here's a question for you, honey. How far did you come in search of your mother?"

"Far. All the way from Philadelphia to Fort Hall, where we were forced to turn off toward California."

"But, really, farther still. Right?" Cookie gave her a pensive look. "Didn't your father come from England to Philadelphia, in part to pacify your mother's desire to flee?"

"Yes." Abby nodded. "I guess we've come a great distance, covered a lot of miles, to win her back."

"And that's my point." Cookie rested her hand on Abby's arm. "As far as you've come, as many miles as you've traveled to bring your mother back home again, God will go that far and farther still to bring His children home again, no matter how far they've roamed, no matter how hard their hearts. He does all of this, out of His great love for us."

"I never thought of it that way."

"He came all the way from heaven to earth—a bit farther than Philadelphia to the Oregon Territory—to woo His children home. And Abby, though it might not seem possible in our minds, these men and women here in San Francisco, they are His children."

"A rowdy lot."

"Definitely." Cookie grinned. "But, what I'm saying is this: He would do it all again, cross miles and miles, just to win one of these ornery fellows back to Himself. So, as you travel the miles to find your mother, as you pray for her homecoming, her peace, her heart, just understand that the Lord has those same longings for every one of His children, male or female. And He hasn't given up on your mama, either. He loves nothing more than restoration."

"Cookie, thank you." Abby slung her arms around her friend's neck. "Thank you for that reminder. As much as I love Mama, God loves her even more." She paused, her thoughts on the goings-on at the saloon. "And I suppose it's for the best that you reminded me about the men and women I saw tonight as well. Sometimes I forget they are as precious to God as we are."

"Every last one of them, lost sheep and all. I can picture the Almighty coming up with ways to tap these fellas on the shoulder and woo them to Himself. And He wants us to win them over with our love too. Not our judgment, but our love."

"Judging them is the very last thing that will work, I suppose. Mama was never won over by harsh words or criticism."

"Which is why we're called to pray and not to beat them over the head with our Bibles. 'By this shall all men know that ye are my disciples, if ye have love one to another.' That's John 13:35."

"I don't know how you do it, Cookie. You always have the scripture I need to hear ready on your heart at a moment's notice."

"It helps to memorize the verses so I can apply them to my life," Cookie responded. "You know, honey, sometimes all these men need is the knowledge that someone is praying for them."

Abby nodded. "And I suppose that's what Mama needs too." A thought hit her all at once. "You know what, Cookie?"

"What, honey?"

"I haven't been praying for Mama. I mean, I've prayed that she would come to her senses. I've prayed that God would drag her home. But I haven't actually prayed for her peace, her security, her heart. Maybe it's time I shifted the direction of my prayers."

"Absolutely. No doubt God is calling you to do just that."

"I was so silly, to let myself be tempted to play the piano at the Lucky Penny. That wicked man flattered me and I fell right into his trap."

"If you have a hankerin' to play the piano, then I have an even better idea."

"What's that?"

"I can't offer you any money, but I can tell you that we need a pianist up at the church. We haven't had one since Mrs. Orchard passed away. And, to be honest, her skills were lacking. We couldn't tell 'Jesus, Lover of my Soul' from 'Blest be the Tie that Binds.' The piano's probably in need of a tuning, and I think it's missing a few keys, but we could find someone in town capable of taking care of all that, if you're willing to give it a go."

"I don't mind playing for the church, and the idea of helping the community holds some appeal. But I don't plan to be here long enough to be of much use, Cookie. Remember? My parents are arriving in short order. They will whisk me away to Philadelphia and this adventure will come to an end."

A wave of sadness washed over her with those words.

From the kitchen door, a voice rang out. "Would you consider it, Abby? In the meantime, I mean."

She turned to discover Sam had entered the room. Hopefully he hadn't been standing there long enough to overhear much.

"Consider what?"

Playing at the church. If so, I think my father would spring for an overhaul of the old piano. Not sure if we have anyone in town who could tune it up, but maybe we'll locate someone."

"Oh, I have the perfect someone," she said. "Neville."

"Did someone call my name?" Neville entered the room and headed straight to the cinnamon rolls to take a nibble. Cookie swatted his hand, but he didn't flinch. "If I can stand up to a fellow like Marcus Denueve, I can handle you, woman."

Cookie's eyes flashed with mischief. "In that case, eat the whole thing." She picked up a cinnamon roll and passed it his way.

"Don't mind if I do." Neville took a bite and turned back toward Abby and Sam. "Now, what were we talking about, again? Ah, yes. I've never met a piano I couldn't tune. My mother always said I had perfect pitch." A somber look came over him. "Always thought it a bit odd that I can't carry a tune in a bucket but can hear notes at exactly the right pitch." He seemed to shake off his pondering and took a big bite of the cinnamon roll. After swallowing he said, "At any rate, I would be happy to give it a try."

"Anything you can do would be a move toward the positive," Sam said. "And we'll pay you for your work, of course."

"Not necessary," Neville said with the wave of a hand. "It will be my pleasure."

The two men headed out of the kitchen, deep in conversation.

"Well, there you go." Cookie's face was awash with sweetness as she gazed after them. "We are surrounded by wonderful men, are we not, Abby?"

"We are." And that thought left her heart feeling more twisted than ever.

Abby said her goodnights and headed upstairs to bed. As she reached the hallway, she came face to face with Jin, who was carrying a load of dirty sheets in his arms.

His face lit into a smile the moment he saw her. "You come back, Miss Abby."

"Well, of course I came back."

"Good." A hint of sadness flickered in his eyes. "We miss you much if you go."

"I would miss you too." She wanted to give him a hug, but the dirty sheets made her think twice.

"Miss Abby, I tell you something."

"Sure, Jin."

He shifted the linens and rested against the stair railing. "You make Miss Les beautiful."

"Why, thank you."

"But she already beautiful." Creases formed between his brows. "Before you turn her into swan, I mean. Always beautiful."

"Yes, I believe she was."

Jin looked at her intently. "Not all woman need pretty dress to show beauty. Some woman need only kindness of heart."

"And she's always been very kind, hasn't she?"

"Yes, like boss man." Jin gestured down toward the dining room, where Sam and Neville sat at a table. "Him good, kind man."

"Yes, Sam is a very good man." Her gaze lingered on the object of their conversation, who glanced her way with a smile.

"Him take good care customers," Jin added. "And me. Give me home. Teach me business."

"Yes, he's the best."

She'd watched Sam in action for some time now, how he laughed with the men. How he'd given up his bed so that she could have a comfortable place to sleep. How he always looked out for the underdog. Somehow Sam had managed to rise above his troubles to become the man God intended him to be.

Abby squared her shoulders, the idea giving her courage. If he could rise above his family's situation—above the pain caused by his mother's death and his father's struggles—she could certainly rise above the divisions between her mother and father. If he could turn his situation around and use it for good, so could she.

Chapter Twenty-One

On the Tuesday night before her parents were set to arrive, Abby prepared herself for her final etiquette class. The past few weeks had given her plenty of opportunity to continue with the work the Lord had given her, shaping the town's men into gentlemen. She felt almost as happy about their progress as she did about her own on the church's piano. How she had summoned the courage to play for Sunday services two weeks in a row was beyond her. Still, she counted it all joy.

"James chapter one, verse two," Abby said aloud. . .and then giggled.

Looked like Cookie was rubbing off on her.

About an hour before class was set to begin, she went to the kitchen to check on the snacks. She caught Cookie in a belly laugh. Jin must've said something funny just before Abby walked in, because Cookie was doubled over. Minutes later, Jin left to gather eggs from the henhouse and Abby took advantage of the moment to talk to Cookie.

"Tell me about Jin," she said.

"Jin?" Cookie's lips curled up in a smile. "What do you want to know?"

"He's just so sweet. I've never heard him say an ugly word to anyone."

"You'll never find a finer soul. He came to the area three years ago, I believe. Looking for gold, like so many from China."

"But he didn't find any?"

"Oh, he found plenty. Sent it all back to his parents and siblings in

China, from what I've been told. And just for the record, his real name isn't Jin."

"It's not?"

"No. But Jin means gold, so his family members gave him that name before he left to come here."

"Do you think he's planning to stay?"

"Ask him yourself. His English is getting better every day."

"I know. I've been amazed at how well he's been able to communicate with me."

"He's a fine man, Abby. A kind man. And I can tell you with certainty that his heart is right with the Lord."

"I'm so glad." She paused to think this through. "You know, Cookie, I'm learning that our preconceived ideas are rarely God's best. Not saying I had any ideas about Jin. . .I just rarely gave him any thought at all. He's been a permanent fixture in this place, a real rock, and I hardly noticed the role he's played. I'm ashamed that I scarcely paid attention to him."

"Plenty of time to notice from now on, honey. And as for our preconceived ideas—about people, places, or things—this is exactly why we need to listen for the voice of the Holy Spirit. He can whisper into our ears and nudge us in the right direction. Often the right direction is the opposite of the way we're headed, which requires an about-face, but turning around is always for the best."

"Yes, I agree." Like she had turned away from the Lucky Penny and bolted toward the door.

Jin entered the kitchen again, with the gathered eggs in a basket. Abby waited until he set the basket down then walked his way and took his hand. "Jin, I just want you to know how much I appreciate you for teaching me so much about kitchen duty over the past few weeks. You've been a real godsend, and I'm very grateful."

"Why, thank you, Miss Abigail." His deep-brown eyes sparkled in obvious delight. "My pleasure."

Abby's heart warmed with kindness toward the man as she headed into the dining room to locate Sam. She found him at the register checking in a new guest, a fellow from Indiana. His words, "Welcome to the Gold Rush Inn" made her smile. In fact, everything about Sam made her smile these days. The way he laughed at Neville's dry jokes. The way he swiped Cookie's Snickerdoodles when she wasn't looking. Even the way he poked fun at her.

Yes, Sam was most certainly growing on her.

Les entered the restaurant at the same moment Sam headed toward the stairs to carry up the guest's bag. Abby turned her attention to her friend and welcomed her with a cheerful, "Good evening, Lesley."

Unfortunately, she only saw concern in Lesley's eyes.

"Are you all right?" Abby asked.

"I don't know if I can do it, Abby."

"Do what?"

Lesley pointed down at her skirt and blouse. "Keep up this charade of dressing like a lady. For one thing, I can't take all the whooping and hollering from the men. They never treated me like that before. What difference does a dress make?"

"To them, a lot, I guess." Abby shrugged.

"It's just the wrapping on the package. I was okay with the wrapping before. And Marcus isn't really paying any more attention to me now than he was before. It's been weeks, and he doesn't even give me a second glance." She plopped down at the table nearest the door and sighed. Loudly.

Abby's heart quickened as she heard Marcus's name. "Would you mind terribly if I shared a story about him, Lesley? I think it might change your mind about the man."

"Sure. Be my guest."

Abby told the whole tale of how things had gone at the saloon two weeks back. Lesley listened quietly, but when she got to the part where Neville punched Marcus in the jaw because of what he'd done to Abby, Lesley sprang from her seat. "That oaf! He put his hand on you...where?"

Abby pointed to her backside. "He's no gentleman, I assure you. And Les, it pains me to tell you this, but he has joined himself with those women at the saloon. I saw him coming down the stairs with two of them, after. . ." She paused and cleared her throat. "Spending time in their company privately."

Lesley groaned. "So much for thinking he was the fella for me. I can't believe I've wasted so much time thinking about him at all."

"Appearances can be deceiving, I guess. Just because a man's in a fine suit doesn't mean he's a gentleman."

"And just because a gal's in a skirt doesn't mean she's a lady." A little sigh followed. "I think my days of pretending to be something I'm not are behind me, to be quite honest. I'll go back to being Les, the hermit who lives alone in the house on the hill. The fellas can admire me for my gold, not my dresses."

"I wouldn't give up just yet, but neither would I encourage you to do anything that makes you uncomfortable." Abby rested her hand on her friend's arm. "Lesley, you were a lady long before I dolled you up. And any man in his right mind would have already taken note of that. So don't get all wound up about Marcus. Pray and ask the Lord to show you who He's got in mind for you. I suspect He will answer sooner than you think."

"Hopefully he won't care if I'm in dungarees or a ball gown."

"He won't care either way," Abby countered, "but just for the record, you look lovely in that skirt, and I adore your hair long and flowing down your back like that."

"Thank you, Abby. You're such a good friend."

Moments later, Neville entered the room. Something about him looked different, but she couldn't place it. Abby narrowed her gaze as she tried to figure it out.

"Well, go ahead and say it." He stroked the sides of his face. "I look more American, wouldn't you say?"

"More American?"

Cookie came out of the kitchen with a tray of sweets in her hand, which she almost dropped when she saw Neville.

"You've done it!"

"Yes." A sly smile turned up the edges of his lips. "I have, indeed." He pointed to the space where his graying sideburns had once resided, and

Abby gasped as the realization hit.

"That's it. You've shaved off your sideburns." A pause followed as she took in his new appearance. "I'm not saying I think that's a bad idea. I'm just surprised."

"Someone convinced me they were too formal for San Francisco." He gave Cookie a nod. "So, I decided to try out a new look."

"It suits you, Neville." Cookie looked amused as she got back to work. "Gracious, but it suits you."

"Thank you." He gave her a wink. "Now, would you happen to have any chocolate cake in that kitchen of yours? I've got a hankerin' for chocolate."

"But. . .I thought you said you didn't like chocolate?" Abby pursed her lips as he disappeared into the kitchen.

A short while later, a rush of local men entered the dining room for their evening lesson. Some of the same fellows who raised such a ruckus at the Lucky Penny a few weeks back, arrived, all sobered up. Abby did her best not to judge, as Cookie had suggested, in the hopes that extending grace would win them over to a better way of life.

The lesson went even better than before, including the dance portion, where she called on Sam to help her demonstrate the waltz. He seemed happy to be of service. Judging from his jovial expression, he had an even better time than she did.

In that moment, as she observed the relaxed expression on his face and the spring in his step, Abby felt convinced that her place of service was right here, offering lessons to these men.

And the women. She couldn't help but notice that Les had a wonderful time on the dance floor as well. With Neville as her partner, she sashayed in 1-2-3 time, over and over, a relaxed smile on her face. Only when Jin cut in did Neville relinquish his spot as Les's dance teacher.

Neville grabbed Cookie in his arms and they took off across the floor in perfect rhythm. Abby was fascinated, watching this newer, freer version of the stiff, proper butler she had once known. How would he respond when the time came to head back to Philadelphia? She couldn't imagine him slipping back into his role as a family servant.

When the lessons ended, Cookie served up slices of cherry pie and told the fellas all about her plans to open the bakery in a few weeks. This got a rousing cheer out of everyone in attendance.

Well, everyone but Jedediah Tucker. As the men quieted down, he raised his hands and got everyone's attention.

"Something you want to say?" Cookie asked.

He nodded. "Yes'm. Just wanted y'all to know that I. . .well. . ." He beamed, as if holding some sort of secret. "I've decided to go back home."

"For your daughter's wedding?" Abby asked.

He nodded and she grabbed his hand and took him for a jig around the room to celebrate.

"I'm so proud of you!" she said when they'd wrapped up the dance.

"Me too." Cookie waggled her finger at him. "Now, shave off that fool beard and present your wife and daughters with a clean-shaven face when you get home. And remember all the things you've learned from Abby over the past few weeks. Don't want to find out all of this was for naught."

"Oh, I will, I will." He flashed Abby a grateful smile and then took a bite of pie.

Abby had to wonder if things could possibly get any better. She caught a glimpse of Sam and gave him an appreciative nod. He was as much to blame for this as she. His efforts with the men were being rewarded, as were hers.

Across the room, Jin and Les chatted about something or another. He must've said something funny, because Les laughed. Abby approached them to offer a thank-you for attending her classes.

She arrived just as Jin pulled back Les's chair. Les thanked him as she took a seat. Then Jin pulled back a chair for Abby as well.

"You're learning a lot," she said as she took a seat. "Such a fine gentleman you're turning out to be, Jin. Truly."

"Thank you, Miss Abby." His gaze shifted to Lesley. "And may I say, you look lovely tonight, Miss Lesley." His words came out crisp and clear. "Like a vision from above, if I might be so bold."

Les's cheeks flushed pink. "Why, thank you, Jin. What a kind and generous thing to say."

"Your eyes are like flowers on hillside in sunshine. I tell Mr. Sam last spring how much your eyes remind me of larkspur."

"Last spring?" She glanced up at him, her blue eyes widening in obvious surprise. "Really? You noticed back then?"

"Of course." He brought his hand to his chest, his words even more serious than before. "Always, they have captivated me." He paused and appeared to be thinking. "Captivated. . .right word?"

"Captivated, right word." Abby and Les spoke in unison, and they both laughed.

Lesley beamed. "A girl could get used to hearing such things. I will have to visit more often." She faced Jin, a twinkle in her eyes. "What's on the menu tomorrow night? Maybe I'll stop in for dinner and we can talk some more. I've had a hankerin' to learn Chinese, Jin."

"Chinese? Yes." His eyes sparkled at this news. "Tomorrow night fried chicken. Plucked by Miss Abigail."

"Then I'll skip dinner and just come for lunch." Les slapped her thigh and released a belly laugh. "The last time I ate chicken plucked by Miss Abigail, I got a mouthful of feathers."

Abby almost fell out of her chair giggling at this one. She managed to get control of herself just as Sam's father entered the room. Judging from the serious expression on the man's face and the fast clip as he headed straight for his son, Mr. Harris had something rather urgent on his mind.

❤

"What is it, Father?" Sam looked up from his spot at the table near the kitchen as his father paced back and forth. "You're making me nervous."

His father took a seat and placed his hands in his lap. "You've seen me coming and going a lot these past few weeks."

"Yes. I. . .I haven't had the heart to bring it up, but I have been concerned."

"The truth is, son, I've been spending time with Maggie O'Callahan."

"Maggie O'Callahan, the washerwoman?"

His father nodded. "Didn't quite know how to tell you, if you want the truth of it. Maggie's been mighty lonely since her husband died last year, and I. . ." His words faded at the same moment his cheeks flamed red. "Well, doggone it, I've been pining away for her for nigh on three months now, so I finally worked up the courage to tell her. We've been seeing each other ever since, but I just didn't know how to tell you."

"Father, I'm stunned. I don't know what to say."

"Say you'll be happy for us, Sam. Say you'll be all right if I choose to up and marry her. That's my plan, anyway, unless she changes her mind."

"You're getting married?"

"Mm-hmm. Middle of August, soon as her son and daughter-in-law can get here from New York. But that isn't all." His father rose and the pacing started again. "Giving thought to selling the inn."

"Selling the inn?" Months ago, this news would have delighted Sam. Now it put a hole in his heart. "Do you have a buyer?"

His father's gaze drifted to the table. "I've had an offer from Marcus Denueve."

Sam's heart plummeted to his stomach. He lowered his voice to a strained whisper so that the others in the room wouldn't overhear. "Father, you can't be serious. You know Marcus Denueve better than anyone. He's trying to take over this town, one business at a time. You'd be playing right into his hand if you sold to him. It wouldn't end well for anyone."

"I didn't say I planned to do it, just that he placed an offer. A generous one."

"You're dead set on retiring after. . ." Sam could barely get the word out. "Marrying?"

"The inn is a lot of work, as you well know. And with prices going up every day, I don't know how I can keep it going. Marcus has painted us into a corner."

"Which is why I'm so shocked you would give thought to selling to him, of all people."

"It's the only thing that makes sense, actually." His father appeared to lose himself to his thoughts. "Sometimes the tide is against you. And right now, my heart just isn't in it. One day you'll understand, son. You'll fall in love."

The words cut deep. Sam was already feeling the emotional tugs of what he believed to be love, only the one he cared for would soon be leaving. She would go, then Father would sell the inn, and Sam would be on his own—with no one. Nothing.

Sam rose and walked toward the kitchen, his thoughts tumbling. Finally, he turned back in his father's direction to speak his mind. "I'm sorry, but this conversation has taken me totally by surprise."

"No doubt. I understand you're surprised. I told Maggie you would be. But don't you see, son? I'm getting older. That's why. A man can't go on working forever."

"Are you giving thought to going back home to Independence after you marry?"

"No, but if I sell the inn—"

"Something I hope you won't do."

"If I sell the inn, I would move into Maggie's place. She's got that nice house on the west end of the district. It's just the right size for the two of us." He flashed Sam a smile. "And big enough for a few grand-kids to visit, when the time comes." Just as quickly, he sobered. "I know how badly you've wanted out of this situation, son. You've hated San Francisco and this inn from the get-go. To be honest, I figured this idea would delight you."

Funny how things had changed, and in such a short time too.

Sam decided to end the conversation on a positive note, so he congratulated his father and then turned to head up the stairs.

Abby approached just as he grabbed hold of the stair railing. "Everything all right, Sam? You don't seem yourself."

He shook his head as he gazed into her beautiful eyes. "No. Not sure I can talk about it right now, though. Maybe tomorrow?"

"Tomorrow, then." She rested her hand on his arm and gave him a tender glance, one that pricked at his heart. "But I'll be praying, Sammy. Whatever it is, God is big enough to handle it."

He wasn't sure which touched him more, that she wanted to share his burdens with him, or that she'd called him Sammy.

He settled into bed a short time later. The noise from downstairs dissipated and he knew all the fellas had left for the night. Still, his father's news kept him wide awake.

The lingering smell of Cookie's cherry pie hovered in the air adding further distraction. Perhaps a trip to the kitchen was in order. Just for a nibble, of course. He could think more clearly with the taste of cherry pie on his lips.

After a while, he couldn't take it anymore. He slipped down the stairs and tiptoed into the kitchen.

What he saw next almost sent him reeling backward, out of the room.

Cookie.

And Neville.

Wrapped in each other's arms.

Chapter Twenty-Two

"What do you mean, Marcus is making a move?" Sam leaned against the kitchen counter and stared at his father, stunned at his news.

His father ran his fingers through his thinning hair, something he only did when nervous. "He stopped by early this morning and put more pressure on me to sell the inn, son. He upped his original offer to one that's hard to resist. With all the changes coming in my life, I have to at least give the offer some consideration."

From her place at the sink, Cookie cleared her throat.

Sam shook his head. "No, you don't. Father, please tell me you're not ready to give in to the pressure just yet. It's only been a few days since you told me about your engagement. We haven't even had a chance to talk this through. And you know how I feel about the man. To lose the inn to him, of all people, would be the ultimate insult."

"We wouldn't be losing, we would be selling. There's a difference. The money would be enough for you to live...and live well, Sammy. I'm talking about a life without the pressures of running a business dependent on Marcus Denueve."

"If we sell to him, I fear we'll never really be free of him." Sam felt his temper rising and it was all he could do not to raise his voice. "Please don't do anything yet. There's no reason to feel forced to do something against your will."

Cookie cleared her throat once again, this time a bit louder.

"The clock is ticking, son. Maggie and I are getting married in a few weeks. After that, I'll be living at her place. If I don't sell the inn to Marcus, then the whole lot falls to you, and I'm of the opinion it's too big a chunk to bite off, especially for someone who's been keen on leaving, anyway."

"My feelings on leaving have changed, Father."

There. He'd spoken the words aloud. Hearing them caused a wave of fear to creep over him, but he would deal with that.

"Really?" His father looked perplexed. "Are you saying you want to stay and manage the inn without me?"

"That's what I'm saying. Unless you're desperate to sell because you need the funds."

"If prices keep going up, we'll be hurting. But it was never really about the money, Sammy." His father gave him an unexpectedly tender glance. "It was always about having something to leave to you, a legacy. But I thought—and please forgive me if I'm wrong—I thought you hated it here. I've had the feeling for some time now that you wanted to return to Independence."

"I. . .I did." Sam shook his head. "But now, I don't."

"Just like that?"

"Just like that."

"I'd made up my mind to sell," his father said. "But you've given me a lot to think about."

"And what about the bakery, Mr. Harris?" Cookie turned to face them, her face ashen. "Have you changed your mind about buying the building next door?"

"Not sure my heart is in it right now, Cookie." He shrugged. "You might say I'm a little distracted. Let me think about it, all right? We can talk later."

"But I've got it all planned out—in my head and on paper. I've even been trying out new recipes on the men. I know it'll be a success. I just know it."

"I don't know, Cookie. I really don't." Sam's father reached across the countertop, grabbed an apple muffin, then took a bite. "Mmm."

"See?" She raised her arms, as if to prove a point. "New recipe. It's good, right?"

"Everything that comes out of your oven is good, Cookie," Sam's father responded.

"And everything that touches Marcus Denueve's hands turns to evil." Sam stood a bit straighter, determined to speak his mind. "Which is why I can't abide the idea of letting the Gold Rush Inn fall into his hands. He would turn it into a den of iniquity."

"I highly doubt that, son."

"What's to keep him from turning it into another dance hall that serves food and offers rooms to accommodate its"—Sam spit out the word—"guests?"

"Don't let your imagination run away with you, Sam."

"I've never been accused of having a runaway imagination, Father. I'm just flabbergasted to think you might be all right with selling to a man like that. Anyone else, I could understand. But him?"

"Just hold steady." His father took another bite of his muffin then turned to face Cookie. "This is one of your best, Cookie."

She squared her shoulders. "Thank you. I'll be serving them in the new bakery, which I still plan to open next month, regardless. Breakfast muffins. Loaded with vitamins to get you going for the day ahead." She muttered something under her breath about how she probably wouldn't be able to afford the ingredients once Marcus took over the town, then stormed to the other side of the kitchen.

"That is my biggest concern, actually," Sam's father interjected. "If I refuse to sell to Marcus now, he'll take revenge by upping the prices on our goods even further." He turned to face Sam. "Don't you see, son? He'll just keep on raising costs until we finally fold. He's got the upper hand and he knows it."

"Then we have to think of a way to get it back."

His father gave him a pensive look. "Can't picture how that will work. As long as we need items from his store, he will have us in his grip. It's as simple as that."

"Then we need another option for goods. Another store."

"The nearest general store is miles away. We can't send Cookie that far for flour and sugar and such."

Cookie rested her hand on the countertop and shook her head. "I don't mind, Mr. Harris. Not if it will keep us here. I'll ride as far as necessary to buy what I need. If it means Sammy can keep this place, it'll be worth it to me."

Sam looked her way and nodded. "We could manage, if we stocked up. Right, Cookie? Jin and I could go with you, once a month, say, and we could buy all we needed. Then we wouldn't be dependent on Marcus anymore. It's not an option we've looked at in the past, because it's inconvenient, but inconvenience is better than highway robbery."

"Whatever it takes." Cookie planted her feet firmly, placed her hands on her hips, and faced them both. "My heart is here. My place is here. I don't want to go back."

Sam's father released a sigh, a defeated look on his face. "I'll leave it up to you for the moment, Sam, but let's talk about this again in a few days. I want to be sure you're up for this, in it for the long haul, as it were."

"Well, I know what I'll be praying for in church tomorrow, anyway." Cookie reached for a mixing bowl and dumped in a mound of sugar. "In the meantime, you'd better up your prayers too, Sammy-boy."

Sam nodded in agreement. What were his other options, really?

♥

Abby didn't mean to snoop, but found herself at the kitchen door at the very same moment Sam and his father were conversing about the fate of the inn. Two things caught her by surprise: First, Mr. Harris planned to marry? This was certainly news to her. And second, he had planned to sell the inn to Marcus Denueve?

The very idea made Abby feel sick to her stomach. Thank goodness Sam had shared his thoughts on the matter. But how would things turn out in the end? Would Marcus really gain control? If so, they could wave good-bye to the whole town, at least their corner of it.

She paced the dining hall, her thoughts tumbling madly. How could she help fix this situation? "Why do I care?" she said aloud to the empty room. "I'm not even staying here. Mother and Father will be here soon, and they'll take me. . ." She couldn't say the word "home." Philadelphia didn't feel like home. Not at all.

No, the only place that truly captured her heart now was San Francisco.

Beautiful San Francisco, with its sparkling waters and scenic overlooks. Exciting San Francisco, with its rowdy cowboys and brawls in the street. Lovely San Francisco, with its precious citizens, including a few who had won her heart fully.

Citizens like Cookie.

And Lesley.

And Sam.

Sam.

Abby's heart began to twist in ways she hadn't known possible. In a flash, she pictured herself seated on the wagon next to him, looking out over the bay. She could almost feel her hand in his, could hear his words, whispered in her ear.

What was it he had called himself, again? Oh, yes. Reliable. Reliable old Sam.

Her heart twisted with a mixture of joy and pain as she pondered her growing feelings for reliable old Sam.

The wave of emotions that hit her was almost more than she could take. How had she overlooked his sweetness? The way he'd cared for her when she arrived. His mother's quilt on her bed. His kindness toward Cookie and his father. His gentlemanly ways around Les, even before her transformation. The way he treated Jin like a brother. The way he gave of himself so freely to the local men like Chet and Adam.

Yes, he was reliable, in every way that mattered. Sam Harris was a prize, one she had almost missed because her eyes were on something—or rather, someone—else. A manipulator, no less. She'd almost fallen into Marcus's trap. And Sam had tried to warn her, hadn't he? Surely he cared about her too, or he wouldn't have bothered.

He cared about her.

Yes, and he'd tried to tell her, hadn't he? Pieces of his heart had shown through that day at the bay. How had she missed his heart? Oh, if only she had listened. She could have avoided so much frustration. And maybe, as Lesley had said, she and Sam would already be courting right now.

The very idea brought a rush of warmth to her face.

It also brought the pain of knowing she would soon have to leave San Francisco.

Leave him.

A lump rose in her throat and she had to sit down. For, while she hadn't truly planned to come to San Francisco in the first place, she could no longer deny the inevitable: she didn't want to leave. Emotion gripped her like an ocean wave and the tears began to flow.

When Mr. Harris passed through the room, she turned the other way and pretended to work. He spoke a couple of words of greeting and she responded, but it was all she could do not to throw her arms around him and beg him not to sell the inn. Would he listen, if she pleaded her case?

Abby didn't have time to think that through. He disappeared out the door and she turned back to her work, determined to dry her tears. All the while she prayed for Sam, for the Gold Rush Inn, and for her parents.

When the lunch hour came, she forced herself to remain attentive and polite as she moved from table to table, waiting on the men. When she reached the table nearest the door, her gaze landed on a familiar young man. She narrowed her gaze to make sure she wasn't seeing things.

"Jimmy Blodgett!"

The young waiter from the train looked her way, his eyes widening as he took her in.

"Remember me?" she asked.

He lifted his coffee cup and stuck out his pinkie finger. "Nottingham."

"Right." She giggled and plopped down into the empty seat next to him. "I can't believe it."

"Me either. What in the world brought you to San Francisco?"

"You, actually," she responded.

"Me?" He looked stunned by this.

"Yes. It was your glowing description of the place. I had to see it—and taste it—for myself."

"Didn't realize my words had that much power. You told me once that you would never see the inside of the Gold Rush Inn, and yet here you are." He cocked his head. "Are my eyes deceiving me? Are you working here?"

"I am." She laughed. "It's a long story, but here I am. The roads to the Oregon Territory were washed out, so we took a different route. But I wasn't joking before. It was your description of San Francisco that won me over."

"And it was your use of the word 'wanderlust' that convinced me to come back. What an amazing stroke of fate, to find you again."

Behind her, Sam cleared his throat. Abby turned, joy flooding her heart as she clamped eyes on his handsome face. Suddenly she could hardly wait to tell him about her feelings for him. That would have to wait, of course. Right now there were introductions to be made.

"Sam, you've heard me talk about the young man on the train who shared his passion about San Francisco. This is him."

"Jimmy Blodgett, sir." Jimmy stood and shook Sam's hand. "I believe we met last time I was here, but it's been some time, so no offense taken if you don't remember me."

"You do look familiar," Sam observed.

"Jimmy is the reason I'm here," Abby reminded him. "He had a lot of wonderful things to say about this place."

"Then you're the one I have to thank." Sam gave the young man an admiring smile. "Not quite sure how we'll go about repaying you for sending Abby to us."

Abby's heart wanted to burst into song at Sam's sweet words. She wanted to dance a waltz. She wanted to play the pianoforte. She wanted to. . .

She could barely control the joy that flooded over her as reality hit. She wanted to give Sam Harris a kiss on those sweet lips.

Oh my.

She wanted to kiss Sam Harris.

Not here, of course. And not now. But. . .soon. She would kiss him soon, and he would know just how she felt about him.

"Miss Abigail, are you all right?" Jimmy looked at her, concern in his eyes.

She startled to attention. "Oh, yes."

"You look a bit overheated."

Abby fanned her face with her apron. "Right. We've been baking all morning. Now, you wanted a slice of pie, is that right?"

"I'll get it, Abby." Sam rested a hand on her arm and gave her a look so tender, she wanted to stop right then and there and tell him she loved him.

She never had the chance. Cookie came out of the kitchen and glanced their way. She took one look at Jimmy and rushed toward him. "Well, as I live and breathe. One of my favorite customers, back to visit."

"Couldn't stay away for long. Had to have some of that cherry pie."

"You came a long way for a piece of pie." She laughed. "Happen to have a big slice in the kitchen. Sit back down, young fella, and I'll fetch it for you."

"Well, I also came back to see about starting a business of my own," he said to Cookie's retreating back. "Not really sure how or where, but I have some. . .ideas. . . ."

Jimmy laughed. "Guess I'll tell her later."

"Looks like it," Abby agreed.

She glanced Sam's way and noticed concern in his expression.

"You still look a little flushed, Abby. Maybe you should sit down."

"No, I'll be fine, I promise." She reached over and gave his hand a squeeze. "Can we talk a little later? I want to tell you some things you might be interested to hear."

"Of course." He gripped her hand, his eyes never leaving hers.

Oh, sweet bliss! Had she ever been this happy? Had a day ever gone as well? Would her heart ever beat normally again?

"Abby? Baby girl?"

Abby turned as she heard the familiar voice.

A gasp escaped, and then one word. "Mama!"

Chapter Twenty-Three

*A*bby ran toward her mother and threw her arms around her neck. She couldn't seem to stop the tears that followed.

For a couple of minutes, neither of them said a word. Abby could feel her mother's shoulders heaving, though, and knew she was crying too. When they finally released one another, Abby stared into her mother's face. She knew that look: bone tired. Mama was exhausted from her journey. Her faint smile held a touch of sadness.

Her mother looked older, somehow. Fine lines had developed around her gray-blue eyes and even around the edges of her lips.

She pulled off her traveling hat and sighed. "Don't know when I've ever accumulated so much dust, and just look at my boots, will you? I stepped straight down into a mud puddle, first thing."

"I did the very same thing my first day." Abby linked arms with her mother. "Guess we have more in common than I thought."

"Let me look at you, baby girl." Her mother stepped back, her eyes filling with tears as she took in Abby's uniform. "You're a working girl now."

"Don't say those words too loudly in San Francisco, Mama." Abby laughed. "Folks might just misunderstand you. I've met a few of those working girls, and they look a bit different from me."

"Oh, I see." Mama's lips curled upward. "Guess I'd better guard what I say then."

"Mm-hmm." Abby got a case of the giggles and couldn't seem to stop herself. My, but her emotions were in a state today. Crying and laughing, all at once? Seemed impossible.

Her mother yawned and placed a gloved hand over her mouth. "Gracious, I'm worn out." She ran her palms down her gray skirt to smooth the wrinkles. "And I must look a fright. But at least I've arrived in one piece. Your auntie and uncle send their love. They wish they could've seen you."

"I wish the same. But don't worry about how you look, Mama. You're lovely. Father will find you as beautiful as ever."

Why Abby spoke those particular words, she could not say, but the wrinkles appeared in mother's forehead again.

"Your father?" Abby's mother blanched. "He's coming. . .here?"

"Yes, Mama. Tomorrow, but please don't fret." She reached for her mother's hand and gave it a squeeze. "Let's just get you settled in. Sam has prepared a room just for you, one of the finest guest rooms. I think you'll be very comfortable."

"Sam?" She cocked her head. "Ah, yes. The owner's son. I remember now, from your letter." She yawned again. "It will be nice to have my own room. The trip was difficult, and I'm worn to a thread."

"I understand. If you like, you can bunk with me after Father arrives." Abby gave her mother a knowing look, a compassionate look. "But for now, I think you need your own space to rest. And a hot bath too. Cookie has thought of everything, right down to calling for Maggie O'Callahan from the laundry to come and fetch your clothes to give them a good washing."

"Lovely. But, who's Cookie?"

Abby slipped her arm over her mother's shoulders. "She's one of the dearest women in the world. You're going to love her, Mama. You'll love everyone here, I promise. In fact, you'll love them so much it might be hard to tear yourself away."

"I had that problem in Oregon too."

At that moment Chet entered the room, whooping and hollering. "Woo-hoo! Just heard Cookie's making cherry pie again tonight. Thought I'd come early and get myself a piece before the others show up." He grabbed Abby and spun her around in circles. "Been practicing the minuet, Miss Abigail. What do you think? Will I win the ladies over with my dancing?"

Mama's eyes grew wide. Chet stopped cold and stared at her. "Oh, beg pardon, ma'am. Didn't mean to leave you out." He grabbed Abby's mother and whisked her around the dance floor as well, finally depositing her in a chair at Jimmy Blodgett's table. Then Chet bounded toward the kitchen, hollering something about cherry pie.

"For pity's sake." Abby's mother fanned herself with her hand. "Are all the men so forward around here?"

"Jimmy Blodgett, ma'am." Jimmy stuck out his hand. "I'm guessin' you're Abby's ma? I hear you've got the wanderlust. I have a case of it, myself. Not sure there's any cure, now that I think on it."

Abby's mother shook his hand and then rose. "Gracious. And I've only been here five minutes. What's in store over the next few days?"

"Hard to tell in San Francisco. Folks around here are very friendly." Abby looked around, confused. "Where's your trunk, Mama?"

"The stagecoach driver said he'd bring it around in a few minutes."

"Fine. Let's go meet the others and then I'll show you to your room." Abby led the way into the kitchen where she found Chet swallowing down a piece of pie. Sam and Jin appeared to be having a discussion about the inn. And Cookie? She and Neville seemed to be up to something in the far corner of the room.

What in the world? Were they holding hands?

Neville took a step away from Cookie as Abby's mother entered the room. He rushed her way. "Mrs. Effingham, welcome to San Francisco. I'm so glad you made it."

Every conversation in the room came to a grinding halt. Abby watched with a smile as Neville made introductions. She paid particular attention to the interaction between Mama and Sam, who extended his hand to welcome her.

Mama looked as if she might fall asleep at any moment. Abby sprang into action and pointed her toward the stairs. She needed to get Mama up to her room for some much-needed rest. It took a few minutes to do just that, but before long Abby was back in the kitchen, hard at work.

"Your mother is beautiful, Abby," Cookie observed.

"Thank you."

"Yes, now I see where you get it from." These words came from Sam. She swung around to face him but was too embarrassed to formulate words.

She somehow made it through the dinner hour, but couldn't stop thinking about all the things she wanted to say to Sam. If only they could have a few quiet moments together. Perhaps after she finished the dishes.

Yes, that would certainly work. She would catch him alone and share her heart.

A short while later, Abby brushed damp hair from her soggy brow as she washed the last of the dinner dishes. Mama was still upstairs sleeping, thank goodness, and Sam was tidying up the dining hall.

As soon as she finished up in the kitchen, she would garner the courage to talk to him. Together, they would come up with a plan to save the inn. Then, tomorrow, when Father arrived, she would present him with her ideas. He would fuss, naturally, but she would talk him into letting her stay in San Francisco.

She hoped.

Abby couldn't stop her thoughts from tumbling as she prepared the speech in her head. Should she come out and tell Sam that she wanted to stay, or just share her feelings for him and see if he asked? Should she put forth a case for saving the inn, or save that conversation for another day?

She stuck her hands back into the sudsy water and reached for the final plate, her thoughts in a whirl. Strange, how comfortable she now felt in front of a sink full of dirty dishes. Odd, to imagine her life before. She'd never so much as taken care of anything. Now she could pretty much cook a meal and clean up after it. Abby had to smile as she thought about how far she'd come.

And how she could never ever go back.

No matter what.

"Abby?"

The familiar voice jarred her to attention.

She turned her head and gasped. "Papa?" Abby dropped the dish in her hands and it landed in the soapy water, which shot up and soaked her apron. She didn't pay it any mind. Instead, she bounded toward her father and threw her arms around his neck. "Oh, Papa!"

He hugged her long and hard, but when he backed away, pulled a handkerchief from his pocket and went to work tidying up the wet, soapy spots on his suit.

She gazed into her father's face, as if seeing him for the first time. He seemed older, tired. Probably just from all the traveling. He'd come a long way to fetch her.

And Mama.

Oh, Mama! She was still upstairs, napping.

Abby dried her hands on her apron and tried to tidy her messy hair. "Father, I'm sorry you've caught me looking such a fright. We didn't expect you until tomorrow."

"Well, that's a fine how-do-you-do. I thought you would be pleased to discover I had arrived early. Should I go away and come back after you've slept?"

"No. Not at all. It's a wonderful surprise." She gave him another warm hug.

After she released him, his gaze lingered on her messy hair. "Abigail Effingham, I hardly recognize you. If I'd passed you on the street, I wouldn't have known you were my daughter. I've never seen you in such a state."

She brushed her hair out of her face. "Life is different here. I'm learning to earn my keep, and this is what I look like while doing that."

"Humph." He crossed his arms over his chest. "Your working days are behind you, sweet girl. Life is about to go back to the way it was. I've come to fetch you and take you home, where you belong." He turned his attention to Neville, who entered the room, tray in hand.

"Mr. Effingham. Sir." Neville stopped cold, as if seeing Abby's father was something akin to seeing a ghost.

"Neville, old man. Thank you for sending for me. I've come to escort you home."

"Right. Yes. Home." Neville looked as if he might be ill.

"There's something's different about you." Her father's eyes squinted. "What have you done to yourself?"

"Well, sir, I've gained a few pounds. The food here is rather good. Very good, actually. And my attire is somewhat different." He pointed to his apron.

"Perhaps, but that's not it." Abby's father stared at Neville. He snapped his fingers. "I see now. You've shaved off the sideburns. Quite a different look for you, I'd say."

Neville nodded, his expression growing more serious. "There are things, sir, that we do out of deep and abiding affection for those we care about." He placed his hand on his chest, as if taking an oath of allegiance. "This is one of those things."

Abby's father turned to face her, confusion registering in his eyes. "Abby, you talked Neville into shaving off his sideburns?"

"No, Father. Cookie did."

"Cookie?" Her father scratched his beard. "Neville shaved because of cookies?"

"Not cookies. Cookie." Neville cleared his throat. "She's. . .she's. . ." He couldn't seem to finish the sentence.

"Cookie works here, Father," Abby explained. "She's the finest woman you'd ever want to meet. Short of Mama, I mean."

"Ah, yes. Your mother. She's. . .here?"

"Yes." Abby paused. "We have a lot to talk about, Father, but I'd like to wait until tomorrow, if you don't mind."

"Don't mind a bit. I'm exhausted. Can you show me to my room, please?"

"O–of course." She paused, her thoughts shifting to Mama. How would she handle the news that Father had arrived?

Only one way to know for sure. Abby had to go upstairs and tell her.

❤

Sam stood in the open doorway leading to the kitchen and watched as Abby embraced her father. His heart twisted as he heard their conversation. Her father planned to take her back to Philadelphia, and from the sound of it, sooner, rather than later. She would disappear as quickly as she'd come.

And it would destroy his heart.

"Everything alright?" Cookie's voice sounded from behind him.

He turned to face her and put his finger to his lips. She peered into the kitchen and her eyes grew wide.

"Oh. The infamous Mr. Effingham. He's early."

Sam nodded. "And he wants to go to his room."

"Oh my. Does he know his wife is already here?"

"Not sure, but I wouldn't want to be in Abby's shoes right now."

"You wouldn't fit in Abby's shoes," Cookie countered. "Your feet are much too big. And they wouldn't match your trousers, either, but that's just my opinion."

Sam fought the temptation to roll his eyes.

Abby turned and saw him standing there. Sam took a step backward as she approached with her father and made introductions. He extended his hand and said, "Mr. Effingham, sir."

Abby's father shook Sam's hand. "Thanks for taking such good care of my girl, Harris."

"You're very welcome. It has been our pleasure to have Abby and Neville with us all these weeks."

"Yes, our distinct pleasure." Cookie slipped her arm around Abby's waist and drew her close, a move Sam would've liked to have made himself. "She's easy to love."

She was. Indeed.

These thoughts wouldn't leave him alone as Sam watched Abby lead her father up the stairs.

Abby.

Abby, who brought a breath of fresh air with her every time she entered a room. Abby, whose very presence made him want to be a better man. Would she really leave and take his heart with her? How could he bear it?

"Sammy? Are you all right?"

"Hmm?" He turned back to face Cookie and saw the concern in her eyes. "What?"

"You look as if you might be ill. Aren't you feeling well?"

"Physically, I'm fit as a fiddle."

"But emotionally?"

"Black plague."

"My goodness. That bad?"

He offered a lame nod. "I'm afraid so. And short of a miracle, I might not make it."

"My poor boy." She rushed his way and put the back of her hand on his forehead. "Well, at least there's no fever. I don't think you'll pass anytime soon, thank goodness."

"I wouldn't be so sure about that." He clutched his hand to his chest, feeling an odd panging sensation from deep within. "How do I keep her from going, Cookie?"

"Ah, I see. I suspected this ailment could not be cured with a tonic."

"Hardly." He paused. "A slice of pie might help, though."

"Honey, a slice of pie is always the answer, at least if it's one of my pies." Cookie turned on her heel and headed toward the kitchen, leaving Sam in the dining hall to tend to his broken heart alone.

❤

Abby knocked on her mother's door and then entered, leaving Father in the hallway.

"Mama?"

Her mother stirred in the bed. "Abby, is that you?"

"Yes, Mama. I'm sorry to wake you, but Father is here."

"Now?" Her mother sat up in bed, eyes widening. "Is it tomorrow already? Have I slept that long?"

"No, he's early."

"Don't bring him in here. Please. I don't want to see him, at least not yet. Not like this. Please tell him that we can talk tomorrow."

"But he needs a place to sleep, Mama."

"Your father can have my room." Sam's voice sounded from the hallway. "I don't mind at all. I can bunk with my father."

Abby swung around to face Sam, her heart in her throat. She whispered the words, "Thank you" and reached for his hand.

Sam had come to her rescue. Again.

Abby owed him so much more than a simple "Thank you." She would somehow find a way to tell him just how much he meant to her. . .as soon as she could.

Sam led her father down the hallway to his room and Abby said her goodnights, then went back to check on Mama. She found her mother in the bed, sobbing.

"Mama? What's happened?"

"Oh, Abby. I'm sorry. I didn't expect to react this way."

"Is it because Father is here?"

"I. . .I just don't know what to do. I thought I had adequately prepared myself for seeing him, but now I'm not so certain."

"Pray about it, Mama." Abby gestured for her mother to lie back on the pillows. "And sleep on it. You're exhausted right now, and no one makes good decisions when they're exhausted."

Her mother nodded and leaned back against the pillows. Abby slipped out of the room and into the hallway, where she ran smack-dab into Sam.

Instead of stepping back to let her pass, he pulled her close and reached to finger a loose tendril of her hair. "Well, that's a lucky coincidence," he whispered.

"Indeed." She fought the urge to giggle. Instead, she cleared her throat. "Do you have a minute to talk?"

He nodded and took her by the hand. Together they walked down the stairs. Cookie and Neville took one look at them and cleared the room, heading straight toward the kitchen. Abby would have to thank them later. Right now, she just needed a few minutes alone with Sam.

When they reached the bottom of the stairs, she led him out to the sidewalk, then across the street.

"Where are we going?" he asked.

"You'll see."

She led him to the same bench where they had shared their very first conversation, just a few weeks ago. Underneath the glow of the lamps, the street looked different somehow. Any minute now she expected one of the men to ride by on horseback, pistol in one hand, whiskey bottle in the other. But the street remained eerily quiet.

Abby shifted her gaze to the Gold Rush Inn's weathered facade. She remembered what she'd said, all those weeks ago—that they should dress up the exterior. Sam had balked at that idea. Now she understood why. Some things—and people—were better just as they were.

She took a seat on the bench and Sam sat next to her. He slipped his arm over her shoulders and pulled her close then placed a couple of kisses in her hair, which brought her great hope that tonight was already headed in the right direction.

There was so much she wanted to say. So many words she'd rehearsed flitted through her mind. But in that moment, as Sam's lips traveled down her cheek to her lips, Abby decided that any conversation—at least tonight—would definitely have to wait.

Chapter Twenty-Four

wo days after sharing sweet kisses with Sam, Abby attended church, just as she'd done in all the weeks prior. This time, however, she approached the building with a weight in her heart. Every time she thought about leaving San Francisco, she felt sick. But every time she thought about telling her father about her decision to stay, she felt even worse. It didn't help matters that Mama had refused to attend service or speak to her father. This only complicated things and caused her heart to ache even more.

Five minutes before the service was set to begin, Abby made her way to the piano. She took her seat and thumbed through the hymnal to locate the first song. She glanced up when Sam took his seat in the front pew. He was so close she could have reached out and touched him. Something else drew her eye too.

"Sam, look." Abby gestured to Chet, who had entered the church with a familiar young woman beside him. "That's Katie."

Sam's eyes widened.

"I met her that night at the grand opening. I can't believe she's come." Abby rose from her spot on the piano bench and approached Chet and Katie. She extended her hand.

"Katie, do you remember me?"

"Remember you?" The woman's eyes sparkled with recognition. "Of course. You're a hard one to forget."

Abby wasn't sure whether that was a compliment. "I'm so glad you're here."

Katie pulled her shawl over her shoulders. "Chet said it'd be all right. I haven't been inside a church since I was a kid. Not sure I belong now, but figured it wouldn't kill me to find out."

"Naturally you belong. We all do. Would you two like to sit by us near the front?"

"Depends." She laughed. "Does the reverend spit brimstones when he preaches?"

"Hardly. Just the opposite, in fact. He's very genial." Abby paused as she realized it was nearly time to begin. "I'll be playing a few hymns, but then I'll join you all when I'm done. Happy to have you."

"You sure?" Chet asked.

"Certainly. We've got plenty of room."

Minutes later, the service began. Abby spent a moment in prayer before the first song started. As she played the introduction, her fingers felt at home on the keys. Oh, how wonderful to lift a song in praise to the Lord. She enjoyed every moment of the service, from the first to the last. When it came to its conclusion, she just had one thought on her mind: I won't get to do this again. Ever.

Her heart nearly broke in two.

As she walked away from the church a short time later, Abby reached for Sam's hand. She didn't mind if people saw. Let them talk. Right now, she needed the stability that his nearness could bring.

When they arrived back at the inn, she followed Cookie and Neville inside, then checked on her parents. Mama was in Abby's room, staring out the window. Papa was in Sam's room, reading a book. Neither seemed very talkative, and her father asked to have his lunch brought to his room. Abby decided to serve Mama in her room as well. For now, it made things easier to keep them apart. Still, she couldn't picture what the journey home would be like, with everyone so standoffish.

Not that she wanted to go home. No, Abby wanted to stay put, right here in San Francisco. But how could she convince her parents this was where she belonged? After the miles they had both traveled to get to her? Father would have her head if she announced San Francisco as her new home. Oh, but it was, and no one could take it away from her. San Francisco had planted itself deep in her heart, the roots impossible to extricate. She would stay, no matter what it took.

After lunch, Abby helped Cookie tidy up the kitchen.

"You're awfully quiet over there," her friend observed as they finished up. "Feeling blue?"

"Mm-hmm. Just can't get over the fact that we're supposed to leave in a few days." A lump rose in her throat. "Has it really only been a few months that I've been here? Feels like I'm home."

"You are, honey." Cookie drew near and slipped her arm over Abby's shoulder. "We're family now, so it's gonna sting—for all of us—when you go."

Neville set down his dishcloth and leaned against the counter. Abby could read the sadness in his eyes.

"Has it always been this way, Neville?" she asked, her heart in her throat. "Did Mother want to run from Father the moment they married?"

The discomfort in the butler's expression was more than evident as he pressed his hands in his pockets. "I dare not say," he added after some time.

"Meaning you don't want to betray any confidences. I understand." Abby paused. "But Mother has hardly spoken since she arrived, and Father's not the only one she's avoiding. If I tell her I want to stay, will she even mind? Father will, I know. He'll have a conniption. But Mama? I just don't know."

Neville's silence felt painful.

"A daughter has a right to know if she was wanted by her mother. It's only right that I should know."

"Oh, you were wanted, Miss Abigail. That was never in question."

"So my father was the unwanted party, then?" She gave Neville a piercing stare. "Mama stayed busy to avoid being with him?"

He slung a dishcloth over his shoulder. "Not everyone is meant for married life, I suppose. Take me, for instance. I've been perfectly content to tool about, a confirmed old bachelor."

Cookie cleared her throat.

Neville reached for a stack of clean dishes and set them on the shelf. "I don't claim to know what goes on inside your mother's heart and mind, Miss Abigail, but I do feel obliged to help mold yours. You cannot let their hurts, their disappointments, shape or define you. No matter how this story ends, you can still have a happy, contented life."

Abby was suddenly overcome. She threw her arms around Neville's neck. "You are a diamond, Neville, and I'm blessed to have you in my life."

He patted her on the shoulder. "The feeling is mutual, Miss Abigail."

"Could you try calling me Abby?" she said.

"Miss Abby," he offered.

"Stop it, you two." Cookie lifted the hem of her apron and dabbed at her eyes. "I've got work to do over here and you're making it impossible."

Abby paced the tiny kitchen, her heart in her throat. She needed to do something. Anything. If she didn't make some sort of move, her parents would never mend their ways. She would be forced to live with them in a quiet, strained home in Philadelphia. She couldn't abide that idea.

"You okay over there?" Cookie's voice sounded. "You've gone quiet on us."

"No. Not okay, Cookie."

She glanced up as Sam entered the kitchen. He walked her way and wrapped her in his arms.

"I see how it is." Cookie looked back and forth between them. "Suspected as much. Do your parents know?"

Abby shook her head. "I don't want to go." Her words came out choked in emotion. "I've got to do something."

"Well of course you do. You're a fixer, honey."

"Beg pardon?"

"You're a fixer. You always come up with ways to fix things, don't you?"

Why did her words sound more like an accusation than affirmation?

"Well, I try," Abby said. "And aren't we all fixers, in our own way?"

Cookie shrugged. "I suppose, to some degree. But there really are some things that only God can fix. Take Sammy's situation with his mother. He tried to fix her when she was ill, tried to heal her. I did too. Showed her all sorts of remedies and ointments. Gave the doctor some of my ideas. But in the end, God healed her in a way that neither of us understood."

"Healed her?"

"By taking her to heaven. I'd say that's an almighty healing, wouldn't you?"

"I...I see."

"But my point is, I had a plan, and I wanted to see it fulfilled. You're a lot like me, Abby." She gestured for Abby to sit on the stool and Abby complied. "You came all this way from Philadelphia to California to fix your parents' marriage."

"Not just that," Abby said. "I missed Mama."

"Right."

"But in your heart you felt you were doing her a favor. Your father, too. Right?"

"Yes."

"Maybe you were never meant to fix it." Cookie gave her a sympathetic look. "Just as we were never meant to heal Sam's mama when she was so sick. Maybe some things really are better off left in God's hands. Perhaps all He requires from us is prayer."

"I do pray." Abby paused. "But it's a little late to turn back now. I'm in California."

"Where God brought you. See what He's done, Abby? He's used you mightily during your time here. But maybe He's not telling you to do anything right now, other than leave your parents in His hands."

"Maybe." Abby pondered Cookie's words and then sighed. "Never thought of it that way."

"What if you just prayed, 'Thy will be done,'" Cookie suggested. "That might free up the Lord to do things His way. And it might relieve you of the burden of telling Him how to do it."

"But, I..." Abby's words drifted off. She cast her glance toward Neville, who had remained painfully silent during this conversation. A quick look at his eyes spoke volumes. He agreed with Sam and Cookie. She needed to back off and let God be God.

♥

As Sam took in the somber look on Abby's face, he wanted to wrap her in his arms and kiss those tears away. In front of the others, though, he didn't dare. Instead, he touched her elbow lightly and she turned toward him.

"Want to go for a walk?" he asked.

She nodded.

When they got to the sidewalk, he took her hand and made a turn to the right, past the empty building that would one day—if Cookie had her way—become the bakery. His gaze traveled to the mercantile, closed up tight this afternoon, and thought about the troubles he'd had with Marcus.

"Cookie was right," he said as they made their way along the sidewalk. "I'm like you. I'm a fixer."

Abby sighed.

"I've tried to fix things with my father, and even the mess with Marcus."

She stopped walking and turned to face him. "Herein lies the dilemma. I don't see that as a bad thing. There are times when someone has to take a stand. Wouldn't you agree?"

"I do. Unfortunately, I'm usually running about three steps ahead of the Lord. That's where I get into trouble most of the time. I'm not keen on waiting on Him."

"So where do we find the balance, Sam?" Abby started walking again, this time faster than before. "God doesn't want us to sit idly by and watch as the enemy takes control. Surely we're not called to pray and do nothing."

"I guess there's a time to move and a time to be still." He felt a smile tug at the edges of his lips. "Pretty sure that's a scripture somewhere, but don't quote me on it. Point is, God does the fixing, but He uses us. The key is to listen and move only when He gives instruction. We've got to trust His timing."

"Trust His timing," Abby echoed and then nodded. "Would it be awful to admit that I'm having trouble with that, since my parents are ready to whisk me off to Pennsylvania in a few days?"

"Not awful at all. I dare say we all go through seasons of not trusting. God is big enough to deal with it."

Sam pulled Abby into his arms, right there on the sidewalk. Let the fellas whoop and holler. He didn't care. He fingered a loose tendril of hair on her cheek and whispered, "I can't help but think He knows what He's doing here, Abby."

She nodded and he placed a kiss on the tip of her nose.

"And I can't help but think the answer is just a prayer away, as Cookie would say."

"Actually, Cookie would quote a verse."

"True."

He took her arm and they began to walk together. Together. A couple. Moving as one. No words need be spoken. They did what came naturally, moving in perfect synchronization.

When they reached the corner, he slipped his arm around Abby's waist. She placed her head against his and he could feel her heartbeat, moving in time with his own. Around them the street remained eerily quiet this afternoon. No brawling. No horses barreling by. No rowdy music coming from the saloon.

Just. . .peaceful. Still.

And in that moment, Sam's heart was stirred as never before. Things that had been fuzzy suddenly came into view. He didn't trust himself to say anything aloud, because little nudges, little whispers from the Lord consumed his thoughts.

Did Abby hear it too?

Was God speaking, giving direction, even now?

Sam's heart felt fuller than ever as he paused and lifted his eyes to the heavens.

Indeed, the Almighty was sharing some rather remarkable instructions, laying out a plan, step by intricate step. Oh, how marvelous, to have the assurance that all would end well.

Now, all Sam had to do was act on what he'd been told.

Chapter Twenty-Five

"Sir, I am in love with your daughter." Sam spoke around the lump in his throat as he delivered the words to Abby's father, who sat on the edge of his bed.

Mr. Effingham blanched. "That's all well and good, son, but—"

"And sir, I plan to ask her to marry me."

He half expected the man to punch him squarely in the jaw, but Abby's father fell silent. He dropped his head into his hands and groaned. Not a good sign.

"Does she feel the same?" Mr. Effingham looked up at him.

"She does, sir. Though she doesn't know I plan to ask for her hand. I wouldn't dream of doing so without your permission." Sam's tone grew more tense as his emotions intensified. "And Mr. Effingham, sir, I beg for your permission. I can't live without her." His voice cracked. "If she leaves, I'll stop breathing. I've already rehearsed what that will feel like and nearly fainted dead away, just thinking about it. She can't go. She just can't."

"I hadn't pegged you for a dramatist, Sam."

"I'm not. Trust me, I'm not. I'm reliable old Sam, the guy who's always holding steady when others are off on a wild-goose chase. If you knew me better—and I hope you'll take the time to do so—you would know that I'm not an emotional man." His voice cracked again. "But your daughter, sir. . ."

"Has driven you to the brink of madness?"

Sam offered a lame nod. "That's the long and short of it, yes."

"Then it must be love."

"Oh, it is." Sam put his hand on his aching belly. "I can't imagine feeling this awful for any other reason. I had influenza last year and it didn't hit me this hard."

Abby's father rose and paced the room. He released a loud sigh as he turned to face Sam. "I know that feeling well, Sam. Pining away for a woman will wreck you." He placed his hand on Sam's shoulder. "If this is true, and if my daughter feels the same, then I will not stop you."

Sam shook his head. "I need more than that, sir."

"All right. I will give you my blessing."

"Thank you, sir. You won't be sorry. I promise I—"

"Just one more thing, Sam, and it's important."

"Anything."

"Do as I say, not as I do."

"Beg your pardon?"

"Do as I say. Love her unconditionally. Don't drive her away by letting your work come first. Give her the attention and love she needs—and trust me when I say that the Effingham women love attention—and you'll never find yourself chasing her halfway across the country to prove you're the same fellow she once fell in love with."

"Oh, I plan to. Trust me, I plan to."

"Good." Mr. Effingham gave him a curt nod. "Now, do me a favor and tell me how to win my sweetheart back. Then we'll both be happy."

"You just told me yourself," Sam countered. "Make sure she knows that she's the most important part of your world, that nothing—short of your relationship with the Lord—will ever come before her." His voice lowered. "I don't mean to nudge myself into your affairs, sir, but have you done that?"

"I have not." Mr. Effingham rose and walked toward the door. He turned back before reaching for the knob. "I've done a thousand other things, but not that."

"Women are interesting creatures," Sam said. "Sometimes they just need to hear the words. In my humble opinion, anyway."

"Right." Mr. Effingham squared his shoulders and released a slow breath. "How do I look, Harris?"

"Like a man in love, sir."

"I was afraid of that." His future father-in-law's shoulders slumped forward. "Now wish me luck."

With a purposeful stride, Mr. Effingham made his way out the door and toward the stairs.

❤

Abby watched in awe as her father made his way down the stairs to the dining room, headed straight for Mama.

"Oh, my." Mama looked as if she might faint as he came near. "He looks determined."

"He does indeed."

In fact, Abby wondered what Sam might've said to her father to put such a serious look on his face.

Father came to an abrupt stop in front of them. "Eleanora, I have something to say, and it won't wait."

"Should I leave?" Abby asked.

Her mother shook her head and pointed to the chair next to her. Like an obedient child, Abby sat.

"Fine, we will do this in front of our daughter. All the better." Father cleared his throat. "Eleanora, there are some things I need to tell you, things I should have said long ago."

"Go ahead, Edward."

"I—I—I—" He paced the area in front of them, his words choppy and frantic. "I've been a fool, Eleanora. I've allowed my work, my business ventures, to take first place in my life. I've been more interested in earning money than earning your love."

"Love shouldn't have to be earned," she responded. "Love is a gift, freely given."

"Yes, and therein lies the problem." He knelt beside her chair. "Sweetheart, I've always thought that if I gave you a fine home and nice things that it would strengthen our relationship, that you would be happy. But the one thing I didn't give you—and what I now see that you needed above all—was me. I was so busy working that I didn't take the time to understand. I've even moved us from place to place, thinking you would find happiness in those places. I believed it would settle your heart."

"It wasn't the location, Edward. That was never the problem." Mama's eyes flooded with tears. "Don't you see? A woman can be just as lonely in a big house in Philadelphia as she is in Nottingham."

"Yes. And a husband can be just as blind in Philadelphia as he is in Nottingham."

"I don't need fine things." Mama's voice lowered as she looked his way. "They are a poor substitute for what I really need. All I've ever really needed was what you couldn't seem to give me. I needed you."

"You've always had my heart, and I offer it to you fully. Completely. If you'll still have an old fool like me, I mean."

Out of the corner of her eye, Abby caught sight of Sam, inching his way down the stairs. He put his finger to his lips and made his way toward the kitchen, where he disappeared through the door.

Abby turned her attention back to her father as he spoke to Mama once more. "You are a rare jewel, Eleanora Effingham, and I promise to treat you as such from now on."

She watched in amazement as her father rose and took her mother by the hand. Mama stood and allowed herself to be swept into his arms. He brushed her tears with his fingertips and planted several kisses on her lips.

Abby's mother began to cry. It started quietly at first, but before long, her wails filled the room.

Cookie popped her head out the kitchen door. "Everything all right out there, folks?"

"Yes, very." Abby rose and eased her way into the kitchen, where she couldn't seem to stop smiling.

"What's going on out there, Abby?" Les asked, after the door closed. "I thought I heard someone crying."

"You did. It's my mother."

"Oh, dear. Is she distraught?"

"I don't believe I've ever seen her in better shape, actually."

"Well, that's good. We were starting to get worried in here." Les took a seat on the stool, her ankles crossed. She looked relaxed and regal, as if she'd been born a lady. Abby couldn't help but notice that Jin paid her particular attention, waiting on her every need. Les seemed to take it all in stride.

Until she saw a spider in the corner of the room. Then she leaped from the stool, barreled across the room, smashed it with her boot, and tossed it out the door.

"Someone in this room has been very busy sharing his advice with my father," Abby observed. "And I owe this person a huge debt of gratitude."

"You're welcome," Neville said, and then grinned.

"I wasn't talking about you, Neville," she countered. "But what have you done?"

"Told your father I'm staying put in San Francisco. Said he'd have to drag me back to Philadelphia, kicking and screaming."

"Really?" Abby turned his way, stunned. "You're staying put?"

He nodded and slipped his arm around Cookie's waist. "I am, Miss Abigail. I've been looking for a way to tell you for days now. You once told me that I should throw caution to the wind and just enjoy life."

"I did?" Abby shook her head. "When was that?"

"On the coach as we pulled into San Francisco. I seem to recall my response was less than enthusiastic." He paused. "To be perfectly honest, I wasn't sure how to throw caution to the wind. Someone had to teach me." He looked at Cookie. "Let's just say I've been thoroughly schooled, here in San Francisco."

"Neville?" Abby stared at him, more than a little perplexed.

"And let's just say we're both starting to enjoy life," Cookie added. She leaned over and gave Neville a kiss on the cheek.

Abby couldn't help herself. She let out a squeal so loud it must've startled everyone else in the room.

"I have fallen in love. . ." Neville sighed. "With coffee."

"Coffee?" Abby laughed. "Truly?"

"Yes. I didn't want to admit it, even to myself, but one sip of Cookie's coffee, and I couldn't look back. So I've decided to stay in San Francisco, where I can have at least one cup. . ." He kissed Cookie soundly on the lips. "Or two." He kissed her twice. "Every day from now on."

Abby got so tickled she couldn't stop laughing.

"No more tea for you, Neville?" Les asked.

He pursed his lips and then responded, "I wouldn't go that far. A good Brit loves his tea. But there is something to be said for a strong cup of Pioneer Steam coffee, brewed by a woman with a loving touch." He gave Cookie a look so tender it melted Abby's heart.

"Since we're talking about coffee and all, I have a confession to make." Cookie's cheeks flushed red. "It's about the secret ingredient in my chocolate cake." She paused and her eyes twinkled with merriment.

Neville stared at her, as if seeing her for the first time. "Cookie, are you telling me I've been shoveling down slices of chocolate cake. . .with coffee as the secret ingredient?"

She nodded. "Mm-hmm. And you have to confess, it's mighty good."

"Best in town." Neville shook his head and then laughed. "But I never would've guessed about the coffee. I'll be."

Abby couldn't help but laugh as she faced Neville. "You told me once that you strive to be content, no matter what state you find yourself in, be it Pennsylvania, Oregon, or California."

"So I did." He pulled Cookie close, barely glancing Abby's way.

"It would appear you've learned to be content in San Francisco, something you once felt impossible."

"Funny, how things work out." He gave Cookie a little kiss on the nose.

It was all Abby could do not to burst into song. "Well, if you're staying, then I'm staying. That's all there is to it. Father will just have to understand. And Mother too."

"Sure you're not secretly aching to go with her to the next destination?" Les asked.

"No." Abby shook her head. "I've been blessed to travel so many places in my young life. I've seen the world." She turned to face Sam.

"Now my world is here, my heart is here. . .in San Francisco."

"There's no place to compare, is there?" Les added. "We've got it all in California: snow-capped mountain peaks, majestic in splendor. Sparkling waters of the Pacific, crashing against the rocks like thunderous applause. Deserts so light and airy they remind me of grains of sugar. God's hand is all over this state. Why, I can almost picture His fingertip, carving out the canyons. I can envision His breath, blowing sand across the desert floor."

The whole room grew silent at such a lovely description.

"My goodness, Lesley, aren't you the poetic one?" Cookie gave her an admiring look. "You should pen those thoughts before they slip away from you."

"Oh, I have." Les nodded. "Trust me. I keep a little book with me and often write things down. It's good for the heart. Some folks compose hymns. I write. It's how I worship."

"And what a lovely way to worship it is." Abby agreed.

"Just for the record, I consider my cooking to be a form of worship." Cookie's eyes twinkled. "And I can't wait to open that bakery. I plan to forge ahead, no matter what. Once I do, I'll be worshipping all day long, up to my elbows in cake batter and cookie dough."

"Indeed." Les nodded. "I know a great many townspeople who would lift a song of praise for one of your Snickerdoodles, Cookie."

This got a laugh out of everyone.

"But, how, Cookie?" Jin asked. "Mr. Harris no buy building for you. Right?"

"Right." Her eyes twinkled with delight. "Don't need him to. My years in San Francisco have been good to me. Going to see that banker fella tomorrow. Have to invest my money somewhere. What better place than the building next door, where I can put my talents to use."

"How will you work in both places at once?" Les asked.

"I'll do the baking here, just as I do now, and shuffle the products to the bakery shelves. There will still be time to cook meals for the fellas. I've got it all worked out in my head."

"But who will man the bakery?" Abby asked. "You can't be in two places simultaneously."

Neville raised his hand. "Me. I'll be the one selling the baked goods."

"Neville, you?" Abby had to laugh at that idea. "This is delightful. I'm thrilled for you both."

"We'll have to ride all the way to the other side of town to buy our goods," Cookie said. "But it'll be worth it."

"If I had the money, I'd open another general store." Sam offered a sympathetic shrug. "That would change everything."

The room grew silent again and it felt as if the wind had gone out of their proverbial sails.

Until Les spoke, her words crisp and firm. "I have the money."

"What?" Everyone looked her way.

"I have the money. It's just sitting over there in the bank, gathering dust. What say I open a general store?"

"You want to run a store?" Sam asked.

Les shrugged. "Not really, but I suppose I could find someone to take care of it for me."

Cookie stared at Jin and shook her head. "Don't even think about it. I need you too much."

Abby startled to attention. "Oh, I have just the person! Jimmy Blodgett. He came back to San Francisco to start a business. Remember? Maybe he would run the new store."

"It boggles my mind to think the Lord had all of this worked out in advance," Abby said, her heart awash with joy. "He's not taken by surprise, but I certainly am."

" 'For I know the thoughts that I think toward you, saith the Lord,' " Cookie piped up. " 'Thoughts of peace, and not of evil, to give you an expected end.' That there's one of my all-time favorites verses. Jeremiah 29:11."

"Well, I don't know if I expected this end." Abby said. "I never would've dreamed I'd end up here."

"Awfully glad you did." Sam slipped his arm around Abby's waist and drew her close. "Right here, next to me." He planted a tiny kiss in her hair and she felt a shiver run down her spine.

"I remind myself that He has called me to this," Cookie said. "And will use me according to His will. As long as I stay submitted to Him, I mean."

"Cookie, you are truly one of the most amazing women I've ever met in my life." Abby then turned her attention to Lesley. "And you, my friend, are one of the most precious and generous women I've ever met." What was the phrase her father had used? Ah, yes. "You're a rare jewel, Lesley."

" 'She is more precious than rubies: and all the things thou canst desire are not to be compared unto her.' "The words came out—in perfect English—from Jin. He stood across the room holding a featherless chicken in hand. "Proverbs 3:17."

"Actually, it's verse fifteen," Sam whispered in Abby's ear, "but at least he got the words right."

Jin dropped the chicken and strode across the kitchen to where Les sat on a stool looking as regal as a princess.

"Did you just say I was more precious than rubies, Jin Xiang?" Les asked as she reached up to brush his hair from his forehead.

He nodded and the most delightful smile lit his face.

"Well, crown me and call me queen of the castle then." Lesley threw her arms around Jin's neck and planted a kiss on his lips.

Abby froze, wondering if—or when—the two of them would come up for air. She wanted to laugh. No, she wanted to dance a jig. No, she wanted to give a shout.

Les and Jin pulled away from each other and then promptly went back to kissing.

"Well, for pity's sake. I want to get in on this action." Cookie turned and threw her arms around Neville's neck and kissed him soundly.

"Oh, my." Abby shifted her gaze to Sam's face. Those eyes. That smile. Her sweet, reliable Sam.

"Feeling a little left out?" he whispered in her ear.

"Mm-hmm." She certainly was.

He took her by the hand and pulled her into the dining room, past her parents, who were still smooching, and through the front door.

When they reached the sidewalk, she looked at him, his eager eyes drawing her in.

"Abby, I need to talk to you about something important."

"Oh?"

"Yes." He paused and looked a bit nervous. "You called Les a rare jewel just now."

"I stole the phrase from my father, if you want the truth of it. But she really is quite a prize."

"Regardless of where the phrase came from, stolen or not, those are the very same words I would use to describe you."

She couldn't help but feel the warmth of his kindness. "You're sweet, Sam."

"It's the truth. That's why the fellas won't leave you alone, Abby. That's why they propose at every turn. It's not just your physical beauty, though that's undeniable. It's your heart. They see a precious treasure and want to snag it, just like they snag those nuggets of gold from the river. First one in wins the prize."

Her cheeks grew warm at the lovely words.

"Only this time, I'm staking my claim." In one swift move, Sam pulled her into his arms.

"You. . .you are?" Her gaze traveled up to his handsome face and she noted his lips curled up in an impish smile.

"I am." He planted a kiss on her forehead. "What do you say, Abby Effingham? Would you do me the honor of becoming Mrs. Reliable Old Sam?"

Abby threw her arms around his neck and squealed so loud, a fellow passing by on his horse had to fight to keep the animal from rearing.

She let go of Sam and laughed. "Oh dear. There I go again, causing trouble for the fine citizens of San Francisco. Are you sure you can put up with me?"

"Put up with you?" Sam tucked a loose tendril behind her ear. "I don't plan to ever let you go." He spread his arms and made a loud proclamation to anyone who might be within hearing distance. "My name is Sam Harris, and I hereby dare any fella in the town of San Francisco to try to steal this treasure away from me! Any man who tries will have a fight on his hands."

This got a rousing cheer from a couple of fellas across the street in front of the barbershop.

"See?" Sam's lips traveled down to Abby's cheek and a delicious shiver ran down her spine. "They wouldn't dare. No man in town wants to fight me."

"Well, I did say I longed for adventure in my marriage," Abby said. "Though not of the fisticuffs variety."

"True." He pulled her close. "Trust me when I say that we'll have adventures aplenty, Abby. I plan to see to that personally. I'm already thinking of places we can go, things we can see."

"Really?" Tilting her head back, she peered at his face. "Then I guess you're stuck with me, Sam Harris. You provide the adventure and I'll be your reliable old wife. But don't ever say you weren't warned. I have it on good authority; I'm quite a handful."

"A handful of blessing, no doubt." He gave her a kiss so sweet it made her head spin. "No, Miss Effingham, you are a rare jewel. But don't you worry."

"Oh? Why is that?" She batted her eyelashes at him.

"Because. . ." He kissed the tip of her nose and then smiled. "*This* is one treasure I plan to take to the bank."

Fun Facts About the California Gold Rush

- The first two nuggets of gold were found in 1848 when a sawmill worker by the name of James Marshall happened to glance down and see something sparkling in the waters of the American River.

- The wealthiest man during the California Gold Rush era wasn't a prospector, but rather a prominent Mormon store owner by the name of Samuel Brannan. He bought up all of the shovels, pans, and pick axes in the area, then sold them for ten to twenty times what they were worth.

- Between 1848 and 1849 the nonnative population of the California Territory grew from just under 1,000 to over 100,000.

- The first batch of prospectors who rushed to California were known as 49ers (Forty-Niners) because they arrived in 1849.

- Many of the 49ers arrived by ship and had not purchased return tickets to their homelands.

- Chinese prospectors arrived in California by the thousands. Many were killed by claim jumpers. Others (worried for their safety) opted to open restaurants and laundries, where they were paid with gold nuggets. In a roundabout way, they got the gold they were seeking.

- Many of the ships that carried prospectors to the California Territory were abandoned and then repurposed as inns/hotels or stores. Some were stripped for lumber.

- Prices in the gold rush territories were outrageous. Hotels, food, and supplies could bankrupt a miner in a hurry.

- Get-rich schemes were rampant during the gold rush era.

- Women were in the minority until long after the gold rush era. Only 3% of California's nonnatives were women. Many of those were saloon girls.

- During the gold rush era, a pound of coffee sold for the equivalent of $1200 in today's market.

- Saloons were found in abundance and their owners often diluted the whiskey with turpentine, ammonia, or gunpowder. These drinks went by some fascinating names: Tanglefoot, Tarantula Juice, Red Eye, or Rotgut.

- The first American "gold rush" took place in North Carolina, fifty years prior to the discovery in the California Territory.

- The San Francisco 49ers, an American football team, was named after the prospectors who came to California during the 1849 rush for gold.

- Pioneer Steam coffee would eventually become the Folgers brand.

AUTHOR'S NOTE

I'm a fixer. There, I've said it. Like Abby, I long to fix both situations and people. I've often "crossed the miles" (symbolically speaking) to rescue others. Oh, the lengths I've gone to when trying to win a loved one back to the Lord or to reconcile loved ones back to their family members.

Were my efforts always rewarded? No. God has had to remind me on more than one occasion that He's the only One capable of doing the rescuing/fixing. It is never my role to save; only the Lord can do that. I've had to learn the hard way that sometimes all God requires of me is my prayers.

Can you relate, reader? Anyone in need of rescuing in your life? Allow the Lord to use you, but be willing to step back if He asks you to. There's nothing worse than getting in God's way or getting ahead of Him with a plan that you have created on your own.

Here's a good scripture to lean on whenever you're troubled over a loved one who's wandered away: "And I am certain that God, who began the good work within you, will continue his work until it is finally finished on the day when Christ Jesus returns" (Philippians 1:6 NLT). As you recite this verse, put your loved one's name in place of the word "you." Speaking this truth aloud will bolster your faith as you wait on the prodigal to return. And remember, God is faithful. He doesn't start a work unless He plans to complete it. Did He start a work in your loved one's life? He'll carry it through, in His time.

Finding it hard to take your hands off? Does it seem impossible to back away? Always remember, God loves that person even more than you do. Even now, He's at work, wooing and drawing wanderers to Him. What heights and depths and lengths He will go to, to prove His love to one on the run.

What a gracious and merciful heavenly Father we serve!

ABOUT THE AUTHOR

Award-winning author Janice Thompson got her start in the industry writing screenplays and musical comedies for the stage. Janice has published over 100 books for the Christian market, crossing genre lines to write cozy mysteries, historicals, romances, nonfiction books, devotionals, children's books, and more. She particularly enjoys writing light-hearted, comedic tales because she enjoys making readers laugh.

Janice was named the 2008 Mentor of the Year for ACFW (American Christian Fiction Writers). She recently served as president of her local ACFW chapter (Writers on the Storm), where she regularly teaches the craft of writing.

Janice is passionate about her faith and does all she can to share the joy of the Lord with others, which is why she particularly enjoys writing. Her tagline, "Love, Laughter, and Happily Ever Afters!" sums up her take on life.

She lives in Spring, Texas, where she leads a rich life with her family, a host of writing friends, and two mischievous dachshunds. When she's not busy writing or playing with her eight grandchildren, Janice can be found in the kitchen, baking specialty cakes and cookies for friends and loved ones. No matter what she's cooking up—books, cakes, cookies, or mischief—she does her best to keep the Lord at the center of it all.

Read the series! How many have you read?

My Heart Belongs

My Heart Belongs in Fort Bliss, Texas

My Heart Belongs in the Superstition Mountains

My Heart Belongs in Ruby City, Idaho

My Heart Belongs on Mackinac Island

My Heart Belongs in the Shenandoah Valley

My Heart Belongs in Castle Gate, Utah

My Heart Belongs in Niagara Falls, New York

☑ My Heart Belongs in San Francisco, California

My Heart Belongs in Glenwood Springs, Colorado (May 2018)

My Heart Belongs in Galveston, Texas (July 2018)

Read More about the Series at
MyHeartBelongs.com

BARBOUR
PUBLISHING